MY
DAUGHTER'S
REVENGE

NATALI
SIMMONDS

MY
DAUGHTER'S
REVENGE

bookouture

Published by Bookouture in 2024

An imprint of Storyfire Ltd.
Carmelite House
50 Victoria Embankment
London EC4Y 0DZ

www.bookouture.com

ISBN: 978-1-83525-951-1
eBook ISBN: 978-1-83525-950-4

This book is a work of fiction. Names, characters, businesses, organizations,
places and events other than those clearly in the public domain, are either the
product of the author's imagination or are used fictitiously. Any resemblance to
actual persons, living or dead, events or locales is entirely coincidental.

To my mother, who loves the most fiercely

ONE
JULES

I didn't expect to see his death on the morning news. Maybe in one of the local papers midweek, hidden away amongst the ads for double-glazing and car showrooms, but not on the TV at seven o'clock on a Monday morning.

It's too soon. I'm not ready.

The newsreader is perky and blonde, wearing a gaudy lime blazer and pearl earrings that don't match her outfit. She's forcing her face into a serious expression as she reads the autocue.

'Respected in the community...'

The news is showing a photo of him collecting a charity award so that everything that follows shocks the viewers more. He was no asset to the community. He was dangerous.

My mobile phone starts vibrating right away.

'Believed to have died by suicide on Saturday...'

Suicide? I look over my shoulder, in case my family has gathered around to watch the horrors, but it's just me standing behind the sofa, leaning on it so I don't fall. Thank God Adam is still asleep and Reece isn't home.

'Wanted in connection with...'

They know more than I thought they would. But they don't know everything.

I'm shaking. I can't think straight. I need a coffee.

There's no skimmed milk left, and I'm on a no-sugar diet, so I take it plain and black.

My phone won't stop buzzing. I can't look at it, not yet. It will only make it all too real.

Suicide. What do they mean 'suicide'?

The coffee is too hot to drink, but I still grasp it with both hands, the aged 'I love my mum' mug with its thin cracks and broken handle that Adam glued back on years ago. If I hold on tight enough, I won't be tempted to glance at the messages I'm getting.

The truth is it makes no difference if I look or not. I already know what they will say.

I put my phone on mute, but it continues to flash, alert after alert after alert. Everyone local has seen the news and they're all relishing in the gossip and speculation and fake concern. Well, of course they are.

I close my eyes, focusing on my slippered feet on the lino, the comfort of my dressing gown, the heat of the mug in my cupped hands. It's about being present, they say, the ones who know how to be good mothers and good wives. I should savour this, the calm before the storm, and allow myself to be suspended in the silence and stillness of a yawning in-between. Every second that I'm not talking about it means one more second where nothing has changed. For now, there's no before and no after, just this. A thin, taut line separating hope from horror.

I blow on my coffee and take a sip. It scorches the roof of my mouth. Too cheap, too bitter. I don't think I can stomach coffee anymore – not after what I've seen.

Sleep is a distant memory. I can't even remember what I did all weekend because all I really did was wait for this. Adam asked me if I was OK last night, said Leah and I seemed out of sorts.

Out of sorts.

Yes, that's what we are. The two of us tiptoeing around one another. Pretending, pretending, pretending.

The WhatsApp notification number keeps climbing. How long is this going to go on for? I take a deep breath, but it does nothing to steady the pain in my stomach. Hands shaking, I press the little green icon on my phone's screen.

Have you seen the news?

And there it is.

The woman posting to the street WhatsApp group is one of my neighbours. I know her well enough to smile at her but not talk at length. She once took my green bin by accident, and we had to swap them over. She's not a friend.

More strangers are replying.

Devastating. And so young!

Poor guy. What happened?

Dot. Dot. Dot. The comments are pouring in. Someone posts an emoji shocked face. Someone else posts a blue heart. Dot. Dot. Dot.

WTF

???

OMG

My friend Lynsey messages me.

Have you seen the news? Did you or Leah know him?

I don't reply. The original group chat poster returns. Everyone is having so much fun.

I don't get why he killed himself.

He didn't.

I keep scrolling through the chat, checking to see if anyone's sharing any details that weren't already on the news. More sad and shocked emojis. More questions. No answers.

My chest aches, my head stuffed with so much cotton wool I can no longer see the phone screen clearly. I drag a breath into my lungs and wipe my sweaty hands on my dressing gown.

I keep scrolling.

Lots of posts on local Facebook groups.

So tragic about that young man!

I'm seeing some terrible accusations against him. You never know who you can trust.

All I can hear is my own heart, my ears thrumming with a deafening *mmph, mmph, mmph* beat. I take another deep breath. It hurts.

Hopefully he didn't suffer.

He did.

I heard they found things in his flat. It's why they're linking him to that terrible business on the news the other day.

What do you think they found?

Yes. What did they find? I swallow but I have no spit. This could mean anything. My finger hovers over the phone keypad. I have to comment on these posts. It will look strange if I don't comment.

I scatter a few broken heart emojis here and there.
The messages don't stop.

I don't want to speculate, but he must have had a reason for offing himself.

My son says he knew him. Jesus, the children!

The children. Think of the children, Jules!
I do. I think of Leah.

I haven't heard her alarm go off. It's nearly seven thirty; she doesn't have long until she leaves for school. I'm hovering outside of my body as I make my way down the hall to her room on legs made from something transparent, something soft.

For once Leah doesn't shout at me for not knocking. Even more surprisingly, she's already wearing her school blazer, sitting on her bed, staring at her phone.

Too late.

She looks up, her face pale and hair unbrushed. She gives me a tight-lipped smile of acknowledgement, and I respond with the same.

There's something almost ethereal about my daughter, standing before that gaping chasm between child and adult. I still remember the impatience I felt at seventeen to grow up, as if casting off the dead skin of my childish years and emerging as a woman would be freeing. Easier. How little I knew. How little we all know.

My baby. She's still in there, somewhere, that little one I vowed to protect forever. Did I protect her, though? Did I do enough?

No matter how hard we try, parenthood is nothing but trying and finding out too late, over and over again.

When they're born, you're prepared for all the firsts – the first smile, first step, first word – but you forget that every day is also full of new lasts. The last bottle, the last gummy smile, the last time they want to hold your hand or sit on your lap or beg for a bedtime story. And you don't know, on that day, that it's the last time. And then it's gone, and it won't happen again, and you realise you didn't hold it close enough and breathe it in and savour it.

What last is this? I wonder.

I pass Leah a hairbrush and watch her run it through her hair.

She may look old for her age, with her t-shirt straining over her chest and her make-up perfectly applied, but Leah is not as grown up as she thinks she is. A grown-up wouldn't have screwed up as badly as she did.

I close my eyes. That's not true. We both screwed up.

'Thanks,' she says, handing me back the brush, her voice impossible to gauge.

God. She's beautiful. A gift. A curse. I should have prepared her better for womanhood, not left her to flounder and fail. I should have warned her that she was too delicate. Too precious. Too deadly, now.

'Have you heard?' I ask.

She nods. No tears, no fear, her expression as closed as ever.

I step closer. She doesn't edge away. 'Are you OK?'

She shrugs and something inside me deflates. I tried, but it's too late. Again.

'I'm fine.'

Was all of this my fault or hers?

His. It was *his* fault.

'He wasn't a nice man, Leah.'

She stares at me for a really long time.

'Mum.' There are only two people who call me Mum. I'm only this person to two people. My heart swells. My babies. Leah and Reece, her older brother. Killing me softly, giving me life, making everything worthwhile.

I cup her face in my hands. 'Don't say anything.'

She shakes her head and I kiss her cheek.

'You'll always be my baby,' I say to her, my veins filling with something sharp and hot, my voice straining at the edges.

I'm glad that bastard is dead.

FOUR WEEKS EARLIER

TWO

JULES

It's 10.30pm on a Friday night and Adam and I are in bed, lights off, our cursory 'good nights' already mumbled to one another. He's not asleep yet, not properly, so I wait for the soft purr of his breathing.

I always ensure Adam is fast asleep before I touch myself.

It wasn't always like this. There was once a time when I only had to kiss my husband and we'd be having sex – feverish, desperate, sweaty tangled sheets and intertwined limbs like we'd only just met and would never see each other again.

My friends used to envy our relationship: the way he'd stare at me across the room, how he couldn't be near me without touching me in some way, and how he'd tell anyone who would listen that he was the luckiest man alive. My single or unhappily married friends thought it was me, that I'd somehow discovered the secret of how to keep a man loving you. And they thought it was them that had somehow failed to do the same. They'd ask me for tips, and I'd happily hand them out like sweets at Halloween, basking in the glow of their respect and awe. I really did think I was doing it all right.

I look at him now, his silhouette in the half-light of the night, waiting for him to still. He looks so untroubled. What must that feel like?

My friends and I became mothers at the same time, more or less. Some of them avoided sex after giving birth, happy and relieved to be finally left alone; others found that motherhood ripped open cracks in their relationship that they'd thought a baby would smooth over. Most of them drifted away from their men, some of them forever.

But not me and Adam.

We were having sex three weeks after Reece was born. Even once we'd had Leah, after two babies had pulled my body and mind into a totally different shape, Adam still found me attractive. Stretch marks, that extra stone I couldn't shift, milky tits I wouldn't let him touch, days full of toddlers and newborns and noise and mess and vomit, and still he would look at me and see the person he'd fallen in love with all those years ago.

I was irritated that he could still see her, the woman I'd once been, because I couldn't. To me she was a woman I'd lost as soon as I got pregnant, someone I'd never see again. But I was grateful she still existed to Adam. Grateful that I always felt wanted.

Then, I don't know what happened. It wasn't sudden. It wasn't as if he came home from work one day, disliked what he saw and refused to touch me. It started with our goodbye kiss before he left the house each morning, a kiss that went from lingering to perfunctory. He stopped noticing when I got my hair cut or had my nails done. He'd say I looked nice when we went out, but he wasn't looking at me. Not properly. Not that hot gaze that said he couldn't wait to get me back home.

At first, I accepted his excuses for not being in the mood for sex. He was tired. He was busy. He was stressed. He owns a large tech company, manages high-profile clients – there's a lot of money tied up in what he does. I don't understand the details of Adam's job, but I do know the hard work it's taken to build his business. Over the years I've done my best to shield him from my own stresses, the inconsequential everyday things I can deal with on my own. I didn't want to be the reason he wanted to be alone.

The feminist in me fought against my desire to provide my husband with a home he'd see as a sanctuary. Where was *my* sanctuary? Yet still I wanted his before and after of work and home to be extreme. I wanted him returning to his family in the evening to be the best part of his day. I told myself he had it harder than me, that he deserved some respite after work, yet the truth was I was scared he'd get bored of me always being the one waiting for him.

Maybe he finally has.

I've worked for the jewellery brand Medusa since the children were born, copywriting, marketing and PR mainly, often from home. Yes, I carried the mental load of two children and the home and work, but I truly believed that it was nothing compared to the pressure Adam was under to keep a roof over our heads. Before we had children I made good money at high-profile comms agencies, double his salary. Then Adam created his tech start-up, Atë Innovations. I got pregnant with Reece and as my stomach grew, so did his profit margins, until he was earning five times what I was. The bigger his company got, the more he was needed. The older the kids got, the less I was needed.

I told myself his disinterest in me was simply a dry patch. Every couple goes through them; everyone knows that stress does bad things to a man's mental health and libido. None of it was his fault. I simply had to try harder. So I made the house pretty and myself prettier, in the vain hope he'd notice. And it wasn't as if we didn't have any sex *at all*. We did. Less than before, but it was still there. And yet, like his kisses in the mornings, over time our lovemaking slowly became a thoughtless habit. Adam knew what positions made me climax, and I knew what he liked, and we stuck to that. He stopped turning the light on; sometimes he wouldn't even switch the TV off – once I even caught him checking the football score over my shoulder.

But I didn't say anything. We weren't the arguing type, and anyway, did I really want to be that woman? The kind that tells her husband off for making love the wrong way?

A year passed before I mentioned it to some of my friends. We'd all had too much Prosecco on a night out and as usual found ourselves in the women's toilets telling one another how the other was more beautiful than them. My friends batted away the compliments, but I was hungry for them. I needed to hear them. At forty-five I was still getting glances on a night out, still getting chatted up. My old schoolmates used to call me 'No Rules Jules' because I still got to be the woman they remembered being. And I could be that woman, the one I thought had vanished, because my husband still saw her.

Adam loved me.

No. More than that, he *desired* me, and that shone from every pore of my wrinkle-free skin. But the glow was dimming.

'We hardly have sex anymore,' I slurred into a friend's ear as we stumbled out of the toilets.

This woman, Cathy, had recently gone 'natural'. She said it like she'd initiated a women's lib movement, like going from blonde to grey and wearing baggy trousers was a power statement.

'Doesn't mean he doesn't love you, Jules,' she said. 'All men our age slow down a bit.'

'He's three years younger than me,' I replied. 'He shouldn't be bored of sex already.'

'Jules, Adam adores you. You've got nothing to worry about.'

She sounded convincing, and maybe she was right, but I couldn't help noticing that smug look in her eye. I knew she was gagging to get back to our other friends and tell them I wasn't immune after all. That Adam had gone off me, or was sleeping with someone else, or that I must have done something to turn him off. They'd all been waiting for the day I finally joined them in their man-hating frenzy of accepted misery.

That was three years ago. I no longer see those women. I only have one real friend now – Lynsey – and we hardly go out. Not *out* out.

When Adam turned forty, I expected a mid-life crisis; instead, he focused on getting fit, building the company and even reading spiritually enlightening books. And with every year he became a better man, I rebelled: cooking too much and eating too much, telling anyone who'd listen that no longer giving a shit was empowering.

But I was lying to myself. I did care. And because I believed Adam was more interested in going for a run than having sex with me – because I was too old, too fat and too boring – that's who I became. Like Cathy and her baggy trousers.

But the worst thing was that Adam didn't even notice that I'd stopped trying. If anything, he seemed relieved that I'd finally ceased asking him about his feelings and why he was never in the mood for sex. God, I hate myself for falling down this pathetic spiral of triviality.

I look over at him. So peaceful, so beautiful. Maybe I should be more realistic about life. I'm forty-eight, relatively fit and healthy, with a wonderful husband, great kids, a big house and a job I enjoy. I have nothing to worry about. So what if we're not bonking like rabbits? I have it all. I'm lucky.

Yet I don't believe it when I think it, because the woman in the mirror is not the woman I want to be – she's the woman my husband sees. The woman the world sees. And I hate her.

Adam's breaths have slowed down and grown deeper, a light snore confirming he's fast asleep. I slip my hand into my pyjama bottoms. It's been fourteen months since we last had sex. More than a year. Which is why I'm lying here gently rubbing myself. Quietly. Secretly. Aching not from desire but from something so deep and so sad that I can't even bear to look at him as I climax.

I turn over and close my eyes. I miss my husband so much, but never more so than when he's right there beside me.

THREE

JULES

It's a warm day and the bird outside the kitchen window has been singing the same three notes on repeat for the last fifteen minutes. I open the window wider. No matter what I do I can't get rid of the acrid stench of burning in this house. Leah and those bloody letters. I light a Jo Malone candle. Now the house smells of bonfires with a hint of jasmine.

Everything is still, so quiet I can hear the hum of the fridge and the scrape of my knife against the toast. I remember, when the kids were small and loud and everywhere, how I'd fantasise about Saturday mornings like this. It's nearly ten o'clock and Leah is still in bed, Adam is getting dressed, and we're not seeing Reece until this afternoon. The house is clean, surfaces clear, no one is crying or screaming or running around. I'm not saying I miss the chaos of my children being little, or the sleepless nights, but after all these years it still feels strange to have been awake for two hours on a Saturday and no one has needed anything from me yet.

'Morning. How did you sleep?'

Adam plants a kiss on the back of my neck, so fleeting it's nothing but the brush of a butterfly wing against my skin.

Does he really want to know how I slept? How I woke up three times in the night from the same anxiety dream, how my t-shirt was soaked through from yet another night sweat, how I can go from horny to silent sobbing in the space of a minute?

I think about answering, but he already has his back to me, fixing himself a coffee.

'What are your plans today?' I ask, adjusting the dressing gown cord around my middle.

What would he do if I wrapped my arms around his waist and placed my cheek flat against his back?

He takes the toast off my plate, bites into it with a crunch and carries it to the living room. Crumbs scatter in his wake.

'Allotment,' he says, sipping his coffee before he's swallowed the toast.

The allotment. His latest obsession. First it was the rowing club, which he never missed for years, every Tuesday and Thursday. Then he came home in April so excited I thought he'd landed a huge client, or we'd won the lottery. According to him we *had* won the lottery. The allotment lottery.

Adam had been waiting for a spot at the local allotments for three years, a simple plot of land a mere ten-minute walk from our house. And, thanks to a recent spate of old-man deaths, all his botanical dreams had come true. His own plot.

'Organic tomatoes and potatoes, Jules!' he kept saying.

It even came with a shed and a lean-to glass thing which he insists is a greenhouse. We went once, as a family, took a picnic and sat on fold-up chairs, agreeing the scrappy patch of land had a lot of potential. And, yes, wasn't it nice to have somewhere to plant things seeing as our house only has a small patio for a garden.

Then Leah started complaining she needed a wee and wasn't going to 'squat in the sodding cabbages', and Reece jokingly asked his dad whether he could grow marijuana next to the tomatoes, and I picked up all the packaging that the wind had scattered amongst the wildflowers, and we all went home.

I never went back again, and neither did Leah. Reece has been a few times. Adam says he has a little rockery, has taken an interest in unusual plants, but I suspect he's just humouring his father. And Adam, he's there all weekend, every weekend. Sometimes he even goes after work during the week. He's even taken the gas heater we once bought for an ill-advised camping holiday, and when it rains, he sits in his shed with his book and a blanket.

He says it's meditative. I tell myself that at least my husband isn't having a torrid affair with his secretary, or spending money on embarrassing sports cars, and isn't it nice to have fresh runner beans.

'Don't forget we're out for dinner tonight,' I say, handing Adam a paper bag containing his sandwich and a packet of crisps.

When did we become these people? We're still too young for this life.

He winks as he takes his lunch and grabs Reece's old Paddington Bear Thermos flask I've filled with tea. Even something as small as a wink makes my guts ache. Adam turned forty-five last year, still my toy-boy and annoyingly more handsome with every year that passes.

I try not to resent him for that too.

His once dark hair is now a salt-and-pepper grey, and he wears it slightly long, but it still looks smart. His stubble, although greying, accentuates his strong jaw. The same jaw our son has inherited. And the lines around his eyes make him look rugged, weathered, like he works on an oil rig or as a war reporter or something outdoorsy.

Adam is tall and broad – all that rowing. And he has avoided the ubiquitous middle-aged paunch – all that digging. And he dresses well because I've been buying his clothes for years now. Because of course he's too tired, too busy, too stressed to do anything as mundane as shop for shirts and jeans. My husband is a very successful, very attractive man in his mid-forties who prefers to sit in his shed drinking tea on a Saturday morning than stay in bed making love to his wife.

'Dinner?' he says. 'Oh, right, yes. Reece's birthday.'

'It's not *any* birthday.' I feel myself bristling so I close my eyes and take a deep breath. 'It's his twenty-first. Shame we have to celebrate it a week early.'

Adam smiles at me. I used to find it indulgent; now I find it patronising.

'Sweetheart, you can't blame him for choosing to spend his big birthday with his friends in Ibiza instead of dinner with us old fogeys.'

Ibiza. My God. Where the hell does my son find the money to finance his party lifestyle?

'But we always eat pasta at Al Fresco for his birthday,' I say. 'It's tradition.'

Leah enters the kitchen. The summer holidays are nearly over, and I rarely see her before noon. She's barefoot, wearing cotton pyjama shorts and a t-shirt that rides up her stomach as she stretches and yawns. Her long hair is tied in a scruffy bun on top of her head. She looks a mess, yet also absolutely breathtaking.

'He'll be having plenty of al fresco *something* in Ibiza,' she says with a laugh.

'I know you think you're funny, Leah, but I worry about him out there with those friends of his.'

'*Those* friends? You mean because he's *gay*?'

My daughter does this. She tries to get a rise out of me, as if I'm some Gen X bigot who doesn't understand her generation. Like she and her friends invented the concept of sexual prefer-ences and partying, even though at her age my friends and I were dropping E at illegal nineties raves in fields and shagging boys in bucket hats whose names we didn't even know. Her generation's idea of pushing boundaries is so mild I don't even have the strength to argue.

'No, Leah. Who your brother sleeps with is none of my business – my only concern is that he stays safe. And I'm not telling you again, will you please stop burning stuff in your room? It's dangerous and it's making the house smell.'

'Only doing what I'm told.'

I grit my teeth.

'Burn the letters on the patio. Like I keep asking you to do.'

She rolls her eyes and pours herself a glass of orange juice. Some of it splashes on the counter and I clench my fists so as not to wipe it away while she's still standing there. She places the juice back in the fridge and slams the door shut. It doesn't stick and stays open a little.

'Reece is so lucky. I can't wait until I'm out of this house,' she mumbles.

Leah's seventeen in three weeks. It's her first day of sixth form week after next. While she's wishing away the next two years, all I can think about is how quiet and empty my life is about to get.

'At least Reece gets to celebrate his birthday in the sun every year. It's so not fair!'

'It's your birthday as well soon!' I shoot back.

She makes a face. 'The tenth of September is a crap time for a birthday. No one wants to go to a party when they've just gone back to school.'

'You won't be at school forever,' Adam says to her, popping a kiss on the crown of her head and waving goodbye as he heads for the door. 'See you all at the restaurant at six. I'll probably go direct.'

'Aren't you going to change before meeting us?' I shout out at him.

'I have spare clothes in the shed,' he says before shutting the front door quietly behind him.

I'm married to a man who keeps clothes in his shed.

'Where's Reece?' Leah asks.

'Don't know. He stayed out last night.'

'He's such a tart.'

'Leah!'

Her brother goes to university two hours away by train. Far enough away that we pay for him to rent a pokey room in a vile flatshare during term time, yet close enough that he's here whenever he wants a proper dinner, or to get his washing done. Reece has been home all summer and is back at school early October, more inequality for Leah to complain about. I wish he could be home with us every day.

'I can't believe you let him study philosophy yet don't think I should go to art school!'

I don't know what my precious daughter is talking about. We haven't even discussed university with her yet. Adam wanted Reece to major in tech or business, follow in his footsteps, but our son has never done what anyone wants him to do. My boy always does what my boy wants to do, and everyone loves him for it because he's the easiest person to be around.

I close my eyes and try not to think about Ibiza or what he gets up to when he's not home. My handsome, hedonistic little shit of a son who gets away with murder because he has his father's smile.

'Mum!'

My eyes snap open. Leah is looking at her phone, which is perpetually glued to her hand.

'Reece texted. He said to tell you he'll meet us at the restaurant.'

Why didn't he text me directly?

'Great.' Leah sighs dramatically. 'Eight more hours of boredom.'

'Maybe you and I could do something nice?'

She looks at me like I've stepped in dog shit.

'Nah. You're all right.'

'We could get our nails done or check out that new clothes shop that opened last week on the high road?'

'I'm going to see if Paige and Summer want to come over.'

She heads back to her bedroom as I wipe the orange juice from the counter, shut the fridge door properly and tighten the cord on my dressing gown.

FOUR

JULES

No sound has a higher decibel than three teenage girls squealing. God knows what they're all laughing about. I have a pounding headache that I can't shift, so whatever hilarity is making them cackle and whoop like that, I wish they'd stop. But also, I don't want them to ever stop laughing.

When Leah first went to secondary school, the sound of her having fun in her room with her friends would make my chest hurt with happiness. I was so relieved. Leah was awkward and gangly for a long time; she was the frizzy-haired kid with bad posture who would sit at the front of the class but be too scared to speak. Every class has a girl like that, and it pained me that she was it. I tried everything on her first day of 'big' school to make sure she wouldn't stand out. I helped her straighten her hair, applied concealer on her pimples, worried she'd be the only girl wearing braces. I was terrified for her.

Adam would say, 'Stop projecting your own school-based trauma on to her.' Which was ridiculous because I loved school. I wasn't popular in an 'American cheerleader' kind of way, but I was pretty and smart, and people liked me. Was it so awful that I wanted the same for my daughter?

'She'll be fine,' Reece said. 'I'll be there. I won't let anyone mess with her.'

I did appreciate that her big brother was four years above her, but it's not like Reece was anyone to be scared of. Even now he's skinny, so relaxed he's horizontal, and outrageously camp. What would he do if some tough boys were mean to his sister?

She didn't know anyone else there but him. I was nervous, but I needn't have been. Paige and Summer became instant friends with her, and the three of them were inseparable. As the girls got older and turned into young women, I began to worry about her less. But even though Leah's skin cleared up and her chest grew, her puppy fat disappearing and her teeth now perfectly straight, for a long time she still acted like the gawky kid. It was both endearing and frustrating. I wanted her to snap out of it – stand up straight, own her youthful looks, enjoy the best years of her life. God knows she'll miss it when it's gone.

I couldn't stop thinking about those movies where, through the power of magic, an adult gets to be young again. What I would give to be a teenager again, knowing what I know now. All I wanted was for my little girl to know how wonderful she was.

I take it all back now. Leah's transformation a few months ago was like something out of a clichéd teen movie. Almost overnight the ugly duckling turned not only into a swan, but the queen of all sexy swans. She can finally see what everyone else can see... and she likes it.

I don't. I'm terrified.

I hold a short red dress up to myself in the full-length mirror and suck my stomach in, but no amount of Spanx is going to hide my gut. I push my Snoopy-shaped breasts up with two hands then let them fall back down. Great, even my tits look depressed. I'm not going to dwell on it. I'll wear the same thing tonight that I wore to my cousin's anniversary party last month.

My long black wraparound dress and some big jewellery. Fail-safe and flattering. It's only Al Fresco, it's not as if it's anywhere fancy.

Leah bursts in and I reach for my dressing gown.

'God, Mum!' She covers her face with her entire arm. 'Put some clothes on!'

'*You* barged into *my* room. What do you want?'

I pull my t-shirt and shorts back on and take my black dress out of the wardrobe.

'I wanted to show my friends your vintage dress collection,' she says.

'My vintage *what*?'

She rolls her eyes and starts to rifle through my clothes.

'This,' she says, holding up a dress I haven't worn for over twenty years.

'That's not vintage.'

'You said you bought it in 1998. It's from the last century.'

What she says is a fact, and I know she's not trying to be mean, but I still want to slap her. I've never hit my kids, yet the urge is so strong I have to place my hands on my hips.

'Paige! Summer!' Leah shouts over her shoulder. 'Check these out.'

Both her friends come running into the room. *My* room. I plaster on a smile, because that's what you do for other people's children, but the smile soon slips because I've caught sight of our reflections in my mirrored wardrobe. All I see is youth, youth, youth and me. Three pairs of perfect breasts facing straight on, towards a bright, exciting future, and my own staring down at the floor because they know all the best days of our life have already happened.

Leah is plucking outfits out of my wardrobe one by one and handing them out like she's a personal shopper at Harvey Nicks.

'Oh my God, Jules, this stuff is so cool!' Summer says,

holding up the dress I wore to my friend's wedding when I was twenty-four.

She turns this way and that, the bright blue of the satin shining against her dark skin. She hands it to Paige, who does the same. Paige, with her honey hair and clear eyes, completing the Benetton ad trio.

'The fashion was way better in the nineties,' Summer says, as if she'd been there.

'It's so cool that you kept all this to hand down to Leah.'

I force myself to smile. The truth is I wasn't saving my Kookai and Morgan dresses for anyone but myself. They're still in my wardrobe after all these years because I truly believed that, one day, I'd be back to a size eight again and fit into them. Yet, even if I was that tiny again, who the hell wants to see a forty-eight-year-old woman wearing a zebra-print mini dress with neon-pink lace edging?

'Can I borrow this one for the festival tomorrow?' Leah asks, holding up my favourite black chiffon dress. It's asymmetrical with ruffles along the hem and spaghetti straps, like they all had back then. It's also what I was wearing New Year's Eve 1999, the night I first met her father.

'No,' I say, holding out my hand.

Paige and Summer quickly return my dresses, but Leah pulls back.

'Please? It will look so cute with my cowboy boots and denim jacket. Like retro Coachella meets, like, Nirvana.'

She has no idea what she's talking about.

'Leah!'

She hands it back begrudgingly and I add it to all the other outfits on my bed.

'Can't wait for Carnage tomorrow,' Paige exclaims. The three of them let out high-pitched squeals and jump up and down, then run out of the room as if I wasn't there. As if they hadn't been playing dress-up with my memories.

I'm not entirely happy about this Carnage music festival they're so excited about. It's a three-day event and tomorrow is the closing act. Some rapper called Little something-or-other is headlining and the girls have had tickets since Leah's birthday last year. I threatened to sell her ticket at first. After all the drama she created at school last term with that older boy, there was no way I was going to reward her behaviour with a festival. Adam then reminded me that the school therapist, Pat, told us it was important we show Leah that we trust her. Apparently teenage girls are prone to obsessive behaviour, and it was probably a phase. I have Pat to thank for my house smelling like burned paper.

'It could have been worse,' she assured us when Adam and I had our final meeting with her. 'Leah recognises what she did was wrong. I have given her coping strategies and tools. Believe me, you should be relieved she didn't direct all those emotions inwardly. She has high self-worth. That's a good thing.'

So we said she could go on the one condition that she stick with her brother. Reece has assured me Sunday is the most chilled day, and because everyone will be hungover and packing up to leave, I have nothing to worry about. Yet my son also said I had nothing to worry about ten minutes before borrowing my car last year and backing it into a lamppost.

Well, at least we'll all be together tonight at the restaurant. I've ordered Reece a special cake in the shape of a twenty-one. He'll love it. He's the only person I know who enjoys having 'Happy Birthday' sung to him.

I close my eyes and focus on that conscious breathing my mindfulness app taught me, then I throw myself back on the bed, landing on all the dresses I can't bear to look at but can't bear to part with either. I grimace at the image of Leah and her friends trying them on like they were in Primark. As if the years that shaped me – the best years of my life – are nothing more to them than a fancy-dress theme.

I reach out for the green dress beside my head, and everything comes rushing back to me. I wore this outfit on my first holiday with Adam to a Greek island, the name of which I've long forgotten. I can still smell that evening, the scent of jasmine and the faint remnants of aniseed on his Raki-damp lips. The sky was full of stars; it looked pretend, like a painting. He kissed me so hard that night, up against the bougainvillea of the hotel wall, that I felt dizzy and had to grasp the back of his head. Then he moaned into my mouth – that's how much he wanted me there and then. So much it hurt.

'You're everything, Jules,' he said. 'Loving you forever is going to be so easy.'

I'd do anything to feel like that again. Anything. I scrunch the dress into a ball, hold it against my mouth and scream.

FIVE

LEAH

'Wasn't your mum once, like, a model or something? She's so pretty.'

Summer is sprawled out on my bed, her braids cascading over her shoulders, her chin resting on her hands. Everything she does looks like she's waiting to have her photo taken.

'She did some catalogue modelling when she was eighteen. Nothing important.' I hand them each a cupcake Mum baked yesterday. She did the icing a mint green because it's my favourite colour. 'God, she was such a cow about me borrowing her dress. Don't you think she was a cow? I mean, it's not like she'll ever get to wear it again.'

They nod in agreement as they chew.

A wispy piece of ash floats through the air and I bat it away. I opened the window earlier, after Mum moaned at me, but my room still smells of burning. I don't know why she's being such a nag about the smell when I'm only doing what that stupid therapist told me to do.

'Butterfly,' I say.

My friends both look up.

'For the matching tattoos.'

Paige screws up her tiny nose. It's really small. She looks like one of those little cartoon pixies.

'Butterflies are a bit cringe. How about a star? On our ankles?' she says.

Summer sits up and brushes crumbs off her top. 'Carnage Festival won't have a tattoo tent. It's not that kind of scene.' She screws up the cupcake case and tosses it on my bedside table.

Summer is really cool and so confident. She was the first girl I spoke to when I started at St Margarette's. She came up to me, put her arm around my shoulder and said, 'You look lost and I'm a collector of lost girls,' then led me to a group of students she already knew from primary school. Paige was one of them. We still hang out with the others sometimes, they're all right, but it's Summer, Paige and I who've been best friends ever since.

The two of them lean back on my bed. Paige tucks my large cuddly Garfield behind her head then lets out a grunt.

'Why's it hard? Is there something inside your weird cat pillow?'

She's poking it and I snatch it out of her hand.

'It used to light up,' I lie. 'It's the battery box.'

Garfield isn't a toy; it was made to keep pyjamas inside and it has a Velcro opening. It's where I hide things. I used to keep my sweets in there so Reece wouldn't eat them, and a few months ago it was full of love letters to Nathan that I planned to send to him but ended up burning. As instructed. Right now, it contains a box and inside is a round wad of dried chewing gum that Nathan spat out at Paige's party, a little football charm that used to hang from his schoolbag and some blank paper. Pat, the stupid therapist Mum said we all had to see, said every time I feel a strong emotion, I should write about it in a letter and burn it. So far, all my letters have been about the therapist and my mum. I know she can't stand the stench of burning, but that's what my anger smells like.

Paige doesn't ask any more questions about Garfield; she

just shrugs and pushes the rest of her cupcake into her rosebud mouth.

'Did I tell you Jacob's going to be there tomorrow?' she says.

She's told us every day for a month. Paige and Jacob have been dating since, like, *forever*. They're the hottest couple in school. Jacob is our age but not an idiot like the other boys in our year. He's sweet but not in a dorky way, smart but not in a boring way. He's not my type – I like older guys – but he and Paige totally match.

Nathan and I matched. Everyone thought we looked cute together. Well, we would have if he hadn't been such a gutless pussy. He was going to be my first. The plan was for me to be the first one of us to have sex with a guy, but then Paige beat me to it.

In May, the week after her sixteenth birthday, she lied to her mum and stayed the night at Jacob's. His dad was away, something to do with his work, and Jacob was meant to be at his grandparents. He lied too, said he had a school trip, and he and Paige lost their virginities to one another on his single bed on top of his Star Wars duvet. She said it was totally romantic, red rose petals on the pillow and pink champagne. He'd even put a Spotify playlist together.

Sounds totally basic to me.

Summer turns to Paige. 'Will Jacob and his friends have their own tent?'

Paige nods, smirking like she and her boyfriend have some dirty weekend planned. They don't – she wasn't allowed to stay all weekend at the festival either.

'Come on! You can't hang about with him all day. There are so many bands to see.' I sound like a whiny brat, but I don't care. Jacob is nice, but I'm not spending all of tomorrow watching those two make out. They do enough of that at school.

'Don't worry, we've already tested out his tent,' she says, widening her eyes at Summer, who laughs.

Paige is always dropping hints that she has this wild sex life, but we all know she doesn't. She says Jacob has made her come twice, but Summer told me she's lying. And she should know because she's the queen of orgasms.

Summer is seventeen in October, a month after me. She plays a lot of sport so she's always meeting girls from other teams – some of them are even eighteen. She says lesbians know their way around a female body better than any guy, and she has no problem hooking up with whoever she likes because she's fierce and hot as hell.

My friends are always sharing smutty stories, then looking awkward when they catch my eye because I'm the opposite of a man magnet. Leah the boy repellent.

'Hey, check this out,' I say, holding up two small bottles of Evian. 'I swapped my mum's vodka with water.'

My friends squeal and I laugh.

'We can buy some Fanta on the way to Carnage tomorrow, then Reece will think we're drinking that, but then we... oops.'

I mime accidentally tipping the bottle into a can of drink and the girls laugh again.

'Hey.' Paige leans forward the way she does when she has gossip. 'Did you hear Aaron asked Vanessa out? I didn't think he liked her.'

'I thought you said Jacob would hook him and Leah up?' Summer says.

I make a face to show that I couldn't care less. 'None of the boys at our school are mature enough for me anyway,' I mumble. 'No offence, Paige.'

I'm the oldest girl in my class, and the tallest. In nine days, we're starting sixth form and I'm the only one who has never been in a proper relationship. It's embarrassing.

Paige does that thing with her mouth that shows how she feels bad for me. 'Yeah. Sorry. I thought Aaron liked you, Leah, but... you know... after the whole Nathan thing.'

The Nathan thing. That's what all the stuff hidden in Garfield is about. It's why Ms Willis called my parents in, and we all had to sit with the school therapist and talk about boundaries and respect. Two years older than me and Nathan still acted like a scared little baby all because I wanted him to be my boyfriend and he preferred to act like he didn't know me.

'We kissed!' I shout at my friends for the hundredth time. 'He definitely liked me.'

It's all Nathan's fault – starting rumours about me, making out like I was some kind of eager psycho. I literally did nothing wrong.

We were at Vanessa's birthday party. I'm not sure what Nathan was doing there, but he was knocking back Jägerbombs and I kissed him and he kissed me back. Properly. With tongues. He even put his hand up my top, so I know he liked me. But then back at school he ignored me. When he finally spoke to me, he made up some excuse about how he had to focus on his A levels and I was too young to date, which was a lie. That's why I kept trying to get his attention, to remind him that we had something special. In the end he grassed on me to Ms Willis, who called it harassment, and she spoke to Mum, who told Dad, who said we should 'nip it in the bud' and get me 'professional help'.

I made out to the therapist like I was really sorry, but I wasn't, because I didn't do anything wrong. It's not like I was boiling his pet bunny! All I did was write him a few letters and wait for him at the school gates. It was all blown out of proportion. Nathan left school a few months later anyway after sitting his exams. I found out he's studying biology at Plymouth University. I know what halls of residence he's in, I even found out his room number, but I'm not a stalker. If I was, I'd have sent him the letters I wrote.

'I don't know why everyone was acting like I was a mad headcase!' I shout.

'I think it was his injury,' Summer says, glancing quickly at Paige.

'Injury?' I scoff. 'Please! I went to take his hand and he pulled away and that's how I scratched him. Big deal. It was an *accident*.'

They both nod quickly, Paige shifting about on my bed. 'Nathan totally wasn't worth it.'

'I know,' I reply. 'Everyone made a big deal out of nothing.'

'It's just that you can be a bit... intense, sometimes,' Summer says quietly, picking at her perfect nails. 'But I'm sure everyone will have forgotten by the time we go back to school.'

Something in my chest coils tight like a rattlesnake ready to pounce but I keep my mouth shut. Instead, I think about what Pat said about projecting emotions on to Nathan, who 'didn't reciprocate my feelings'. She said it wasn't healthy to pursue a love interest if it was one-sided.

'I can speak to Jacob and see if any of his other friends like you if you want, Leah,' Paige continues.

When are my friends going to stop treating me like a child? Like I don't know how to get my own boyfriend. I've kissed plenty of boys. I had my first proper kiss when I was fourteen playing 'spin the bottle', way before Paige did. And Alfie in our year asked me out after Christmas and we met up a few times. I told my friends he'd fingered me in the park, but the truth is I let him put his hand down my jeans then pulled his hand out once it touched my pubes. But they don't know that. I thought boys were always up for it, that it would be way easier than this to get a boyfriend. Maybe I'm looking in the wrong places.

'I'm going to hook up with someone tomorrow!'

I say it just like that, blurt it out like it's nothing. Summer and Paige look at one another.

'What? Like kiss?' Paige asks.

'No. Like, hook up properly. Like, sex.'

'How?' Summer has shuffled closer. 'Your brother will be with us.'

'Reece is so dreamy,' Paige says.

'He's gay.'

'I know.'

'And he's only going there so he can sell weed.'

'*I know.*'

I roll my eyes. 'Reece is a tart. Believe me, he'll drop us as soon as he sees his mates or spots a cute ass. Then I'll be free to find my own hottie.'

My friends look at one another again then back at me.

'Seriously, I'm going to have sex with an older guy,' I say again, making it clear I have higher standards than any of Jacob's stupid mates. 'Like... uni age.'

'Nice!' Paige says. She's impressed. I like that. 'You know you look much older than sixteen.'

'Seventeen,' I say. 'Well, nearly.'

'You could totally pass for twenty,' Summer says.

'Or even twenty-one,' Paige adds.

I know they're trying to be nice after the Nathan comments, but they're right. I do look older than my age. It's time to find a real man.

There's a knock at my bedroom door. My mum's saying something.

'What?' I shout.

'We're leaving in twenty minutes.'

I roll my eyes at my friends and they grab their bags. I'm not even going to get changed. It's only Reece's lame birthday dinner. Another embarrassing family thing where Mum gets to make a fuss of her golden boy, and everyone ignores me.

'I'm sure you'll find the perfect guy tomorrow,' Paige whispers as they leave my room.

'Oh, I'm going to make sure I do,' I reply.

Because I'm not letting another one slip through my fingers. This time I'm serious.

SIX

JULES

Al Fresco hasn't changed in the twenty years we've been coming here, and that's one of the reasons I love it. Too many things change. Not enough remains the same. The owner, Antonio, knows us all by name and always remarks on how much the kids have grown.

'Twenty-one?' he exclaims as I tell him why we're here. 'I remember Reece eating spaghetti in a high chair by the window, there. And this can't be Leah? Mamma mia, she's a woman now.'

I don't like the way he says that. How his eyes linger on her new chest for a fraction too long, the way Leah smiles because that's what's expected of her, and how I stand there and smile too. She's only in a short top and jeans yet still looks like a supermodel. How does she do that? Antonio doesn't take his eyes off her behind as she makes her way to the table, our table, but Leah's too busy looking at her phone to notice. Adam certainly hasn't noticed, and I hate myself for knowing that I'm not going to say anything either.

As Adam and Leah take a seat, Antonio's attention snaps

back to me and I covertly hand him the cake I had specially made for my son.

'Reece will love this,' Antonio whispers.

He will. I smile and he smiles, and I don't know why I'm smiling at him. Maybe this will be our last visit.

Adam and Leah are waiting for me as I weave my way to the back of the restaurant and sit down. It's a square table yet, somehow, I still feel like I'm sitting at the head. At mealtimes I like to do this thing where I look at my family and count my blessings. I read an article once about how the secret to a happy life is being present and thankful.

Adam. He didn't bother to get changed after digging in his filthy outdoor trousers all day, but I'm thankful that he's here and that he placed his hand over mine as I sat down.

Leah. She keeps scrolling through her phone and rolling her eyes at everything her father says, but I'm thankful that I have a strong and bright daughter.

Reece isn't here yet. He's late. But that's OK. It's OK to be late to your own party. I'm always thankful to have my boy.

'Hey!'

It's him. My chest swells. I knew he wouldn't keep us waiting. I watch as Reece bounds over to us in that puppy-dog way of his.

My son lights up every room. I can see it in the faces of each person he passes as he winds his way to our table. He sits with a thump, draping his arm over the back of my chair as he pecks me on the cheek.

'Hello, my darling,' I say.

He's wearing shorts and his hair is a mess.

Reece. I'm thankful for my son and for how much he loves his mama.

I breathe deeply. I'm present. I'm here. This is my family. I love my family. They love me. We are all very lucky to have one another.

I glance at the menu, which hasn't changed for over twenty years either. I know exactly what I'm going to eat tonight. Leah has finally put her phone away and is laughing at something her brother has said. I smile at Adam, and he smiles back at me, and I try to ignore the stench of compost emanating from his shirt. This is Reece's birthday dinner and it's going to be a wonderful evening.

SEVEN

LEAH

Reece's birthday dinner was shit.

I know Mum wanted to make it extra special, but hasn't she ever heard of less is more? She was wearing the same plain black dress she always wears, but this time with too much jewellery like it was the Oscars or something. Which was embarrassing because not only is that restaurant dry and boring, with a creepy owner, but Dad turned up in the clothes he wore to the allotment. Predictably Mum got stroppy with him, mumbling about how he smelled of greenhouses, and he had to be all apologetic. I hate that he's always saying sorry to her. Sorry for what? Existing? It wasn't like anyone even wanted to be at her lame dinner. The whole thing was a waste of time.

Then she had this surprise cake made which was like something you'd get at a six-year-old's birthday party – two big numbers, 2 and 1 – and Reece had to act all happy that he had a toddler's sprinkle cake. Mum sang 'Happy Birthday' loudly *and* clapped, and everyone was looking. Seriously, I nearly died, and it wasn't even my birthday. She better not pull that crap for my seventeenth. Reece was cool though, he always is. He sat there grinning, probably thinking about what he's going to get up to at

Carnage tomorrow – or how many guys he's going to hook up with in Ibiza next week.

The car ride home took forever. We all sat in silence, Mum occasionally saying things like 'well, wasn't that nice!' in that fake voice of hers. When we eventually got home, I said I had some emails from school to read before new term starts and ran to my room. I wasn't going to spend another second with any of them. It was obvious she was mad at Dad. I don't know why they don't just have a big argument and say what they think. When they get like that it's like being trapped outside on a hot day before it rains.

As soon as I shut the bedroom door behind me, I could hear Mum say, 'Let's play a family game of Uno. I'm sure Leah will join us in a bit,' in that voice again. I tried not to laugh that I'd left Reece behind with them. Happy birthday, bro.

Of course I don't have any important stuff from school to read – I need to plan my outfit for Carnage. I'm thinking of wearing my ripped denim shorts and retro Guns N' Roses t-shirt with my leather jacket, but I'm not sure it's working. Mum should have lent me her dress. Tomorrow is going to be amazing, and I don't want my friends to look better than me. This is my first festival, but I know exactly what it will be like: a big field full of hot guys sitting around listening to music, chilling; maybe someone will have a guitar and someone else will be passing around a joint. I might try some weed if Reece isn't watching.

When we were twelve, Summer, Paige and I watched *The Craft* for the first time and convinced ourselves we could be witches. We'd write notes about the people we liked and then burn them while chanting incantations. I smile at the memory because our spells never worked. Now my therapist says I have to write letters about my feelings and burn them. I'm going to write about the festival and the man I want to find. Excitement is a feeling, isn't it? Maybe this time the spell will work.

I start to sketch what my dream guy will look like. If I close my eyes, I can practically feel him standing next to me. There's a whole TikTok trend about positive thinking and the law of attraction. People are saying that if you think about something enough, you can bring it into reality. Manifest it. I'm going to bring this perfect man to me because I know he's out there, and when I find him, I'm going to make sure he wants me just as much.

I finish my drawing of a guy sitting on the ground with a guitar; he has messy brown hair and his eyes are closed. I'm good at drawing – art is the only subject I get As in. Then I write words in capital letters around him.

WE ARE DESTINY. FOR ONE DAY THE UNIVERSE WILL UNITE US. FOR ONE SUSPENDED MOMENT IN TIME, YOU WILL BE MY WORLD AND I WILL NEVER FORGET YOU. WE BELONG TOGETHER.

I colour it in, taking time to draw the grass and hearts and musical notes, then I fold it in three, hold it to my heart and whisper, 'I manifest you,' before pulling the metal bin out from under my bed, holding the paper over it and setting it alight. The edges curl black, like the man I want to make real is slowly disappearing off the page and into reality. As the flame reaches my fingers, I drop it into the bin, fragments of ash peppering the air like tiny moths.

The room stinks, so I open my window and the door. The sound of muffled voices drifts up the stairs. I guess Mum finally convinced Reece to play Uno with them, and weirdly I feel left out now. I stuff my lighter back into my giant Garfield, go downstairs quietly and listen at the living room door. They're ribbing Dad for having to pick up four cards.

OK. Fine. I'll join them for one round.

I reach for the door handle but then I hear Mum's voice.

'Is she up there burning those bloody letters again? The house stinks. It's bad enough your clothes always smell of bonfires, Adam, but now *this*? Our family is going up in smoke!'

I hear Dad's low laugh. I wish he'd tell her to go to hell. I go to open the door, but Mum hasn't finished yet.

'Why hasn't Leah come back down? Honestly, I don't know what's got into her lately. She's become so self-obsessed.'

I freeze, eyebrows raised, fingers still hovering over the handle.

'You better keep an eye on her tomorrow, Reece. I don't trust her one bit. Not after everything that happened with that Nathan boy.'

My brother has a deep voice so I can't hear what he says in reply, but whatever it is they all laugh. My face itches as I feel heat rise from my chest to my cheeks. My friends think my mum's so nice, so cool, but it's all fake. Even *she* thinks I'm an obsessive psycho.

It wasn't always like this; we used to be close. Not like besties or anything, but we'd chat and watch movies together. Sometimes I'd give her a pedicure while we watched reruns of *Lost*, or we'd go for a jog together even though I'm faster than her. She was OK. Then she became a real cow. I can't say exactly when – it wasn't like it happened on a specific day – but it was around the time Reece started uni two years ago. Mum acted like she couldn't wait to get him out of the house, but as soon as he moved in with his scummy mates, she changed and started making bitchy comments about me wearing make-up or my skirt being too short.

Yet at the same time, she also wanted to act like my bestie, asking loads of questions about where I was going or who said what to me at a party. Like, that stuff was fun to talk about when I was thirteen but I'm nearly seventeen now. I have a life and it's not any of her business. And now there she is laughing about me with Dad and Reece, saying that *I'm* self-obsessed, like she's not the one always staring in the mirror and pulling at the skin on her face until her wrinkles disappear.

She already thinks I'm a nightmare daughter, so what do I have to lose?

Quietly, I head up to Mum and Dad's bedroom, take the black ruffled dress out of her wardrobe and stuff it into my rucksack for Carnage. I'll change once I'm out the house. Reece won't notice that it's not my dress, and Mum will never know. It's not like she's ever going to wear it again.

Back in my room I try it on and grin at my reflection in the mirror. It's crazy to think that the perfect man for me is out there and he has no idea he's going to fall for me tomorrow.

I can already feel the magic working.

I can already feel my power.

EIGHT

JULES

'It's six thirty on a Sunday morning, Adam.'

My husband is already dressed, tiptoeing around the room as if the sunlight from the partially opened curtains didn't already wake me up.

'The earlier I get to the allotment, the sooner I can get back.'

'You know the kids are out all day and night today?' I say, hooking my bare leg over the duvet.

He glances at my thigh. I've been doing yoga lately. Can he tell? He reaches down and I breathe in, imagining him running his hand up my bare leg, kissing me, holding me down.

He picks up his phone beside me and I breathe back out.

'I wanted to spend some time with you,' he says.

I stretch my leg out and rub the coarse denim of his jeans above the knee.

'Yes. And what would you like to do?'

He steps back and starts scrolling through his phone. 'It's about that financial portfolio I told you about.' He doesn't look up. 'We need to discuss investing the money your mum left you into some bonds or stocks.'

I lie back down and pull the covers up to my neck.

It's the first anniversary of my mother's death in a few weeks. Adam hasn't mentioned it, and neither have I. He was there for me when she died – he said the right things and did the right things, but then he stopped. No one wants to hear you talk about your loss forever. Although, clearly, it's OK to keep talking about her money.

My father left us when I was four so my mother, for as long as I can remember, was my everything. She was a paediatric nurse, looking after children day and night, yet she still had time and energy for me. She didn't have anyone around to help her – no cleaner or husband to lend a hand – yet I never once heard her complain. She was both my parents, every sibling I never had, and my best friend all rolled into one. When I lost her, I lost more than one person.

'Jules? Did you hear me?' Adam asks. 'Want me to explain the advantages of bonds during a fluctuating market again? They're not as risky as stocks.'

He's talking about the money I made from the sale of my mother's two-bedroom flat. The sole advantage of being an only child is that there's no one to fight over a will with. There's also no one to take the reins when your hands are full. Dementia trickled in so slowly that I didn't realise my mother was drowning until it was too late. Then it was my turn to drown in the constant cycle of children and work and caring for her. Dementia stole her soul and replaced it with someone scared and angry, someone I didn't know, until every one of my fond memories of us was overlapped with the horror that came from caring for a stranger. I have to remind myself that I had a good mother. The best. It's a shame she didn't stay inside her body long enough to show me how to be one too. By the time cancer got her, she'd been dead for years.

'Eighty-two. That's a good age to get to,' people told me the day of her funeral, like we'd won a competition.

I never told anyone this, not even Adam, but I was relieved

when she died. As I stood on the soggy ground before her casket, my grown-up children on either side of me, I remember thinking, *Good. I'm finally free.*

Yet life always has the last laugh, because as soon as I had the time to spend with Adam and the kids, they were no longer there waiting for me. I no longer mattered.

Now that a year has passed, a respectable amount of time, Adam keeps mentioning the money from my mother's flat: the money that's languishing in our current account and 'not being put to good use'.

But he doesn't know about the secret money. The money I've been hiding from him.

'Sorry,' I reply. 'I haven't read that thing you sent me. I'll look at it later.'

After my mother died, I was left to clear out her flat by myself. Adam was busy with his business, there was talk of potential buyers, Reece was at university, and Leah said it would be 'too depressing'. I had one week to get all my mum's things out of a two-bedroom flat – the only home I'd ever known as a child.

Everything smelled of her: talc, polo mints and lavender. How does a person's scent survive longer than they do? I felt her there, watching me, telling me I'd be fine without her. I didn't believe her. Everything in that flat was about me. Every keepsake, every drawing, every book somehow led back to me and her role as my mother and grandmother to my children. Everything she owned had been important to her at some point, every item had a meaning, but not anymore. Now her belongings were nothing but musty clothes people would be buying in Oxfam next week, assorted bric-a-brac to be labelled 50p and rummaged through by curious strangers.

As I sorted things into bags and boxes, I wondered what stories my own children would tell about me as they stuffed bin bags with nineties lace-trimmed dresses and notebooks I'd never written in. Did my belongings lead back to them too? I know Adam's wouldn't, and I know he wouldn't hate himself for that.

I kept my mother's jewellery, a few books and the nice Le Creuset dish she'd inherited from her own mother; the rest I donated to charity. But as I sorted out the books, of which she had hundreds, a ten-pound note fluttered out of the pages followed by a fifty-pound note. I called the charity and postponed their pickup by a day, then proceeded to have the most curious of treasure hunts all on my own.

Turned out my mother had been hiding money for years, long before she'd been diagnosed with dementia. I'll never know if that money had been for her, her own self-care, or for me to find one day. Either way, she'd managed to look after me long after she'd gone. I found £11,770, which I've been keeping in a hat box under our bed. Nobody knows about it. It's mine and Mum's last little secret.

'I know talking about investments is boring, Jules. But we need to think about the future.'

Why is everything we do for the future? Why is it never about now?

'We might be close to selling the business,' he continues. 'That will be life-changing if we pull it off, but there's still a lot of work we need to do before then. You and I need to be smart with what we have.'

His own parents weren't. When they died, they hadn't even put anything away for their own funeral costs, leading to an argument that resulted in us paying for two lavish funerals and Adam no longer speaking to his brother.

It's just us now. Me, him, the kids – our entire family.

'I'll look into it,' I say. 'Promise.'

Adam pats me on the shoulder like I'm a good dog, then stands to tuck his t-shirt in.

No kiss goodbye this time, nothing but a nod and the gentle

click of the bedroom door closing then footsteps on the path outside.

I let out a groan, thinking of the feel of his jeans beneath my toes and what could have happened had I had the courage to persevere. What if this time I'd run my foot higher, and he'd hardened under my touch? Just the idea that we might have had sex fills my head with vivid images of all the things I want to do. All the things we used to do. I squeeze my legs together but it's no use, I can't ignore it.

I never used to take sex seriously when I was younger. It was always there for the taking, so easy to find. I don't know if that was the nineties or because I was in my twenties, but it was everywhere. As the first millennium drew to a close, the air was feverish, there was so much hope and excitement, we really thought the noughties were going to be magical.

My 1999 New Year's plans were cancelled at the last minute. I was meant to go to a private club with a sub-editor I'd been dating, then he dumped me the day before. I don't remember being upset about losing him – I don't even recall his name – but I do remember feeling devastated about missing out on celebrating the biggest New Year's Eve ever.

I'd started working at the local newspaper, which is where I met my best friend, Lynsey. She was training to be a teacher but needed money over the Christmas holidays so was doing some temp work. I was a journalist, although all I ever covered was local council news or the opening of a new restaurant. My journalism career was short-lived once I discovered copywriting for big brands paid better.

'Join me and the gang,' Lynsey had said, when I'd remarked on my bad luck.

'Where are you going?'

'Only place worth going. Trafalgar Square. We'll take some bottles with us and party like it's 1999.'

Everyone was sick of that Prince song, but I laughed

anyway. I wore my black dress with the ruffles. It was a bit
flimsy for London in December, and I'd been stupid to wear
heels, but I was excited. I met up with Lynsey and her friends.
We never made it into town. The Tube was heaving. Even the
streets of Camden, where I was sharing a flat with four other
girls at the time, were already full of wasted revellers dancing
and vomiting and pissing in the street. It wasn't even nine
o'clock yet.

'Let's have a drink first then try the Tube in an hour,'
Lynsey shouted over the din.

That's when I spotted Adam, leaning against a phone box.
He was smoking and staring up at the sky, the only still figure in
a landscape of surging, drunken partygoers. I never did ask him
what he'd been doing, if he'd been waiting for friends or had
gone out by himself. He caught my eye and straightened up. I
asked him for a light – I used to smoke back then too. He smiled
at me and that was that.

Well, that's the version we tell the kids. They used to love
the part where I said I'd left my friends to see in the new millennium with the man I would spend the rest of my life with. But I
wasn't to know that then; Adam had simply been one of my
many impulsive decisions.

We got chatting and I discovered he was from some small
town outside of London but was staying at his cousin's empty
flat near Camden Lock. He suggested we watch the fireworks
from there, that at least we wouldn't get cold or vomited on, and
off we went. But as soon as we stepped through his front door,
we were ripping our coats off. He didn't even bother to remove
my dress, pushing it up over my waist, taking me in the hallway.
We couldn't get enough of one another. We only realised it had
turned midnight when the city exploded with an almighty roar
of colour and merriment, everyone outside cheering and
singing, and we held each other and laughed until tears poured
down our faces.

They say no one fantasises about their husband, that illicit thoughts are reserved for the things you wish you could have but never will. Yet thinking about that night feels like the ultimate fantasy as I bring myself to climax, even though I've slept beside that same man for the last twenty-five years. Does Adam think of me when he masturbates? Does he think of me at all?

I wonder who's keeping the most secrets from the other.

NINE

JULES

Reece and Leah are still asleep at 9.30am – so much for leaving for the festival early so they wouldn't miss out. I bang on their doors, wait for their 'I'm up' grunts, then press Lynsey's name on my phone. It may be early for anyone else on a Sunday morning, but not the mother of two kids under the age of four. For as long as I have known Lynsey, she never wanted children. As a teacher she said her life was already full of kids, and as deputy head of a fancy school in Potters Bar she had enough on her plate. Until, aged forty-one, she decided she really did want kids and went on to have two back-to-back. Now she resents her partner because being an older dad is never as tough as being an older mum.

'Thank God you called,' she hisses down the phone. 'It's the bank, love. I have to take this,' she shouts out.

I hear the rustle of her moving, the clonk of the bathroom lock sliding, and she lets out a deep breath.

'Are you pretending I'm NatWest again?' I say, curling up on my bed, thankful for the millionth time that I don't have little kids running around the house anymore.

She chuckles. 'There's only so much *Paw Patrol* one woman

can take. Oh my God, I can't believe we haven't spoken since last month. Chickenpox is Satan's work. I swear I'm still traumatised. So, tell me something new and exciting.'

New and exciting. She still thinks my life is exciting.

I have nothing.

'Reece is twenty-one next week.'

'No way!'

'I know. It's depressing.'

'What's depressing is that I still have to wait sixteen years until I have this house to myself.'

'Well, I'm not totally free yet. Leah is still being a pain in the arse.'

'She's nearly seventeen. That's normal.'

'She's gone from being a sweet kid to walking around as if she's in a girl band or something. All she talks about is boys, clothes and her friends.'

'Are you telling me you can't remember being a gorgeous teenager? How it felt to walk into a room and turn the heads of every guy in there?'

I do, but it's not so much fun on the other side.

'Honestly, Lynsey, she's sucking all my energy up like some kind of manicured Dementor.'

'Don't talk to me about kids sucking the life out of you.'

We fall silent.

'I have nothing interesting to say,' I offer after a few seconds.

'Me neither.'

'Any gossip?'

Lynsey hums as she thinks. 'Oh, yeah. Remember my friend Fiona? The one who left her husband after he started getting obsessed with raising ducks?'

I can't help snorting but she keeps going.

'Well, she was telling me about a new app she's started using called Kandid. Have you heard of it?'

'No. Is it a dating app?'

'Not quite. It's like a secret confessional thing, but you can filter it by location, age, gender and topics. She said it's full of single guys being vulnerable and opening up, so loads of women go on there to find a match. Although she said it can get pretty X-rated.'

'And it's anonymous?'

'Yeah, you can't show your face.'

'So how do people know if they like one another?'

'*Personality*, Jules. Remember personality?'

'Didn't exist in our day.'

She laughs.

'So who's she been chatting to?'

'Loads of guys. She said there are so many crazy stories on there, which goes to show you never know what your neighbours are really like. She said someone within one kilometre of her house is a furry.'

'What the hell is that?'

'You know... likes to dress up as ponies and bunnies and stuff during sex.'

'Wasn't one animal-obsessed man enough for her?'

'That's what she said. Apparently, she searches for the word duck and if anyone mentions them in their confession, she blocks them.'

We both laugh until the screech of Lynsey's sons interrupts us and her toddler starts banging on the bathroom door.

'I have to go,' she says. 'I've been rumbled. NatWest is never this amusing.'

'May the odds be forever in your favour,' I shout, and I hear a faint chuckle as she hangs up.

My curiosity gets the better of me and I search 'Kandid confessions' on my phone. There are a few articles about scams and lonely hearts, which I ignore, and I keep scrolling until the logo for the app appears. Lynsey said it was full of juicy local gossip and I have nothing better to do today.

I download the app.

Poor Fiona. Thank God I'm not as desperate as her. Am I?

TEN

JULES

Motherhood is a strange beast.

Most of the time it's about survival, feeding and sleeping and protecting your babies until they reach another year safe and well. No time to look up. Yet other times you get such an immense surge of love for them it makes you feel sick to the stomach. I'm feeling it now, looking at Reece and Leah in the kitchen, squabbling over the last of the milk.

Reece looks like a Renaissance cherub, albeit as sinewy and languid as his father. Everything about him is like water – the way he moves and walks and talks, like he has all the time in the world. His hair is messy and dark blonde, like mine was before I convinced myself highlights were worth the money. His eyes are a piercing blue, like the colour of the forget-me-not flowers my grandmother had in her garden. That's what I want to scream at him: *Don't forget me, son. Don't forget me.* Sometimes I imagine he can feel that fear emanating off me like static, and it has the adverse effect. The more I need him, the more steps back he takes, as if I'm an overeager saleswoman peddling my love for him.

His sister, on the other hand, looks so much like me at

sixteen it's unsettling, but with Adam's colouring. Tall, strong, sharp, dark. Leah's hair is thick and a deep mahogany that doesn't need synthetic highlights to make it shine, but with eyes just like mine and her brother's. She's wearing a Guns N' Roses crop top and ripped denim shorts that accentuate her pert bum, although she keeps tugging the hem down as if she likes that it's provocative but doesn't know what to do about it. It's always struck me as terribly unfair how by the time a woman finds the confidence to be herself on the inside, her outside has changed irrevocably.

God, I love these kids. I can't stop marvelling at how beautiful and strong and amazing they are. I'm so lucky to be their mother.

'Why are you staring at us like that?' Leah says, her face twisted in disgust. 'You're being creepy.'

They can also be huge arseholes.

'I was wondering what you have in that giant backpack,' I say. 'I don't know how you don't have a crooked back with those heavy bags you're always lugging about.'

Leah huffs through her nose and pulls out two bottles of water, some cereal bars and a toiletry bag containing deodorant and sunscreen.

'Happy?' she says. 'Or do you want to frisk us too?'

Reece is eating his breakfast at the table and interrupts me before I have a chance to reply. 'No need for frisking, sis, your Daisy Dukes are so tiny we can already see everything.'

Leah tugs at her shorts again then slaps her brother around the head playfully. Milk dribbles out of his mouth until he chokes with laughter, splattering specks of white all over the kitchen table.

'Slut era,' he whispers.

'You're the only whore around here,' she counter-attacks.

I wipe down the counter. 'I hate the way you two speak to one another. It's so ugly.'

Leah ruffles Reece's hair and he pulls her down, planting a kiss on the top of her head. A pain shoots through my chest again. Jealousy. How awful of me. It's the same feeling I had when Reece bought Leah a gaudy gold ring with an L on it for Christmas and all I got was a boring John Lewis voucher. She never takes that ring off. I should be happy my kids love one another so much, yet all I feel is left out.

'So, Leah, are you looking forward to seeing Little Face? He sounds good.'

She looks at her brother and they both burst out laughing again.

'It's Lil *Bass*,' Leah says. 'And *she's* amazing. There's going to be, like, seventy thousand people there.'

My heart squeezes with fear but I stay silent, smiling encouragingly instead. She doesn't notice; she's already pulling on her battered cowboy boots.

'Look after your sister,' I say to Reece as he straightens up and grabs a jacket he's not going to need. It's baking hot outside, the sky a thick film of grey cloud making everything sticky and humid. 'Please stay together.'

'You worry too much,' he says, planting a kiss on my forehead. And that's enough to quieten me and believe everything he tells me. My beguiling little angel.

'I don't mind driving you both.' I pick up my car keys. 'Come on, it's only forty minutes away and it will save you money.'

Leah is already at the door. 'We're picking my friends up on the way. Reece already ordered an Uber, and he's paying.'

Where does my boy get all his money? Reece has done some bar work over the summer, and he has his student loan, but that's not enough for all the exciting things he gets up to. Adam tells me I need to stop worrying about everything, but I've done the maths. I push a fifty-pound note into my son's hand and make a face that says, *Look after your sister*.

He grins and glances at his phone. 'Uber's here. Don't wait up, Mum.'

'Be home by midnight!' I shout down the garden path at their retreating backs. 'And stick together!'

Leah doesn't even turn around, let alone say goodbye.

The kids left three hours ago, and in that time I've cleaned the house, plucked my chin hairs, stacked the dishwasher, curled my hair, watched a YouTube tutorial on how to draw the perfect eyeliner, googled 'Slut Era' (to no avail) and done a few squats. I even considered opening my work email, but none of my colleagues work on a Sunday so I don't see why I should.

God, I really need a hobby.

I dial Adam again, expecting it to go to voicemail as usual, but this time he picks up.

'Hey, when are you coming home for lunch?' I ask. The sounds of birdsong and a lawnmower hum in the distance. 'I thought we could go to that new pub down the road?'

'Sorry, love. I've already eaten. Bert's having a barbeque.'

'Who?'

'Bert. You know, the old guy in the plot next to mine. He and Rashid invited me to have some burgers with them. They have beers too and an icebox.'

Adam has chosen Bert's burgers over me? I wait for him to invite me, not that I want to have a stupid barbeque over at his stupid allotment, but he doesn't say anything further. All I can hear is chewing.

'The kids have left for the festival,' I say. It sounds pathetic, even to me.

'That's nice, you're always saying how you never get any quiet time to yourself. Have fun.'

'What time are you home?'

'I have some seedlings to plant later, so I won't be back until dinner. What are you cooking?'

I haven't planned to cook anything but I say, 'Chicken.'

'Lovely. Oh, and don't forget, if you get bored later, why don't you do a spreadsheet of our finances so we can go through them tonight?'

I don't answer. Tears are stinging my eyes and whatever I plan to say next sticks in the back of my throat. I don't even know why I'm upset.

'Hello? Jules? Reception's pretty bad here,' he says. 'I'll see you tonight.'

He's gone and I stay rooted to the spot, staring at my phone as if I'll be able to see Adam, Bert and Rashid with their juicy burgers through my screen. I don't care that Adam's made new friends, or that we won't be eating at the fancy gastropub tonight; I care that he sounds happier than he's been for a long time.

I'm a terrible person.

I go back to the bedroom, throw myself on the bed and scroll through my phone. I hate social media. I have an account on most platforms, even though all I do is mindlessly flick through pictures of people I hardly know sharing news about things I don't really care about. There's a new app on my home screen. A big orange K. For a moment I don't recognise it, then I remember. Kandid. Desperate Fiona's confessions app.

I open it, but without my own account I can only read a few examples of people's posts. From the little I can see, it's pretty amusing. One woman works in a bar and every time her ex-boyfriend orders a drink, she spits in it. A straight mother of six is confessing to having a crush on her female Pilates teacher. And some old man has been throwing slugs and caterpillars over his garden fence because he hates his neighbour. So far, so harmless, but I want to read more.

To sign up all you need to do is create a username and

attach it to an email address; that's easy enough. No photo is required; in fact, anonymity is the rule and your username can't be your actual name. I sign up and call myself BoredAndCurious. There's space for a short bio asking who I am and how I spend my free time. Free time? I don't do anything besides work and be a mum.

I write the first thing that comes to my head: 'I love my family, reading, sunflowers and gin and tonics.' I may sound boring but it's better than sounding too interesting and attracting attention. I'm only here to be nosey. With a final click on the Save button, I sit on my bed and get comfortable. At least reading about other people's pathetic lives will make me feel better about my own.

I've been scrolling for ten minutes, but nothing is that entertaining; if anything, it's full of too many sad and lonely people. I want to be amused, not read about people like me. Lynsey said Fiona had narrowed down her searches to within her local area. Now *that* could be interesting. I'm pretty sure the guy at number thirty-five is leading a double life; it's not normal for someone to change their outfit that many times in one day.

I go to the filter section and choose users within ten miles of my house. There are also categories: Relationships, Sex, Family, Work, Hobbies and Other. Can all of human existence, our fears and hopes and joys, really be subcategorised so easily? I guess they can.

I click on Sex and start to read.

My boyfriend doesn't know this, but every time we make love, I imagine what it would be like to murder him.

Well, that's disturbing. I wonder how local this psycho is. The responses to her post are a mixed bag, a smattering of concern alongside comments from men telling her the poor boyfriend is clearly not satisfying her and then describing what they would do to keep her keen. I'm ashamed by how aroused I feel reading their lewd replies. Instead of ignoring them, as any sane woman on any other app would do, the original poster is responding to the pervs. And then it hits me: most of these confessions are probably made up. The woman wants attention, and the men want an excuse to describe their fantasies to a stranger in extreme detail.

So that's how Fiona has been meeting men on here. I wonder what she posted to get attention. Perhaps chemistry isn't physical; perhaps it's cerebral. Other dating apps start with a picture of someone's face and a list of interests, whereas this app lets you filter locally then bond over your deepest, darkest secrets without knowing who you're talking to.

Well, as my username implies, I'm certainly bored and curious. Let's see what kind of replies my post gets.

I start to type...

I'm in my late 40s and I don't think my husband finds me attractive anymore.

I stop, swallow and put my phone down.

This is a terrible idea and really bloody sad. I came on here to read other people's confessions, have a bit of fun, not use it like therapy. But is it really that terrible to crave a bit of attention? It's not real. It's not like anyone knows it's me. I bet people will tell me I'm being silly and that of course my husband still loves me. I'm forty-eight, for God's sake. I'm not *meant* to be sexy; I'm meant to be too busy, too confident, too important by now for any of that shallow nonsense to matter.

But what I really need to hear is that I'm right and Adam needs to appreciate me more. Perhaps someone on this sad little app will tell me how great I am, and I'll believe them. I take a deep breath and pick up my phone again.

We haven't had sex in over a year, and even though he clearly cares about me, every time I've hinted at it, he's completely ignored me. I'm scared to say how I feel out loud in case he admits that he no longer wants me. I wouldn't be able to deal with that. Am I really that unattractive?

Much like the other social media apps, you can add a picture. You're not allowed to upload photos of faces on Kandid – not your own or other people's – or any nudity (I think some kind of AI recognition picks that up), but you can add photos of your clothed body.

I took some lingerie selfies for Adam last year. It was during my lacy underwear phase, back when I thought some marital sexting could make a difference. My favourite photo was of me bending over in black suspenders, my buttocks perfectly round with just a hint of a thong visible. When I sent that one to Adam last year, his reply was one word: *Nice*. That was it. And he never mentioned it again.

I add the picture, close my eyes and hit Send. My phone begins to ping immediately. Thirty-two hearts and five comments. Seven. Ten. Fifteen. What the hell is happening? In under three minutes hundreds of people have liked my post, dozens have commented and I have five direct messages from various men.

I shuffle up my bed, plump up the pillows and get comfortable.

ELEVEN

LEAH

'One spliff.'

I'm trying to keep up with Reece, who's pushing his way through the crowds, Paige and Summer stumbling behind. Jacob texted Paige twenty minutes ago to say he's by the red tent, but all the music tents are red and looking for him is getting tedious now.

Reece stops. 'Leah, dude, back off.'

'Tell me how you sneaked them in.'

They checked our belongings when we entered the festival. Reece has a big bag full of food and drink – you're allowed to bring your own stuff as long as it's not alcohol – but I know he's dealing. How did he sneak drugs past security?

He raises his eyebrows and I cross my arms.

I'm wearing Mum's dress. I changed into it at Summer's house when we stopped to pick her up, but it's tighter than I realised with this bra and my boobs are spilling out.

Reece lowers his voice. 'Fine. I pre-rolled the joints and they're in the Pringles packets under a few crisps. But I'm not giving you any.'

I've never bought or taken drugs before; I just think it would look cool if I turned up with some when we reach Jacob and his mates.

'It's for my friends. They only want some Molly or coke or something.'

'What the hell, Leah!' Reece pulls me closer to him so no one can hear us. 'You know I only do natural stuff, weed and shrooms. I don't mess with any of that nasty crap.'

Well, *excuse me*, Mr Botany the organic dealer. I know he's growing weird plants over at Dad's allotment.

'Your friends take pills though,' I whisper back. 'Maybe I'll ask *them* for some.'

Reece grabs me by my wrist, and I make out he's hurting me. He's not. He's about as strong as a five-year-old.

'Not all of them are my friends,' he hisses. 'Some are really bad news. Keep away from them.'

'Fine, *you* sell me some, then. How much are mushrooms?'

'You're mental.'

'I'll tell Mum you're dealing.'

His mouth sets into a hard line. 'Then I'll tell her you're wearing her favourite dress that you clearly *stole* from her room.'

Touché. Prick.

Reece's face softens. 'You're going to have to stop following me. You're a big girl now, go watch the bands. That's why we're here, isn't it?'

No, I'm here to find my perfect man and Reece is here to make money.

Reece has this grand plan of making big bucks then going backpacking after uni and, according to him, drug-dealing is the fastest way to raise the cash. It also helps that he looks more like some Californian surfer than a middle-class philosophy student from Hertfordshire.

We're heading away from the music tents towards the chill-out area, not far from the camping ground. Reece loves camping, he's even taking his sleeping bag to Ibiza next week. He thinks he's some kind of Bear Grylls with his plant obsession and organic lifestyle. Weirdo.

Reece's friends have been here all weekend; we're the only ones who came only for the last day. That's Mum's fault. Dad was fine about me getting a Saturday ticket too and staying the night, but Mum had to keep bringing up the Nathan thing and saying how I need to understand the repercussions of my actions and can't be trusted. What actions? I liked a boy who didn't like me back. Big deal. She's acting like I'm a serial killer or something. They were going to make me sell my ticket until valiant Reece, the big brother hero, insisted that he'd go to Carnage just for the Sunday and he'd take me – even though I know he wanted to be here all weekend. But that's Reece for you. Always the golden boy.

A cheer goes up as we reach my brother's friends. There are loads of them. Some I recognise from his Instagram posts, most of them I don't. None of them have normal names; they're all called things like Bunny, Dronk and Jug Head. A speaker is hooked up to someone's phone and it's blasting old-school indie music.

'Here,' Reece says, handing me something. I think it's going to be a joint but it's a packet of plain M&Ms. I prefer the peanut ones. 'Go and play with your friends.'

Knobhead.

Reece's friends don't acknowledge me or my friends standing behind him, looking like a gaggle of stupid kids waiting to be invited to the grown-ups' table. Within a minute my brother is already surrounded by guys passing him food and drink and buying weed off him. I've never seen him look so happy.

Paige's phone pings. She leans close to me, her mouth by my ear.

'Jacob and the rest of them are waiting by the green flag

now,' she says, pointing at something in the distance. 'I said we'd go and meet them there.'

Summer is also checking her phone, probably texting a bunch of girls she knows. No way am I going to trail behind either of them like some third wheel when all they care about is getting felt up before the Lil Bass set.

'Beer?' Someone is holding a bottle out to me.

It's a boy. Well, more of a man. He looks in his early twenties. My stomach flips as I take him in. He's sitting on an upturned bucket, cradling a guitar, his dark hair held back with a red bandana. I accept the beer but just hold it. It's cold and sweating in my hands, threatening to slip through my fingers. I grip tighter.

It's him.

This is the guy I drew a picture of in the letter I burned.

Destiny. Fate. Magic. My spell worked.

TWELVE

LEAH

'I'm going to stay,' I say to my friends, opening the M&Ms and putting one in my mouth. 'Go ahead, I'll catch up with you later. Lil Bass isn't on until seven anyway.'

They look at me, at Bucket Boy, then back at me again.

Summer nods once. She approves.

Paige goes to say something then stops herself. 'Cool,' she says. 'You got everything?'

I nod. The guy with the guitar is no longer looking at me, so he has no idea we're talking about condoms, but I'm fully prepared.

'I'll call you when I'm done,' I say. 'I won't be long.'

Summer sniggers. 'Well, for your sake, I hope that's not true.' Then, with a parting wave, they're gone.

Reece has his back to me, talking to his friends, so I sit down next to Bucket Boy, who's plucking a few chords on his guitar.

'Cheers,' I say, tapping my bottle against the empty one by his feet. 'Want some chocolate?'

He hasn't heard me. He has his eyes closed, like the music he's playing is too unbearably sweet. It sounds like an Oasis song. My dad listens to Oasis. I think all their songs sound the same. A few more people wander over. One wraps her arms around Bucket Boy's neck and nuzzles him.

'I got you a bean burger,' she says.

He hooks his arm around the back of her head and pulls her close until they're making out over his shoulder. Big slurpy kisses, wet tongues, groans, right in front of me. I take a swig of my beer and look away. I don't think I like beer. It tastes of wet bread.

After a few more seconds of uncomfortable kissing, the guy with the guitar and his girlfriend wander off with their bean burgers and I'm left sitting on the dry grass beside an upturned bucket and dozens of empty beer bottles full of cigarette butts. Paige and Summer have already melted into the crowd, and I no longer know where my brother is.

'Can I sit down?'

I look up but can't see who's talking because the sun is shining in my eyes. The hazy silhouette plonks himself down on the bucket and I blink until he comes into focus. He laughs softly, looking over his shoulder at the boy in the bandana. 'There's always some prick with a guitar.'

The silhouette hardens into the shape of a man with a kind face. I think he's one of the guys who was buying weed off Reece earlier. His hair is a halo of dark curls, his skin tanned, his shorts baggy and frayed around the edges. He pushes his hair away from his face and gives me a lazy smile.

He's holding a camping mug. It smells like coffee.

'Dylan,' he says.

My mouth goes dry. I take a gulp from my beer bottle and swallow.

'Leah.'

He puts his coffee down, pulls something out of his pocket and starts to skin up.

'You with them?' he asks, nodding over at Reece's friends.

I shrug. 'Yeah. Kind of.' I test out my first lie. 'Uni friends.'

Dylan doesn't even flinch. Summer and Paige were right, I *do* look older than nearly seventeen.

'Do you go to uni with any of them?' I ask.

I take in his perfectly bowed lips and strong hands and clean fingernails. He runs the tip of his tongue along the Rizla paper, and I feel my cheeks tingle.

'No, I hardly know them. I'm friends with Bunny's brother's friend,' he says. 'We all went to Leeds together years ago. What about you? You in your last year?'

I nod. What does that make me? Twenty-one? He must be twenty-four or twenty-five. He doesn't appear to know my brother, so that's good. I squint into the distance at Reece laughing at something someone has said. What if he sees me and comes over and says something? He'll give the game away, probably do something embarrassing like tell this guy to stay away from me. I keep one eye on my brother, but he's so wrapped up in what his friend is saying he's totally forgotten about babysitting me. I smile at the thought of what our mum would think if she saw us both right now, witnessing how her perfect boy is actually an irresponsible, selfish dick.

'You drinking coffee?' I ask, pointing at the mug at Dylan's feet.

He gives a light laugh, a rumble that hits me straight in the belly. 'Yeah. Heavy night last night.' He leans closer to me. 'I'll let you into a little secret: I'm a bit of a coffee wanker. I only drink certain blends, so I brought my own. I'm an addict.' He holds up the perfectly rolled joint. 'Coffee and weed.'

'Chocolate is mine. M&M?' I hold out the near-empty packet.

He recoils. 'Are they peanut?'

I shake my head, and he smiles.

'I'll stick to weed, thanks.'

I look down at the dry grass, water droplets trickling down my half-empty beer at my feet, my cheeks stinging red. Why did

I ever think this grown man would be interested in a kid like me?

Dylan lights up his spliff and takes a long, deep drag.

'Want some?'

'I'm not... I don't know...'

Oh God, I sound like such a baby. It's not that I don't want any, I do, but the one time I tried, I coughed so much my throat felt like singed paper. I don't want to do it wrong and look stupid in front of someone who has the most kissable lips ever.

'I'm not very good at smoking,' I say.

Dylan smiles again, making two deep lines appear on his cheeks. He has light stubble, and his eyes are three shades lighter when he's facing the sun. I thought they were brown but now they look like amber.

He beckons me over with the crook of his finger and I sit up on my knees.

'Open your mouth,' he says.

My heart is racing. I look behind me, but Reece still has his back to me. Dylan leans closer and gently blows the smoke into my mouth.

'Hold it,' he says. 'Hold it a bit longer. That's right. Now breathe out.'

I grin as smoke escapes between my teeth.

'You nervous?' he asks. 'You keep looking behind you.'

Great, now I look like some pathetic kid scared to do drugs in the open.

I need to think of something believable. 'My ex is here.'

Dylan isn't at all fazed.

'Want to go to my tent?' He takes another drag. 'We can smoke in private there.'

Five minutes sitting beside a total stranger and it's that easy to get him alone? He's waiting for an answer, his gaze flickering from my eyes to my mouth to my cleavage. I can see why Mum really liked this dress.

I jump up, hold out my hand, and he takes it. My chest burns from the smoke, my throat is scratchy, and I'm dizzy with anticipation.

'Here,' he says, handing me a daisy he plucked from the grass.

Who is this guy? I grasp the stem of the delicate flower. I want to keep it, but I don't have a pocket. I contemplate putting it in my bag, but Dylan is already leading me away from everyone and the daisy falls to the floor. There's no way a man who gives a girl flowers and brings his own coffee to a music festival is dangerous.

'This way,' he says, leading us farther away from the rest of the gang towards a sea of different-sized tents. His hand is smooth in mine. Like it belongs there.

People talk about turning points, life's crossroads, but they never recognise when they're at them. I can. This is the part where my life changes forever and I can't turn back. I'm about to lose my virginity and Dylan has absolutely no idea that I've chosen him to be my first. The thrill of my lie emboldens me, and as we slow down outside a shiny blue tent big enough for four people, I tell him we should get inside. He gives me a wolfish smile, making my insides turn to molten lava and spill into a hot pool between my legs.

Inside, the tent smells of sweat and dirty underwear and hot grass, but I ignore it as I sit beside him on a sleeping bag. My heart is beating so fast I feel like I'm going to vomit. I could really do with some water. There are some bottles of Evian in my bag. No, there aren't, they're vodka and I forgot to buy Fanta.

Dylan motions for me to move closer. He runs his thumb over my lips until they part, cupping my face with both hands as he blows more smoke into my mouth. I'm light-headed and this time I don't know if it's from the weed or my mouth being so close to his. He really thinks I'm twenty-one. This hot guy thinks I'm experienced and wild and fun.

As I breathe in the smoke, I lean forward until I'm kissing him. It's perfection. Nothing like the 'spin the bottle' games I've played in the past, or any of the inexperienced boys I've dated who practically ate my face. Dylan kisses slowly, like he wants to savour me. He tastes of coffee and weed mixed with the chocolate I've been eating.

Then his hands are in my hair, slipping my dress straps over my shoulders, tugging at them until the dress and my bra are around my waist and I can feel the warm air on my chest. He still hasn't broken contact with my lips, and I don't want to open my eyes. He moves his hands along my legs and over my hips, pushing up my dress, and the whole time I'm thinking I should be doing something back. Should I pull at his t-shirt? Should I say something? But at the same time, I want to stay present in this moment. I want to remember it all, every detail, because I know I might never see him again.

His hands gently part my legs. 'You sure?' he mumbles as his mouth moves down my neck, over my collarbone, and closes in over my left nipple.

I suck in air and nod.

'We're both stoned, Leah,' he says. 'I need to hear you say the words.'

I push him back a little and look into his eyes. His beautiful eyes.

'I want this,' I say. 'I want you, Dylan. Right now. All of it.'

We lie down on the sleeping bags, and I don't care that they're damp and stink of stale beer; his hands and lips are soft against my skin, and I feel safe. He takes his t-shirt off and pulls down his shorts, but I don't have the chance to wonder what I should be doing or if he thinks I'm inexperienced or bad at this because he's already sliding down my underwear.

This is it.

The condom is on.

I hold my breath.

He gets into position, he's inside me, but it's nothing like the movies. He moves in and out and it's OK, not too painful, but I'm not seeing fireworks. It's all a bit repetitive, to be honest.

We keep kissing, I like that part, and he keeps mumbling my name over and over in time with each stride. He half-heartedly tries to stroke between my legs, but everything is numb from the weed and all I keep thinking is, *I'm having sex. I'm actually having sex.* By the time I decide to try and enjoy it, he's already groaned into my hair and rolled off me.

'Sorry,' he mumbles. 'I'm so high.'

He slips the condom off, expertly ties a knot at the end, and lies there with his arm over his face. Completely naked. Like we've been together forever. He's got the body of a man. I want to stare at it, every sinewy muscle and hair and the way his tan marks stop at his biceps and neck, but he's gone quiet and I'm not sure what I'm meant to do now. Do I stay and talk? Maybe I should kiss him, and we can go again. He's breathing heavily, his eyes drooping like he's trying not to fall asleep.

The condom is coiled up by my head like the gelatinous skin of a snake. I poke at it. It's still warm. Without Dylan seeing, I pick it up and slip it into my bag – proof that I didn't imagine the most important moment of my life.

'I better go,' I say, pulling on my dress. 'My friends are waiting for me.'

He turns to me, his pupils big and round.

'You're going? Wait. What's your Insta?'

'I don't have an account.' It's a lie. I love Instagram, but he'll know as soon as he looks at it that I lied about my age.

He props himself up on his elbows, his head tipping to one side as he takes me in properly for the first time. I think he still likes what he sees. 'Where do you live?'

'Hestington in Hertfordshire.'

He smiles. 'I don't live far from there.' My stomach is fizzing. This has got to be a sign.

'Leave me your number,' he says, handing me his phone.

I type in my name and number then hand it back. Good job I didn't make one up because he calls me and grins.

'Now you have mine.'

He's serious about me. The magic worked.

I shuffle out of the tent, adjusting my clothes as I go. The strap of my dress is hanging on by a thread where he couldn't get it over my chest, but it doesn't matter, I'll fix it before I put it back in my mum's wardrobe.

At the entrance to the tent, I turn around to say goodbye, but Dylan's already asleep. He looks like a slumbering angel. I take a photo of him, just his top half. His arm and hair are covering most of his handsome face, but I still manage to capture a moment. A snapshot in time. The first man who wanted me and had me and enjoyed it.

I now have another token of those I've loved to add to my collection.

THIRTEEN
JULES

The last week has gone fast and it's the weekend again. Most people live for the weekends, but I actually enjoy weekdays. I like going to work Monday to Thursday, feeling like a human being with ideas – not just the person who knows what we're all having for dinner. And I especially like Fridays, my non-working day. I tell myself that's the day I clean and do admin, but the truth is I normally spend it reading or occasionally enjoying a solo cinema treat.

It's the weekends that are hard. The two days a week when I'm reminded my kids and husband hate me. While everyone else is having fun, Facebook-worthy days out, I'm normally stuck at home alone doing all the boring stuff I should have got done on Friday but couldn't be bothered with.

I've been on Kandid every evening this week, distracting myself from Leah acting even more weird than normal and Reece flying off to Ibiza yesterday to celebrate his twenty-first without us. I got a lot of responses to my post. Some were genuine and helpful – women sharing their own marital issues or telling me that I should talk to Adam or leave him. Two things I'm equally scared of doing. But I didn't post for advice; I posted because I wanted a reaction to my photo, and I didn't have to wait long for that.

The app doesn't give you a lot of space for comments, so most replies are emojis or a short sentence. This means that if you want to write more than a few words, you need to send that person a direct message. Within a few hours my inbox was flooded with messages from men.

> If I had an ass like that in my bed, I'd never let you go. Leave your husband and let's meet up.

> You need a good fuck. You know what I'd do to you? First of all...

> I can't believe there are men out there with good-looking women they can't satisfy. BoredAndCurious, you won't be either of those things when I get hold of you.

It's not cheating if the messages are just one way and I don't reply to any of them. I'm not here to have an affair.

Some of the messages describe in detail how each man would pleasure me, and they worked. These strangers, men who only live a few miles from me, have no idea their words make me feel attractive in a way my husband hasn't managed to do in a long time. But none of this means I don't love Adam or would ever leave him. If anything, my little experiment proves that I'm better off miserable at home with a husband who only notices me when we run out of loo roll than having to make an effort with dead-beat divorcees who write erotic fan fiction to strangers on confessions apps.

'What do you think?' Leah asks, whipping back the curtain of the changing room cubicle. She's standing before me in a little tight gold dress looking like a Victoria's Secret model. I don't think I'll ever get used to my sixteen-year-old daughter being a fully grown woman already. When did her chest get bigger than mine?

'Where on earth would you wear that?' I say.

She rolls her eyes but agrees, shutting the curtain again. Leah has been acting strange since coming back from Carnage Festival. Strange in a good way. She's still glued to her phone, as usual, but she's been in a less grumpy mood. Positively chirpy, in fact. So much so she suggested this shopping day together.

She comes back out again, this time in a crop top and skirt so short it skims her knicker line.

'Seriously?'

She groans. 'You don't know what's fashionable anymore.'

'Shoes, Leah. You said you needed new shoes for school.'

'Well, there aren't many shoe shops in this place.'

I hold in a sigh. We arrived at the new shopping mall early because I said I'd only take her if we went before the hordes of teen girls descended, and she agreed as long as we had lunch at Wagamama. But so far all I've done is sit in changing rooms telling my daughter I'm not buying her clothes that look like they came from the costume department of *Hustlers*.

'We should have gone to that place in Watford. They have a wider selection,' I say.

'But the shops here are cooler.'

They are exactly the same shops.

'You don't even need this many clothes,' I say, holding up the three paper bags I've somehow ended up paying for *and* carrying. 'You'll still have to wear a uniform in sixth form.'

She sticks her head out between the two curtains. Even though she's wearing no make-up and hasn't brushed her hair today, just gathered it up into a ball on top of her head and secured it with a scrunchie, she still looks radiant. It's irritating.

'There isn't a uniform, just a blazer while in class. I can wear what I want under it.'

'Not that,' I say, pointing at yet another crotch-skimming number.

She's not listening to me. She's scrolling through her phone again, smiling.

Leah and I have hardly spent any time together this summer, so I jumped at her suggestion of a day out together. I saw it as a chance to re-enact all those mother–daughter bonding dreams I had from the day I found out our second child was going to be a girl. I imagined us walking through the mall, arms linked, slurping boba tea or licking ice cream. Maybe even getting sushi together while she tells me about her latest crush.

Instead, she's been texting her friends non-stop and the only time she's paid me any attention has been when she's needed me to pay for something.

'Fine, I'll get you the top,' I say so I can see her face light up. It does, but not for long.

We leave the blaring music of the shop and head past the food hall. Wagamama isn't far from here and my stomach is already grumbling. I went without breakfast because I read somewhere that fasting from dinner to lunch the next day helps shed the last few pounds. So far all it's done is make me light-headed and hangry.

'Here.' I pass Leah the hairbrush I keep in my bag. I have no idea how she can walk and text without knocking into anyone. 'Sort your hair out, it's going to get knotted.'

She waves my hand away, looking agitated.

'You still haven't told me about the festival,' I say. 'Did you have fun?'

'Yeah. It was good.'

Maybe she met a boy there. Is that why she's been holed up in her room all week? She's never mentioned boys to me before. Not even when she got totally obsessed by that Nathan kid. The idea of a boy touching my baby makes my skin itch.

'Are you and your friends OK?' I ask.

'Yeah.'

'You've not seen them all week.'

'Paige has been with Jacob loads because he's leaving school to go to that sixth form college in Stevenage. And Summer went to France with her mum for the week.'

'Excited about school on Monday?'

She shrugs, her thumbs still a blur as she keeps typing. Two men in their early thirties walk past us then look back. For a moment I think it's me they're checking out, then realise it's my child. They've melted into the crowd before I have a chance to say something.

'Does that happen often?' I ask.

'What?' she says without looking up from her screen.

'Men eyeing you up?'

She gives a light laugh. 'Yeah, loads. Old men are perverts.'

Old men. They were at least fifteen years younger than me.

'You know I'd never let anything happen to you, right? Leah! Are you even listening to me?'

There's a queue outside the restaurant, but it's only a few people. We join the back. If Leah isn't going to get off her phone, then I may as well check mine. Adam has messaged me.

Please grab some milk on your way home

Romantic.

There's an email from work too. It was sent yesterday by my boss, Steve. He's in a flap because we're launching the new necklace collection in the spring, and he wants to discuss some things with me and the marketing team on Monday before we get the ball rolling. He's sent a meeting request. I don't reply. It's Saturday. I'm exerting my boundaries.

'I've got to go,' Leah says, rifling through the bags at my feet and stuffing something into the pocket of her tracksuit bottoms.

'What? Where?' I say.

'Can I have that hairbrush, please?'

I pass it to her, and she frantically pulls at her hair, holding it at the roots so it doesn't snag.

'Where are you going?'

'Seeing my friends.'

'Now? But we're about to have lunch!'

We've reached the front of the queue.

'Table for two?' the woman in the black t-shirt asks us.

I nod, but Leah is still speed-typing with one thumb while brushing her hair with the other.

I head towards a table, but Leah doesn't follow.

'I really have to go,' she says.

'Where are you going? And how are you going to get there?'

She drops my hairbrush in one of the shopping bags I'm carrying and gives me a one-armed hug.

'Bus. I won't be late,' she says.

'But you said your friends were busy. Is this about a boy?' I shout out at her retreating back, but she's already disappeared.

'Table for one,' I say to the server.

She takes away the other paper place mat and cutlery and gives me a sad look.

I take out my phone. I've received five more messages on Kandid.

My kid isn't the only one with secrets on her phone.

FOURTEEN
LEAH

Dylan texted me on Monday. Literally the day after Carnage. It was only a 'Hey' and I thought he'd mistook me for someone else. There was no point replying anyway – it's not like we could ever be a couple after I lied about my age.

Then on Wednesday he texted again.

Leah. I can't stop thinking about you.

I couldn't ignore that. We started texting back and forth, and he was so funny and flirty. On Thursday he asked me for a topless selfie. I'm not basic so I sent him one of me in a red bra. I mean, it's not like he's not seen my body before. I'm also not stupid so didn't show my face. I'm still paranoid he might know people who know my brother.

I kept telling myself it was only a bit of fun, that I won't fall for him, but it's hard not to when he keeps telling me how beautiful I am, and how he wishes he could have a chance to make love to me again, but properly this time. I think he feels bad about how crap it was at the festival. Not that it was his fault – we were both stoned.

I keep thinking back to what Pat, the school therapist, told me about making sure that my infatuation is reciprocated, so I asked Dylan when his birthday is and did our star sign compatibility. I'm a Virgo and he's a Scorpio! Everyone knows that means we're *really* compatible, especially sexually. He's really into me *and* it's written in the stars. So suck on that, Pat.

Dylan kept inviting me to his house and I said no. There was no point us meeting again when our relationship has no future. But then this morning in the changing room, while Mum was being a nag about what I can and can't wear, Dylan left me a voice note. As soon as I heard his voice, my stomach twisted into a giant knot. He promised me his message would be the last time he'd ask to see me then he'd leave me alone as he was obviously annoying me.

I texted him back straight away asking for his address. Poor Dylan, thinking I don't like him when I'm just nervous that our relationship is based on a lie. But what if he doesn't care? I'm nearly seventeen. We're not breaking any laws.

Luckily Mum had already bought me all the clothes I needed, so our day together was more or less over. Getting away from her was easy. I lied about seeing my friends, grabbed the nice underwear and crop top she'd bought me, and ran to the bus stop. His road is literally one of the stops on my route home.

On the way out of the shopping centre I stopped at Boots to put on some make-up using their samples, got changed in the toilets, and now here I am outside his house on a Saturday lunchtime smelling of free perfume and wearing new knickers.

Except I don't feel so brave now. I actually feel a bit sick.

What if he didn't mean it? What if it was all a joke and he's looking at me through the window of his flat right now laughing at how stupid I am? What if this isn't even his house?

A head pokes out of the top-floor window. It's him.

'Push the door,' he shouts. 'The lock's broken.'

Dylan lives in a tall townhouse converted into three flats.

He said in his texts that he has a small studio on the top floor with views over the rooftops of town. A proper adult.

The stairs are covered in worn green carpet, the walls tinted a faint yellow with age, and the air smells of curry and flowery air freshener. My legs are aching by the time I reach the top floor and then suddenly there's Dylan, taking up the entire doorway, his hair a riot of curls framing his stubbly face. He's barefoot, wearing baggy shorts and a faded Sex Pistols t-shirt.

I didn't expect to, but I feel shy. This man had his lips on my chest, his tongue in my mouth. He was literally inside of me, yet I'm standing here like I've never met him before.

'Hi,' he says.

'Hi.'

FIFTEEN

LEAH

'Sorry it's a bit of a mess,' Dylan says as we step into his flat. 'I just moved in.'

It's a studio flat with a kitchen in one corner and the bed and sofa separated by a bookshelf. He has a chess board set up, and a guitar propped up in the corner, and the whole place is covered in art. There are paintings waiting to be framed, and canvases hanging or leaning against the walls, with jam jars of water and paintbrushes scattered nearby.

I wander around the room, smelling the pots of turpentine and peering closer at the artwork.

'Michelangelo?' I say, running my finger over a framed print of the ceiling of the Sistine Chapel.

'I'm a big fan.'

I sense him watching me. It feels so different to when we were sitting in the sunshine at Carnage, chatting, flirting, breathing in the smoke he was blowing into my mouth. That was laid back; this is coiled tight. I shiver.

'Are these your paintings?' I ask.

I want to tell him I also love art, and that I can draw too, but

I don't want to be one of those 'pick me' girls. I don't know what I'm meant to do, or what will impress him the most.

'Yeah, I like to paint,' he says. 'When I like things, I get a bit obsessed. Art, coffee...'

'Weed?' I add, pointing at the table where he's been skinning up.

Dylan laughs. 'Don't you get obsessed with anything?'

He has no idea.

He offers me a coffee from some fancy coffee machine in his kitchen – one of those complicated ones you see in cafés. It takes up half the counter.

'Smell,' he says, holding out a handful of beans.

I sniff and make an appreciative noise, but it just smells of coffee. He then goes on about how Guatemalan beans are better than Colombian, or something. I don't know, I'm not really listening because I'm transfixed by the curve of his lips and the way his dimples appear and disappear as he speaks.

He pours the beans into the top of the machine, and they start to whizz around.

'How do you like your coffee?'

I'm not going to tell him the only drinks I order in Starbucks are covered in cream and three different syrups.

'Black, no sugar,' I say, my tummy clenching because he looks really impressed with my answer.

'That's how I like it too.'

I grin. I got it right.

'So? What do you think?' he asks as I take a sip.

I make a face like I'm really amazed by the intricate flavours, when in reality it's bitter and tastes of burned earth.

'Every morning at seven o'clock, after my run, I have two cups of my favourite blend. Even on the weekends,' he says. 'And I take a thermal cup to work with me too. I can't stand that instant stuff. That's not real coffee.'

Did he invite me over just to talk about coffee? I take

another sip of my scalding, acrid drink, trying to think of something to say. Anything. After what feels like forever, he signals that we move to the sofa, and we sit down side by side. My knee is touching his, but he isn't doing anything. Maybe he doesn't like me anymore. Maybe I shouldn't be here, alone, with a grown man.

'You look pretty,' he says.

He's lying because I'm wearing tracksuit bottoms and my new top, nothing special, and my hair isn't even brushed properly. We sit in silence, drinking, staring at nothing. But as the minutes pass I notice his glances at me are becoming more frequent, more intense, his eyes growing as dark as his coffee. He does want more. I can feel it, like a buzz emanating off him, as if my sitting next to him is enough to turn him on.

I finish my coffee and edge closer, my leg pressing against his, and his jaw tenses and twitches. I knew I wasn't imagining it.

Maybe he's waiting for *me* to make the first move. I stroke his cheek and he leans into it, his breathing deepening, his eyelids drooping.

'Kiss me,' I say, and he does.

He pushes me against the sofa and he's heavy and strong and this time he means it with his whole body.

When I push him away, his eyes widen, but he doesn't say anything.

I smile and he relaxes. OK, so this is a game.

'Stand up.'

And he does. I join him but keep my distance, his gaze never leaving mine. He steps closer and I step back. He tries to kiss me, but I shake my head. His smile widens.

'On your knees,' I whisper.

'Anything for you, Leah.'

Really? Anything? We'll see about that.

SIXTEEN

JULES

I've made too much spaghetti.

Leah texted and said to save her dinner as she was staying at Paige's a bit longer. Didn't she say her friend was in France? Or was that Summer? Maybe it's a boy she's gone to meet. Oh no, please don't let her do anything stupid again. I called but she didn't answer, as usual.

The crunch of the key in the door signals Adam is home. He walks into the kitchen and kisses the top of my head. He smells of tomatoes and fresh dirt.

'Where are the kids?'

He never knows where our children are. It astounds me that he, the other half of the parental unit, can wander through life so free and easy without a constant checklist in his head of what our children are doing, where they are and what they need. I guess that burden only needs to be carried by one of us. Me.

'Reece is in Ibiza.'

'Oh, right, of course. Did he have a nice birthday yesterday?'

Did Adam not message him? I did, but Reece only sent a smiley face back. No message.

'It looks like he's having fun. Leah showed me some photos he sent her of a giant punch bowl with sparklers. She's at Paige's house.'

Adam has already left the room, even though I'm halfway through a sentence. I follow him into the bedroom, where he's stripping off his gardening clothes. From behind, you'd never guess he was in his mid-forties. His back is tanned where he's been digging in the sun all summer, his arms thick and strong. He can sense me watching and looks over his shoulder. This would be the perfect time to reach out for me. To pull me into a lingering kiss as we stumble into the shower together. He doesn't.

'I made spaghetti,' I say.

God. Everything that comes out of my mouth is so dull.

Adam is down to his boxer shorts. What would he do if I reached into his underwear and told him how much I wanted him? But I can't stand the thought of him pushing me away, so I do nothing. All those men on my phone thirsting over me, men probably younger than my husband telling me what they would like to do to me based on nothing more than a photo of my bottom adorned in black lace, yet my own husband sticks to small talk and polite formalities.

'Did you say spaghetti?' he says. 'Sorry. I'm not hungry. Rashid has a pizza oven on his allotment. He brought home-made dough and mozzarella with him then we picked tomatoes and basil from the greenhouses and made our own pizzas. Isn't that incredible? You should come over one weekend, Jules. You'll love it.'

Rashid has a pizza oven. Well, who can compete with that?

I don't say anything as I walk back to the kitchen, put the dinner I made into the largest Tupperware we have and put it in the fridge.

I place two slices of stale bread in the toaster and look for the Marmite. There's only a dribble left inside, but it will do. I wasn't that hungry anyway.

Adam is watching one of his documentaries on the History Channel while I scroll through my phone beside him on the sofa. Why hasn't Leah texted me? She should be home by now. I look at TikTok to see what she's been up to. She doesn't know I have an account – it isn't in my name and there's nothing on it. I don't even follow her, but every day I look at her page. I've never told anyone I do this. I know it's dishonest but after what happened with that boy Nathan, I like to keep an eye on her. I'm her mum; it's important I know what's happening in her life. Every time I ask her how she is, she shrugs or gives me a monosyllabic answer. Then I go on TikTok and see her having the time of her life dancing with friends, making videos about her days out, sharing her innermost thoughts with millions of strangers. I shouldn't have to check bloody social media to understand my own child.

She's been quiet online this week though. She made a few videos at Carnage Festival, which were fun to watch, but since then she's not posted anything. Surely if she's been with her friends all day, she'd have created some funny skit or recorded a dance or something?

'Has Leah texted you?' I ask Adam.

He looks confused, like he doesn't know who I'm talking about.

'No, why?'

Indeed. Why should he need to worry when I do enough for the both of us? I change the subject.

'What's the show about?'

He mutters something about Cleopatra without taking his eyes off the screen.

I go back to my phone. The BBC news site is nothing but

doom and gloom: murder rates are rising, and online extortion has become the new mugging. I flick through all social media, nothing interesting, then hover over the Kandid logo. I've been trying to ignore it, but I find myself yearning for the hit of a new message. The validation. The thrill of someone finally seeing me.

There's a green dot beside my inbox. I click on it. It's someone going by the name of Viper.

> Your husband is mad. If you were in my bed every night, those tiny little panties wouldn't be on for long. I can see you live local. Let's go for a drink. Instead of telling you what I'd do to you, I could bend you over and show you.

I glance at Adam, his gaze transfixed on the re-enactment of Egyptian burial customs. I read the message again, crossing my legs and squeezing them together. There's a man, somewhere nearby, who finds me attractive.

Whereas Adam, who is right there beside me, hasn't glanced in my direction for twenty minutes. Every inch of my body is tingling with the thought of what this stranger wants to do to me. Where did things go so wrong that I'm reading lascivious messages from men I don't know while sitting next to my husband?

Someone has added another comment beneath my photo.

> Her husband is probably cheating on her lol

'Jules?'

I jump at the sound of his voice. He's nodding at the remote control, which I pass to him with a weak smile. It's fine. Adam and I are fine. It's just a passing blip. Viper and his smutty fan fiction is a phase, and I'll get over it soon enough.

I place my phone on the sofa beside me.

'Have you thought about Leah's birthday?' I ask my husband, knowing full well he doesn't even know when his daughter's seventeenth birthday is.

He puts the TV on mute.

'Her birthday isn't for another two months,' he says.

'Tenth of September. Tomorrow's the last day of August, it's not far away.'

He makes a face as if to say that's news to him.

'Are you thinking of throwing a party?' he asks.

'Yes, with balloons, a clown and a bouncy castle in the garden. Adam, are you even listening?'

He turns the volume of the documentary back up. My sarcasm is lost on him.

'I bought her tickets to that band she likes,' I shout over the commentary. 'Maybe I should book the same restaurant we went to last year. The Golden Orchid, wasn't it? Or maybe invite her friends over for a takeaway?'

'Whatever you want,' he mumbles.

I glance at my phone. There's a response to the last comment.

Doubt he's cheating. Why would anyone go out for a burger when they have steak at home?

That ain't steak, mate. That's some old bit of chunky mutton!

Mutton. That's me they're talking about. That's my lumpy body I asked complete strangers to judge me by. Three dots appear below Viper's sordid private message, which he clearly hasn't finished writing yet. I wait, re-reading the mutton message again. People are adding the laughing emoji below it.

My phone buzzes. Viper again. I scan what he's written, something about pussy and tongues and fingers. None of this is sexy anymore. I feel dirty. Stupid. Pathetic. These people don't know me; they don't even care about the person behind the salacious photo. I'm nothing but a worthless old woman to them, someone so in need of attention she's offered herself up for their amusement.

I put my phone down and turn my attention back to Adam's programme, words washing over me, my eyes blurring with tears. I blink, and blink, and blink. My husband doesn't move. I'm invisible. Adam would probably be happier watching his documentary alone. I can't even think of something to talk about that will make him as animated as Cleopatra or Rashid and his organic pizzas.

My phone buzzes next to me again and I pick it back up.

No wonder her husband doesn't want her anymore. Imagine being married to someone this desperate. Embarrassing.

A pained yelp escapes my mouth as I throw my phone on the sofa and run to the toilet. I can't let Adam see me cry.

SEVENTEEN

LEAH

Dylan's arm is snaked around my waist. He pulls me towards him until my back is flush with his chest.

'What are you doing to me?' he murmurs into my neck. 'You're driving me crazy.'

I close my eyes and smile. He can't see that I'm smiling but I know he knows. We've been making love all afternoon. Not like at the festival, but properly, slowly like I was actually there. I finally get it. I get what all the fuss is about.

And now, curled up together in his huge bed, all I want to do is fall asleep wrapped in his arms, but I can't. Mum has called three times already and she's going to totally lose it if I'm not back before dark.

'Crazy about me, huh?' I say, twisting in his arms to face him.

He kisses me, hard and deep, and I feel drunk with all this power he's given me.

'I have to go,' I say.

His arms tighten around my waist.

'Stay.'

What we have, what I'm feeling right now, this is it. Not

whatever stupid things Paige gets up to with Jacob or Summer with her crushes. This is the real thing. I normally tell my best friends everything. With Nathan, I updated them on every glance and everything he'd ever said to me. But what Dylan and I have already feels too sacred, too private, too delicate to risk handing over to my friends. All I told them was that I'd had sex with some stoner at Carnage and that it was fine; they probably still think it's Bucket Boy. I showed them the condom – they told me I was disgusting and to throw it away, and they've not mentioned it since. If I go into detail about what Dylan and I have been up to today, I know they'll judge me for leading him on and say that it will end badly because he doesn't know my real age. But they wouldn't understand. They never understood about Nathan.

'I have to go. I'm going back to uni tomorrow,' I say.

'Already? I thought classes don't start until late September.'

Crap. I stay silent and he doesn't press me for an answer, just holds me tighter.

'How long will I have to wait until we can do this again?'

My stomach clenches. He has no idea how much I want to stay here forever and never let him go.

'I thought you have a new job to get ready for,' I say, rubbing my nose against his. 'Didn't you say you start on Monday?'

He flips on to his back and groans.

'Yeah. I'm getting my hair cut tomorrow.'

'No! Don't cut it. Your hair is so cute.' I run my fingers through it, and he leans into my touch.

'Cute,' he says, and laughs.

I watch him as he gets out of bed and heads for the shower. I take it all in for the last time: the dip of his waist, the ripple of muscle across his shoulder blades, the way his hair is damp and sticking to the back of his neck.

'Want to join me?' he says.

Can he feel the weight of my stare?

I get up to follow, but then my phone lights up, Mum's name flashing across the screen. Does she ever give up?

The water is already running, Dylan is waiting for me, but I can't. It's already getting dark. I'm not sure if he hears me as I shout goodbye, but I can't say it to his face because I know I won't be able to resist him. If I don't go now, I'll never be able to walk away from him. Today has been perfect and I want to keep it that way. If I fall for him any more than I already have, he'll end up learning the truth, and it will break his heart.

I go to close the front door behind me and that's when I see it – a key hanging off a wooden keyring shaped like a marijuana leaf. It's not his door key; that one is still in the door. This one must be a spare or something. I pick it up and place it in my pocket. The leaf reminds me of when we met and of his love of weed, and the key is symbolic because he'll always have the key to my heart. I may not get to keep Dylan, but at least I'll always have this small part of him.

Something else to add to my collection.

EIGHTEEN
JULES

Saturday night Leah came home a lot later than she said she would, then slept most of Sunday. When she wasn't in bed, she was grinning into her phone and giggling at whatever she was reading. I asked her if she'd met someone, and if so not to rush into anything. She rolled her eyes and slammed the bedroom door behind her. Now it's Monday and she's rushing for school as if she hasn't had six weeks to get her act together.

'Do you have everything you need?' I ask. 'I made you some sandwiches.'

'I'm in sixth form now,' she replies. 'We can go out at lunch. I'll grab something at Starbucks.'

Great, more money wasted.

'It's strange to see you going to school without a uniform on,' I say. She's wearing tight jeans, an even tighter white top and chunky boots.

'I still have to wear this nasty blazer,' she replies, shrugging it on then hooking her heavy backpack over one shoulder. I wish she'd think of her posture and put it on both shoulders.

'You look nice.' She looks more than nice; she looks radiant.

I haven't seen her look this happy in a long time. If a boy is making her glow like this, then I hope he treats her well. I can't bear the idea of someone breaking my baby's heart.

'Would you like a lift? I have an important meeting at work later, but I have time. We're launching the new—'

'It's fine. I'm meeting Paige and Summer at the bus stop.'

Why did I think Leah would care about my job? When she was younger, twelve or thirteen, she really loved that I worked in PR for Medusa. Everyone in her class envied her when I'd bring home the latest necklace or ring for her to wear to school. I even got matching bracelets for her and her friends, which they wore the entire summer. No idea what they did with them after that. The brand was cool back then, and so was I. Now Leah says it's 'basic' and 'cheap' and no one other than 'chavvy millennials' wear it.

I told Steve, the CEO, but he said the opinions of teens don't matter. I think they do, seeing as that's who he's always trying to appeal to. Why not target the jewellery at older women? The ones who have money and would actually wear it? But he never listens to me. If I ran that company, it would be thriving by now.

'Have a lovely first day of sixth form,' I say.

I lean in to give Leah a kiss but get a mouthful of her hair instead. I shut the door behind her, and as I turn around I bump into Adam, who's rushing past with a piece of toast clamped between his teeth, crumbs scattering around him.

'Gotta go,' he mumbles.

No kiss from anyone this morning, then.

I don't start work until ten o'clock on a Monday, so I clean up the mess everyone has made and take my time getting ready. It takes so much longer than it used to. Staring into the magnifying mirror is an evil necessity. I have no idea where all this chin hair has come from, and putting on eyeliner is near on impossible. I remember when it used to glide over my eyelids, but now the skin around my eyes is papery and crumpled and I have to pull it to the side to achieve a straight line.

My phone buzzes. It's a Kandid alert, probably another message from another horny guy. This is ridiculous. I should be fixing my own life instead of wasting time reading about the messed-up lives of others while looking for validation from strangers. I'm going to delete the app. I click on the alert but the message that pops up isn't a nasty comment or a smutty DM. It's from someone I haven't seen on here before: Curious2. His bio says he's sporty and I can see he's local. That tells me nothing.

Are you OK? I saw your post and you sound sad.

A lump forms in my throat. This is the first time anyone has asked me if I'm all right. Perhaps he's genuinely being nice. Or maybe this is some weird 'knight in shining armour' fetish and he writes messages like this to every needy woman he sees.

I stare at it. Should I reply? I haven't replied to anyone on here yet; I'm not interested in leading anyone on or making new friends. I go to the settings menu and hover over 'delete my profile'. My phone buzzes again.

You don't have to reply. I simply wanted to let you know that I'm sure you are loved, and I hope you are happy.

I should say something; he's being nice. I should thank the stranger for not being rude or crude, for seeing me as a human being. No. I'm not doing it. I joined Kandid for a laugh. I didn't come here for therapy. I put my phone in my handbag, slip on my sandals and dab some lip gloss on. But as I get in the car, all I keep thinking is... am I happy? Am I?

. . .

'Julia!'

Steve is my boss and the owner of Medusa. I've worked in PR and marketing for him since Leah was four years old, and no matter how many times I tell him to call me Jules he still refuses. Over the years, Steve and I have seen his company grow into a recognisable brand, and I've been by his side since the beginning. He used to flirt with me all the time when I first started, before he met his wife. It was only a bit of fun. It was different twelve years ago – we didn't have an HR manager and I didn't know any better. Neither did he. Now the office is full of younger, prettier girls who would rip him apart if he so much as winked at them. He knows to keep his mouth shut, and I'm glad. But I can't help wondering whether he still finds me attractive – not because I've ever been romantically interested in him, but because the thought of him seeing me differently now I'm older is too depressing.

'How was your weekend?' I say, placing some lemon drizzle cupcakes on the meeting room table. I've hardly slept all weekend so I baked for everyone in the office. 'Did the twins have a nice birthday on Saturday?'

'Yes. I believe so. I had a conference call with Hong Kong, but I was there for the candle-blowing. Six years old already. Who would have thought it?'

Not you, I think. *You only had those kids to stop your wife from leaving you.*

'Ah, you made cakes, Julia. Fabulous. We can have them with our coffee as we discuss the new launch.'

The company only employs thirty people. It was five when I started: Steve, his secretary, sales, finance and me writing all the marketing copy and dealing with the press. But as the brand grew, along with global distribution, the team got bigger... and younger. Steve and I are the only ones left over the age of forty and the only ones with children. Although my salary has gone up a bit, my position in the company hasn't. I still write the press releases and website copy, but we outsource advertising to a big agency.

Everyone starts to file into the meeting room. It's sunny today but not that hot, yet you'd think we were all on our way to Saint-Tropez the way some of my colleagues are dressed. Kimberley heads international sales, speaks four languages and looks like she just stepped off a catwalk. Devon is our brand director. He's six foot three with manicured stubble and not a hair out of place. As for Ameera, she never smiles, just glides around in long, floaty dresses. I'm not even sure what Ameera does. They all refer to their jobs as 'working in fashion' and are young enough to be my children. I absent-mindedly listen to them talk about *Love Island* and how unfair it is that their land-lord has put the rent up and have you heard the latest song by Lil Bass, and I sit there quietly because I have absolutely nothing to contribute.

I stifle a yawn. God, I'm so tired. Not only can I not stop thinking about the cruel comments men have been sending me on Kandid, but I had another night of sweats that drenched my pyjamas and left me lying in a cold wet patch because I didn't want to wake Adam up to change the sheets.

I eye the coffee and the cakes I made. Sugar and caffeine would certainly help, but I've spent months trying to cut out sugar to minimise the rubber ring spreading around my middle and I've already had my caffeine quota for the day. I take a swig of my water instead and ignore the rumble of my empty stomach.

The only one presenting at this meeting today is Steve, as he explains his vision for the new collection so we can work on the approach, brief the designers and get the ad team to start booking magazine space. I'm glad all I have to do is listen as it's a struggle to stay awake. Pictures of the new collection flash up on the screen behind him and we all make the right noises. I like it. It's elegant, feminine, understated for a change. It's the kind of thing my friends would wear.

'What keywords are you thinking of regarding copy?' I ask.

Steve looks confused. 'Oh, don't worry, Julia. You won't be working on the copy for this one. You can assist with the press releases.'

I notice Devon's and Ameera's eyes drop to the tabletop. What do they know that I don't?

'Why aren't I working on this one?'

Steve clears his throat. 'It's a much younger line this time, so we need a more... refreshing voice.'

Refreshing? What am I? Stagnant?

'I know this brand inside out,' I say. 'I've been here since the beginning.'

'Exactly!' Steve says, pointing at me like I've hit the nail on the head. 'And that's why we need a new direction. Ameera and Devon have been working with some TikTok and Instagram influencers to get the new collection noticed by a younger demographic.'

Younger? Why?

'But most of our customers are my age,' I say. 'Not that we ever target them.'

Women like me are invisible. Always overlooked. Can Steve even see me sitting at the meeting table right now, or is he as blind as my own husband? The only time anyone notices me is when I'm posting scantily clad photos of my arse.

'You're right!' Steve exclaims. 'New age bracket means new approach. You're fab at writing copy, Julia, but this collection needs an invigorating new team, one that has their finger on the pulse.'

I'm shaky and light-headed. I should have had a bloody cupcake, but I keep thinking about the Kandid comments from Saturday night. I'm a chunky mutton. I'm embarrassing. I'm past it.

You need to be younger, Jules. Be younger and thinner and less needy.

Steve is still talking. 'Devon and I have been looking to expand in-house so we don't have to keep working with those expensive agencies. There's a girl I've heard of, freelance designer, she sounds good.'

I explode. 'A girl? Is she actually a *girl*, Steve?'

Kimberley and Ameera turn their heads to me in unison, their perfectly lined eyes widening in surprise. I'm the only one who ever contributes to meetings, but that doesn't mean I normally speak to Steve like that. I don't normally speak to *anyone* like that. But why should I allow him to sideline me and choose kids straight out of uni to do a job I've been doing since they were in primary school?

Steve sighs. 'What do you mean, Julia?'

'Is that what our company is made of? Men and girls? Am I the only *woman* around here?'

Not a woman, Jules, just mutton. Nothing but invisible chunky mutton.

Steve looks like I've slapped him. 'I didn't mean it like that, I was just—'

'Infantilising women in business? Is that what women in the office are to you? Either girls you'd like to sleep with or tired, *stagnant* old women who make your life difficult?'

'Not at all! All I'm saying is we need to start targeting a younger demographic.'

'We sell necklaces, Steve! Women over the age of thirty have necks too, you know. Let's be honest with ourselves here. The only reason we work with teen influencers and use young women in our advertising – even though our price bracket is too high for most of them and they think we're shit – is because girls aspire to be these teen models and older women wish they were still young. And the men? They just want to *fuck them!*'

I stand up, my legs shaking and my breaths coming in ragged starts.

'Excuse me,' I say, staggering out of the room.

I've gone too far now. Steve wants to push me out and now I've given him the perfect excuse to get rid of me.

But no one says anything, no one follows me out, and the meeting carries on without me. Like I don't even exist.

NINETEEN

LEAH

I hold Dylan's key in my hand as I walk down the corridor towards my locker, feeling the cool of the metal against my palm, the jagged edges leaving the imprint of a mountain top on my skin. I know it was stupid to take it, but it's something to remember him by. A connection to the soulmate I can't ever see again.

I had a video chat with my friends yesterday and, although I wasn't going to, I told them about Dylan. Not everything, of course. I said I'd met up with the older guy from Carnage again and I showed them his photo. They complained they couldn't see his face in the photo and said he looked older than the Bucket Boy they saw me with originally, and now I'm beginning to regret telling them anything. Dylan is more than a crush to analyse and dissect like a science project. He's *the one*.

He messaged me last night, said he wished I was beside him in bed again. I texted him this morning to wish him luck at his new job. This is what we do. This is what a proper relationship looks like. I don't know how I'll eventually tell Dylan I can't see him again, but for now I'm enjoying our relationship while I fake being at uni.

In the group chat Paige asked me if I was over Nathan. To be honest I've hardly thought of Nathan all week. I can't believe I was so wrapped up in him. I think of his masticated chewing gum ball in the box inside Garfield and I'm glad I didn't tell my friends about Dylan's key, or that I kept the condom. They wouldn't understand.

'Is this new guy your boyfriend, then?' Summer added.

I said no. She said something about how a bunch of new boys will be starting sixth form this week, that maybe one of them will be cute. I pretended to sound interested, but I can't see how any teenager is ever going to compare to Dylan.

Sixth form is better than I thought it would be. I don't share many classes with Paige and Summer, but lunch at Starbucks was cool – even though I could only afford a smoothie – and it's warm enough to take my blazer off when not in class so it practically feels like we're no longer in school. My last period of the day is triple art, the only class I share with Summer. I squint at my new timetable. I don't know who half these new teachers are.

'Do you know who Ward is?' I ask as we head down the corridor towards the art block.

Summer shakes her head. She no longer has her hair in braids; it's now tight corkscrews interspersed with red. She looks fierce.

'Male or female?' she asks, finishing the muffin she bought in Starbucks.

I shrug in response. I wish I'd taken the sandwiches Mum made me because I'm still hungry.

The door of the art studio is open, so we go inside. There's already someone in there. A boy I don't recognise. I pull Summer back into the corridor.

'Who's that?' I whisper.

'Cute, huh?'

I roll my eyes, but he kind of is.

'That's Santi. New boy. Used to go to that St Bart's school that doesn't have a sixth form. He was in my Spanish class this morning.'

More students push in behind us. Santi is studying the artwork on the wall, his shoulders hunched like he's trying to make himself small.

'He looks nervous,' I whisper to my friend as we take a seat at the back of the class. She gets up. I try to stop her, but she's already putting an arm around the new boy.

'You look lost,' she says. 'And I'm a collector of lost boys. Come and sit with us.'

Summer has really strong arms – I know how tight her grip can be – but Santi doesn't even flinch.

'Hey. I remember you,' he says to her. He has a deep, husky voice, and his hair hangs in nineties curtains like a younger, darker Leonardo DiCaprio.

'Meet the delicious Leah,' Summer says, steering him to our table. 'She's very nice, I promise she won't bite. Not unless you ask her to.'

I widen my eyes at Summer, who's trying not to laugh, and I smooth down my ponytail as Santi sits next to me. I smile at him. He smiles back. He has nice teeth.

'Good afternoon,' says a voice from the front of the class-room. A man in jeans, with closely cropped hair, is standing with his back to us as he adjusts the light of the projector. A large mug of coffee sits on his desk.

Everyone stops taking things out of their bags and settles down.

'I'm Mr Ward,' he says. 'Your new art teacher.'

He turns around and my breath catches at the back of my throat.

Fuck, fuck, *fuck*!

TWENTY

LEAH

Dylan is Mr Ward. Dylan's surname is Ward. Standing at the front of the classroom is Dylan Ward, the man I've had sex with. More than once. And he's my teacher.

I feel dizzy. I can't breathe.

'Today's my first day, so you'll have to excuse me if I don't remember your names. I promise to try my best. Let's start by going around the classroom. I'd like you to introduce yourselves, tell me why you're in this class and who your favourite artists are. Let's start at the front.'

Dylan, *my* Dylan, looks totally different. He's shaved off his stubble and his hair is really short. You can't even tell he ever had curls. It makes him look older, his face sharper.

I sink down in my seat but I'm right at the back, so he's not seen me yet.

'I'm Jasmine and I took art because I want to be a fashion designer. My favourite designer is Galliano.'

'I'm Mel. I like studying art because I enjoy drawing manga cartoons. I'd like to be an illustrator, but I don't know any comic book artists.'

Dylan is working his way through the class, one by one, jotting down names in a notebook. He's done a diagram of the class. It makes my chest ache. I need to get out of here. I can't let him see me.

'Are you OK?' Santi whispers.

I dab at my top lip. It's so hot in here but we're not allowed to take our stupid blazers off in class. What if I faint? I started my period this morning; that always makes me feel a bit light-headed. What if I fall off my stool and Dylan notices me? Maybe, when it's my turn to speak, I can make up a different name or change my voice, so it sounds different. No, that's not going to work. All my classmates know who I am, and Dylan is my teacher for the rest of the year.

Fuck!

Summer is looking over at me, her brow creased in concern, but seeing as Santi is sitting between us, I can't reach over to tell her what's going on. She never saw Dylan at the festival, just that blurry photo I took where his face is covered. He looks different now anyway, without so much hair. There's no way she will have connected the dots.

It's Abdul's turn next, then Isabelle, then Olivia. Most of my classmates have finished introducing themselves. We're the last table.

'My name is Summer, and I love to paint. I don't want to do anything creative as a job, I just enjoy it. My favourite artists are Caravaggio and Banksy.'

'Good choices,' Dylan says in a voice I've never heard him use before. All jolly and encouraging. He writes down her name and looks back up.

Our eyes meet and I watch as the colour drains from his face, the pen in his hand shaking as he stares back at me. Santi is telling the class why he's a big fan of some Colombian artist called Fernando Botero, but Dylan won't take his eyes off me.

He hasn't blinked for over a minute. It's my turn to introduce myself. I adjust my blazer and smooth down my ponytail.

'My name is Leah,' I say. My chin is wobbling, and I have to bite down on my bottom lip to make it stop. Tears are collecting and I blink to clear them. 'And I like drawing. I'm thinking of doing an art foundation course before university. I really like Michelangelo, especially the Sistine Chapel.'

He definitely knows now.

'Leah.'

I don't know how many times he's said my name before, his lips against mine, his fingers in my hair. It was only two days ago that I watched as his tongue flickered at the letter L, lips parting at the A sound, my mouth crashing against his.

'Right, then.' His voice is croaky and hoarse now. Both familiar and alien. He shakes his head a little and clears his throat. 'Nice to meet you all. So pleased we have such an eclectic mix of artists here. Let me introduce our first project. This term we're going to be looking at plants and flowers and how they've been depicted in art through the ages – everything from Monet to O'Keeffe. Who would like to share with me what they know about these artists?'

Someone in the front starts talking so I use the opportunity to take out my phone and text Summer.

THAT'S DYLAN!! OUR NEW TEACHER IS THE GUY I HAD SEX WITH AT CARNAGE!!

I can see Summer's phone in her bag by her feet light up, but it's on silent. Of course it is, we're not allowed to have phones in class.

I try to get her attention but she's listening to Dylan, *Mr Ward*, and doesn't notice me waving at her.

'Leah?' Dylan says.

I jump. The sight of him makes me want to cry. This can't

be happening. He looks angry. I've never seen him look angry before.

'I'll take your phone, thank you,' he says, walking to the back of the class. He holds out his hand, closing his eyes for a split second as my fingers brush his. 'See me after class, please.'

TWENTY-ONE

LEAH

Art class passes in a blur. I haven't been listening to a word Dylan's been saying. My ears have been humming the whole time, my heart beating so fast that at one point I swallow down a bit of sick. For the last ninety minutes I've been running through all the different ways to get out of this mess, but there's no way out; I have to tell him the truth.

Which I'm sure he's already figured out.

Summer is the last student to leave the classroom. Dylan is holding my phone and she gives me a tight-lipped smile as if to say she hopes I'm not in too much trouble.

She has no idea.

I go to shut the door behind her, but Dylan stops me.

'Leave it open,' he says, beckoning me to the back of the classroom out of view. He runs his hand through his hair, momentarily surprised at how short it is.

'What the hell is going on, Leah? Please tell me you've been held back four years or you're a trainee teacher or an under-cover cop or... *something*.'

'I'm just a normal student,' I mumble.

When he speaks next, he sounds like someone has their hands around his throat. 'How old are you, Leah?'

'Nearly seventeen.'

'Oh my God.' He crouches down into a ball, his back against the wall and his hands over his face. 'You're *sixteen?*' he moans into his hands. 'Jesus. What the *fuck* have you done?'

'I'm seventeen in nine days.'

'Leah!' he cries, jumping back up. He looks like he wants to punch something or cry or scream. The tips of his ears have gone red, and he keeps clenching and unclenching his fists. 'Did you know I was going to be your teacher?'

My voice comes out in a warbly whine. 'No! Of course not. I only lied to you at Carnage because I wanted to lose my virginity to someone older.'

'Your vir— *Fuck.*'

'But then you invited me to your flat and... I didn't mean for any of this to happen.'

Dylan keeps rubbing his hands over his face. 'This is the first day of my job – you get that, right? Not only could my career be ruined before it's even started but I could go to prison.'

Prison? But he didn't do anything wrong. I'm over sixteen, it's legal. I start crying. Big, ugly sobs, tears rolling down my cheeks and splashing on to my top. Dylan steps forward, like he wants to hug me, then steps back again and picks up my phone. I cringe that my lock screen is a photo of me and my mum. I should change it.

'Unlock it.'

I do as I'm told, and he deletes all the WhatsApp conversations between us along with his phone number. I hold my breath, but he doesn't see my text to Summer. Next, he checks my photos and stops at the one of him in the tent.

'When did you take that?'

'At the festival. After we...' I swipe at my wet cheeks with the back of my hand. 'You looked so cute, and I wanted something to remember you by.'

'Leah.' He blows out his cheeks and lowers his voice, like he's talking to a small child. 'What you did was wrong, and it ends right now. Forget anything ever happened between us. You can't breathe a word of it to anyone, OK? Do any of your friends know?'

I think about Summer and shake my head.

'No one knows it's you.'

His face relaxes a little and he goes back to breathing normally. He looks more like the man I know. I want to feel his arms around me again.

'Can I at least get a goodbye hug?' I say quietly.

He shakes his head, making me cry again.

'Just go.' He takes another deep breath. 'From now on you call me Mr Ward and you never, *ever* mention that you knew me before. Promise?'

'Yes.'

I glance at the empty corridor then run my hand over his cheek.

'You still like me though, right?'

He closes his eyes.

'Go.'

TWENTY-TWO

JULES

'Are you OK, Julia?'

Steve pulls a chair up beside me at my desk, where I've been eating a limp sandwich, the one Leah didn't want. I didn't realise most of the team had gone to the pub for lunch until the office fell silent. No one invites me anymore. I used to be good friends with a few women at Medusa, but one by one they all left to have children, never to return, replaced by younger, more eager models. I'm now the token middle-aged woman. It doesn't normally bother me as I work from home a lot of the time, but on days like these, when I storm out of a meeting and no one follows, I'm reminded of how little my input in this company matters.

'I'm fine,' I reply, biting down on my lip to stop my eyes welling up with tears of embarrassment. I went too far and now I'm going to get reprimanded.

'Come on. It's me you're talking to.' Steve lays a hand on my arm, and I let him. I sniff and he smiles, patting me like a small child.

I was in my mid-thirties when I first started working for him. Twelve years younger than I am now and at least eighteen pounds lighter. He always used to tell me how great I looked, how I was the perfect face for Medusa, sophisticated and elegant. The only women at the company back then were me and Hillary, who was both his aunt and his secretary. She's dead now.

'Are things all right at home?' he asks.

I hate the genuine concern in his voice; it makes a hard lump form in my throat.

No, of course nothing is right at home, Steve! My husband finds me repulsive, my daughter hates me, and my son doesn't even remember I exist.

He's the second man today to ask if I'm OK – neither of whom were Adam.

'Hormones,' I mutter. 'I'm sorry about my outburst earlier. It was unprofessional.'

He rubs my arm again. 'Come to me direct next time you have an issue, eh?'

Since reading all the confessions on Kandid, I now find myself studying the faces of strangers in the street and people I work with. Who wants to sleep with me and who finds me repulsive? Steve's hand stays on my arm. He could be Viper. He could be Curious2. I'd never know if he had a secret too.

'I hate to see you like this, Julia. I know you've had a tough year.'

My boss thinks this has to do with my mother passing. I'm embarrassed that I'm more shallow than that.

I wish I could quiz everyone I know about their relationships. Ask them how often they have sex, how happy they really are, whether they regret any of it. It's impossible to know if my marriage is normal or doomed.

I doubt Steve has been faithful to his wife – men like him rarely are. But would he go on a site like Kandid? I also doubt she cares about what he gets up to. They live in a huge house in St John's Wood and have another house in Mallorca, where she spends all summer with the kids. She got what she wanted, so I guess Steve is free to stick his dick anywhere he wants. I wonder if they're both OK with that. Maybe that's how some marriages work. Maybe it's simply two people living side by side, getting what they want from the other. But what is it I actually want?

'I'm fine,' I mumble.

'Are you, though?' Steve asks. 'Are you really happy?'

The hair on the back of my neck stands on end. There it is again. Am I happy?

I look up. He has kind eyes. 'I don't know anymore. Are you?'

Steve laughs. 'You know I'm never happy. And don't stress about the new campaign, I've given it to Ameera to oversee. Take it easy – you helped me get Medusa to where it is today, no need to fight for every little thing. She'll let you know about the newsletter copy soon.'

He thinks he's doing me a favour. I swallow down all the things I want to say and give him a weak smile instead. Why can't I be relieved that someone else is doing all the hard work? I'm on a decent salary, it helps pay the bills, I can do this job standing on my head, and I'm no longer at an age where I have to learn more, prove myself or be hungry to reach the top. I should kick back and do the bare minimum, yet it still irks me that Steve has decided it's time for me to fade away. As if every woman's ambition is to relax as much as possible. As if staying at home and not having to work is a life goal. When, in reality, I want to be the one making the important decisions he gets to make.

A babble of voices signals that everyone is back from lunch already. They all head to their desks, not one of them looking in my direction. I tell myself that I don't care what any of those kids think. But, as usual, I'm lying to myself.

TWENTY-THREE

JULES

I get home from work to find Leah sprawled on the sofa staring at her phone, a can of Coke leaving a wet ring on the coffee table and crisp crumbs on the floor I vacuumed that morning. She looks like she's been crying. I want to say something about the mess, but I don't; instead, I move her legs to the side and sit beside her.

'What's up?'

I expect her to push me away or storm off to her room, but she doesn't. In one sudden movement she throws her arms around me, and I instinctively hold her tight as she shudders against me, her breath ragged with tears. All the hours of my life I've spent holding this child to me, telling her everything will be all right, passing every last ounce of energy and hope and love I possess like osmosis from my soul to hers. Does it still work? Can she still feel it?

'Shhh,' I hush into her ear.

Guilt seeps like water beneath my skin because instead of worrying about what latest high school drama has made my youngest so inconsolable, I'm enjoying that Leah needs me.

I smooth down her hair. 'Is it about a boy?'

She nods against my shoulder and my chest floods with grief. First that Nathan guy and now some little prick from the festival. I bet he dumped her today after meeting up on Saturday. She gets too obsessed with these boys. Why can't my beautiful, smart, brilliant daughter see how special she is? She shouldn't need the attention of others to feel good about herself.

'Do we need to see that therapist again?' I whisper.

She shakes her head. 'It's not like that. It's over. There's no point being into someone if they're not fully committed.'

OK. Good. I know it's normal for girls her age to be interested in boys, but Leah is an all-or-nothing kid and her intensity gets her into trouble. As we've already witnessed this year. But she walked away from this one before she got too invested. That's a good thing.

'If it's meant to be, it's meant to be. Some boys take a while to realise what's right in front of them,' I say, thinking of her father. I hold her tighter. 'Have you heard from your brother?'

She nods and sniffs. 'He was at Pacha yesterday.'

I don't know what that means, but I doubt it's anything good. I try not to think of the debauchery that boy has been up to in Ibiza.

Leah is still sobbing into my shoulder. The crook of my neck is wet and starting to itch.

'He hates me,' she keeps saying, over and over again. It takes me a moment to realise she's talking about the boy and not her brother.

I stroke the back of her head.

'He's not worth it. No guy is worth crying over.'

I think about Adam, and about the men who've been messaging me on Kandid, and the one who asked me if I was OK this morning. I haven't replied to him yet. Every one of these men have made me cry in some way – even Steve made me cry at work today. Men think our tears are full of sadness, but they're not. They're full of anger and frustration. Little drops of water carrying every futile thing we wish we could say or do but can't or won't. Then we simply wipe them away like it never happened.

'Don't make your skin blotchy over some idiot,' I say. 'If you're mad, do something about it.'

With one final sniff Leah unravels herself from my embrace, gives a slow nod, then slopes off to her room. I think about following her, offering to cook her favourite dinner or seeing if she wants to watch a movie together, but then Adam walks through the front door and the moment is lost. I'm not going to mention this to him. I like that Leah and I have secrets again.

'Hi, darling,' I say to Adam, forcing a smile on my face.

He nods at me and heads for the stairs. No words, no welcome home kiss.

'How was work?' I call out.

'Busy,' he shouts over his shoulder. 'Don't forget we have that dinner with my clients tomorrow night.'

I'd forgotten.

I lie on the sofa where Leah was and eat a stray crisp from the cushion while scrolling through my phone.

Am I OK? No, Mr Kandid Stranger, I'm not.

I haven't been happy for a long time. This isn't the life I planned to have. You?

Curious2 replies straight away.

No. I never expected life to be this hard either.

I wonder if he has kids, or a wife, or if he's a teenage boy letting off steam.

Are you happy?

I'm happy now, talking to you. Your husband's an idiot for not seeing how lucky he is, by the way.

My husband hates me.

I'm sure he doesn't.

I've never admitted my fears about my marriage to anyone before. Not even to Lynsey. I tell her stupid things, like how Adam annoys me when he puts empty cartons of milk back in the fridge, or how he always takes most of the duvet while I'm sleeping, but not the serious stuff. Not the fact that every time I lie beside him at night, my throat aches with tears because all I want to do is feel his arms around me, and how the gap between us has grown so wide the mattress has a literal bump in the middle.

But talking to a stranger is easy. There's no judgement or patronising sympathy. He doesn't know my life in any way – he only knows what I tell him. Plus, I bet his life is as screwed up as mine, otherwise why else would he be scrolling through Kandid?

One thing I do know is that my husband doesn't find me attractive. We haven't had sex in over a year and sometimes I feel like I never will again.

Are you saying you want to sleep with someone else?

Ah. Right. So we've reached the part where he starts flirting with me. Something heavy sinks into the pit of my stomach. Here I am, thinking someone genuinely cares about how I am, yet he's no different to the other guys. He was just taking his time to soften me up first.

No! Not at all. I love my husband. That's the problem.

Loving someone should never be a problem. You sound really frustrated.

I need to tell someone the truth for once.

I am! I'm so frustrated that sometimes I touch myself while he's asleep beside me and imagine it's him. Is it bad that I want to be desirable again?

It feels good to admit to my sins; perhaps this is why Catholics love going to confession. It's safe. This man has no idea who I am; I can say anything.

I wait. No little dots. No response.

Great. If he didn't think I was a desperate old bag before, he definitely does now.

Hours pass. I cook dinner and eat it with Leah and Adam, then clear up, but Curious2 still hasn't replied.

That man could have been anyone and I told him my deepest, darkest secrets. A stranger, who lives locally, who may already know who I am.

TWENTY-FOUR

JULES

I've been staring at my naked body for five minutes now. Who is this? Sometimes I walk past a shop window and catch sight of myself, and I don't even realise it's me.

I pull at the skin around my eyes and let go, watching the thin lines etch their way back on my face. I smooth a finger around the sides of my mouth. How are my laughter lines so deep when I can't remember the last time I laughed? Maybe wrinkles are my penance for having had such a good time when I was younger.

The rest of me looks like it's attached to clear strings pulling me down: stomach, tits, even the skin under my arms is sagging. I pinch the crumpled, deflated balloon that was once my stomach and marvel at how, nearly seventeen years after I was last pregnant, I still have stretch marks. As for my bikini line, twenty-year-old me would be disgusted to see the state of my seventies porno pubic hair. Even if no one has seen me naked for a year, I should probably still give it a trim.

There are no nail scissors in the bathroom, so I rummage through Adam's underwear drawer, where he keeps the male grooming set I bought him years ago but has never used. As I search under a mound of socks, my hand closes around a small box. It's flat and leather. I've never seen it before. Adam is still in our en-suite shower, the bedroom filling with steam, so I peek inside the box. It's a bracelet: gold with a tiny diamond in the centre. Adam has never bought me a fancy gift like this before; last year for Christmas he bought me an air fryer. Our anniversary and my birthday have already passed this year. It doesn't make sense. And why a bracelet? I work for a jewellery company, for goodness' sake. I also didn't see any large amounts of money come out of the account. I take it out of the box, studying the way the light bounces off the diamond, something hard and sharp forming in my stomach. What if it's not for me?

Adam turns off the shower and I shove the box under his socks again, shutting the drawer quickly. I scramble into my Spanx, yanking them up over my stomach, then scooping my boobs into my push-up bra. There. Everything in the right place. I step into my trusty black wraparound dress and give another sigh. I'm sighing a lot lately. Maybe I need to learn to breathe properly. Maybe I should wear something else for a bloody change.

Adam walks into the bedroom, a towel wrapped around his waist, his wet hair leaving rivulets of water down his strong shoulders. I steal a glance at him then look away, my face prickling with something close to anger or shame or resentment. Why did he not mention the bracelet? Why is my husband keeping secrets from me? And how come he got to have two children yet not an inch of his body was forced to change? If anything, he looks better now than he did before the kids were born.

'Oh, you're wearing that dress again,' he says.

I pull it off, throw it on to the bed and stomp off to the bathroom to do my make-up.

. . .

'Are you going to be ignoring me all night?' Adam whispers in the back of the taxi. We're not driving because we both intend to drink tonight, plus parking in Highgate is a nightmare.

I'm not giving him the silent treatment; I just don't know what to say without crying or shouting, so I opt for saying nothing.

'Cedric has had some serious offers for the business,' he says.

Adam and his business partner built Atë Innovations from scratch. I have never fully understood what they do but it's something to do with Web3 and tech, and Adam said a few big brands have been making noises about buying them out. This is what tonight is about.

I make an impressed noise as I adjust the neckline of my dress. I ended up wearing the black dress after all, the same outfit I wore to Reece's dinner, because it's the only thing that I feel good in. But now I'm worried it's too low.

'You look nice,' Adam adds.

Nice. Not hot or sexy or ravishing, just *nice* – the same word he used when I showed him the new tea towels I bought in Ikea last week. I mumble a thank you and stare out of the window at the blur of north London as it passes by. It's still warm for September and the streets are buzzing with life. It's a Tuesday night and there are gaggles of young women out for drinks, couples draped over one another, and families making their way home. I wonder what people see as Adam and I step out of the taxi. Do we look smart and sophisticated, a happy couple off to an expensive restaurant to be wined and dined by my important husband's business associates? Or will they see the cracks in our marriage, running deep and silver like the lines climbing up my sagging stomach?

'I've heard this place makes a great tarte Tatin,' Adam says.

'Nice.'

Everyone is already at the table when we enter the restaurant. I instantly count the men-to-women ratio: three women, five men, including us. I wonder who's paired with whom.

'Jules, you already know Cedric. This is his wife, Cynthia.'

I smile and shake their hands across the table. I've met Adam's business partner a few times – the last time was four years ago at a company event when he said, 'Hello, Jenny,' then we didn't speak for the rest of the night. Partners rarely get invited out, so this is the first time I've met his wife. She looks exactly as I expected her to.

I have no idea who the other woman is. She's in her early thirties, dark hair in a smart bob, a thin gold necklace at her throat with a singular diamond pendant, similar to the bracelet Adam was hiding from me. The woman is wearing a strappy red satin dress which hangs off her like it's made of oil. Satin is a bold choice. It's not that kind of restaurant.

Adam works his way around the table. 'And this is Baz, Jope and Sietze, from MazTech in the Netherlands. They flew over from Amsterdam this morning.'

But what about the woman? Who the hell is that woman, Adam?

I shake hands with the three very tall men and smile politely at the woman in red, who no one has mentioned yet.

'I'm Bea,' she says, pronouncing it 'be-ah'. She has an accent, but I can't tell where she's from. She walks around the table and plants a kiss on each of my cheeks. 'Nice to meet you, Jules. And look at you,' she says, turning to my husband and placing a hand on his chest. 'I don't think I've ever seen you in a suit, Adam. Very smart.' She kisses him on both cheeks, his fingers lightly brushing her waist as he leans in.

We sit down and I accept a menu, but I can't see any of the words.

'I recommend the steak,' Cedric booms. 'And the burrata is very good indeed.'

Cedric has one of those voices that resonates like he's inside a tunnel. Our table is round, and he's seated to my left; beside him is his wife, who looks so out of her comfort zone I feel a bit sorry for her, then the three Dutch men, then Bea sitting on my husband's right. I have no option but to speak to either Cedric or Adam all evening. Except Adam's attention has already been taken by Bea, who's saying something that's making him laugh so hard he's tipped his head back and closed his eyes.

Why has Adam never mentioned her before?

'This is Jules, Adam's wife,' Cedric says to his wife. 'She's a jewellery designer.'

She leans over him and pats my arm. 'How glam. And you have the perfect name for it, too.'

I've not heard that one before. I give them a tight smile. 'No, not a designer. I'm no Suzanne Belperron.' They don't know who I'm talking about. 'I work for Medusa, the jewellery brand.' They don't know what that is either, but they nod their heads politely.

'What about you, Cynthia? Do you work in tech like Cedric?'

Her laugh is like a tiny little bell. 'Goodness, no. We have three children, so I chose to focus on them instead. They're grown up now but there's plenty to keep me busy indoors. Hopefully they'll have their own children soon. I can't wait to have grandchildren. Are you excited about having grandchildren, Jules?'

Adam and the woman in red are talking in hushed whispers, their faces so close together their foreheads are virtually touching. I smile politely at Cynthia and signal for the waiter to fill up my wine glass.

TWENTY-FIVE

JULES

'Did you have a nice time tonight?' Adam asks, sliding into bed beside me. Our bed is so big our bodies don't even touch.

'Yes, you work with some great people.'

We were out for all of three hours. It felt like three days. I had the burrata, the steak and the tarte Tatin. It was all very nondescript and expensive. I talked about pets and children with Cynthia – Cedric swapped places with his wife within five minutes – and I watched on as the others all discussed things I didn't understand, Bea like a bright red flame amongst the dark of their suits.

Does she know how beautiful she is? Did she sense every head that swivelled as she got up to use the bathroom? I watched her too, staring at the way her bottom shifted under the red satin. She was either wearing a thong under there or nothing at all. She certainly wasn't wearing huge gripper knickers that were rolling down her stomach like mine were all evening.

A minute after she left the table, Adam got up to use the bathroom too. I had images of them having sex in the disabled toilet, her red dress pooled around her feet, her lacy underwear as light to the touch as a spider's web. He came back from the bathroom before she did and launched straight into a conversation about the importance of regulating AI, and when she returned, she didn't have a hair out of place. Women like Bea know how to screw without sweating. I bet you could slit her throat and she'd still look beautiful.

'I knew you'd get on with Cynthia,' Adam says, adjusting his earbuds. 'You two have a lot in common.'

Is that how he sees me?

'I don't have anything in common with Bea?'

He takes out the earbuds. 'Sorry, what was that?'

'Nothing.'

He settles down to listen to his nightly podcast and closes his eyes. I pick up my phone and click on the Kandid app. Curious2 hasn't replied to my last message, the one where I told him I masturbate beside my sleeping husband. I'm not surprised. Who wants to chat to a perverted psycho?

I glance at my husband, eyes closed, no clue about how I'm feeling right now. Cheating on him would be so easy. I could message any one of these desperate, lonely men and suggest meeting up. I could flirt and kiss and shag my way around the bloody country if I wanted to and Adam wouldn't notice. Would he even care?

But I wouldn't do that. I don't want to. The only man I'm interested in is the man I promised to spend my whole life with. The man who spent all night pressed up against a beautiful woman but won't even look me in the eye. When I think of Bea, all I feel is hate. It should be Adam I hate, but it's not. It's her. I hate her nearly as much as I hate myself.

TWENTY-SIX
LEAH

I hold my door keys in my hand, Dylan's key glinting the shiniest of all. It gives me a thrill that he has no idea I have it nestled amongst my own, his weed keyring hidden inside Garfield with my other mementos. I stroke the key between my fingers, enjoying the tangy metallic scent it leaves on my fingertips. It smells like blood.

It's Wednesday morning and I got to school early to catch Dylan before the start of first period.

'What do you want?' he says, looking anywhere but at me.

'I need to talk to you.'

I step in front of him, forcing him to look at me. His eyes widen and he stills, like I'm a wild animal he can't decide whether to run away from or pet.

Yesterday I made sure I looked really pretty but I didn't see him all day, so this morning I put on my heeled boots and a cute outfit. My skirt is so short that with my blazer on, it looks like I don't have anything on underneath. I know he's thinking the same thing because his gaze keeps flicking to the hem of my jacket.

He deleted his telephone number from my phone, but I'd

already memorised it. Every night I check on my keepsakes, including the condom which I placed in a plastic bag. It's curled up and hard now. Something warm pools in my stomach at the thought of having Dylan's DNA in my bedroom. I like that I have a piece of him beside me every night.

I've been writing him letters too, then burning them. Mum had another fit about the house smelling badly so I'm hiding the rest of the letters in Garfield until I can burn them somewhere else. The spell worked last time; maybe it will work again.

He leads us to the corner of the classroom, out of sight, and leans against the wall with his arms folded. He's trying to act like he doesn't care about me, but I can see in his gaze that he still thinks I'm pretty. I want to press myself against him, wrap his strong arms around my waist. I can smell his aftershave from here and it's making me think of his bedsheets. If only he'd step a bit closer, he'd know that what we have is real, that it's worth taking a risk for.

'Leah, I mean it,' he says. 'You're my student and I'm your teacher. There's nothing more between us.'

I don't know why he's making such a big deal out of this. I'm seventeen in exactly one week and I look older anyway. If we both keep it a secret, there's nothing stopping us from seeing each other like we did before. As Mum said, if it's meant to be, it's meant to be. Dylan just needs to understand that you don't throw away a connection like ours.

'I messaged you loads, why haven't you answered?'

He breathes out hard through his nose. No response.

'Did you block my number?'

'Of course I did!' he hisses.

I've texted him five times since Monday and sent loads of WhatsApp messages, but he didn't reply, so I looked him up on social media and found his Facebook page. I hope he's seen the photo I sent him on Messenger. I didn't show my face again, but he will know it's me. I took all my underwear off this time.

'How have you been messaging me? I deleted my number off your phone.'

'I already knew it off by heart.'

He sighs and reaches for my hands. I hold my breath.

'Stop,' he says.

He holds my wrists tightly – not my hands, my wrists – and stares into my eyes for a really long time. I want to kiss him so badly.

'You have to leave me alone, Leah. When you see me, act like you do with any other teacher.'

His grip is strong and my skin stings. I like it.

'But you're not just anyone, Dylan.' I step closer to him until our chests are touching. 'You wanted me on Saturday.'

'That was before I realised you were a *child*!'

I yank my wrists out of his grasp, a self-defence move I learned online. 'A *child*?' I shout. He glances over his shoulder but there's no one in the hallway. 'You weren't saying that when you had your head between my legs.'

Dylan lets out a strangled kind of sound and storms over to the classroom door, shutting it quietly but firmly. He looks like he's going to hit me or start crying but he does neither. Instead, he runs a hand over his short hair, standing as far away from me as possible. I miss his curls.

'Leah, please. You're going to ruin me.'

'I don't know why you're acting like this,' I say. I'm trying not to cry because it's important he sees I have my shit together. He needs to know I'm mature, that I can be that woman he thought I was on the weekend, the woman he made proper love to. 'We could keep meeting up and no one would know. I could come to your house on weekends. I won't tell anyone – I haven't mentioned anything to my friends.'

And I haven't. I deleted the message I sent Summer. They know about Dylan, but not that he's Mr Ward.

'Please.' I walk towards him and take his hand, and this time he lets me. 'You mean so much to me. We had something special; you know we did. We don't have to lose it.'

His thumb strokes my fingers, each movement tugging at my chest like someone's squeezing me too tight. Then he shakes his head and lets go.

'No. You're being selfish, Leah. It's not only my career at stake here, it's my mental health too.'

I'm making him ill? I don't want to make him ill.

'How?'

'I'm on meds. I've had bouts of... Leah, seriously, this is making me really anxious.'

I don't know if he's telling the truth or he's just scared, but there's no need to fight it. It doesn't have to be the big deal he's making it out to be.

'Don't get upset.' I stroke his cheek, rough like sandpaper beneath my fingertips. 'I can make you feel better, baby.'

The outline of my classmates walking down the corridor can be seen through the glass in the door. I pull my hand away from Dylan's face as Santi enters the room.

'Sorry. I should have knocked,' he mumbles.

Dylan takes a step back from me. 'Come in, Santi,' he says, acting as if we were having a normal student–teacher chat.

Santi sits at the back of the class like we did on Monday. He gives me a little smile and it takes all my strength to smile back.

Dylan is practically whispering now. 'Being around you is making me feel ill and, unlike you, I'm an adult. An adult that needs to keep a clear head. So please, Leah, leave me alone before you make things worse.'

It breaks my heart that he's struggling. I just want to help him.

'Take a seat, everyone,' Dylan says loudly over my shoulder, then drops his voice so low I can hardly hear him. 'It's over. Keep away, keep quiet and get on with your life so I can get on with mine.'

With shoulders pulled back, he walks to the front of the class, leaving me blinking furiously until my tears clear. I join Summer at the back of the room, where she's sitting beside Santi.

'What were you talking to Mr Ward about?' she whispers.

'My portfolio. I was telling him about the unis I plan to apply for.'

Santi keeps smiling at me. I haven't said a word to him yet, but he seems nice. Maybe he likes Summer. I wonder if she's told him she's a lesbian.

While Dylan drones on about Monet's water lilies, I think about how I can win him back. He still likes me – I could tell by the way he held my hand and stroked my fingers with his thumb. He's scared. But I know if we kissed, he'd realise we can't fight this.

The bell rings. Paige is waiting in the corridor for us both.

'Lunch in the park later?' She looks at my skirt. 'What are you wearing?'

'What?'

'Nothing. I mean, it's very short.'

I'm trying to act casual, but Dylan just walked past us like he's never seen me before and I want to cry. 'So now you're body-shaming me?'

Paige looks affronted, and Summer nudges me. 'What's going on, Leah? You've been acting really weird since we came back to school.'

I want to tell them everything, but how can I? If Dylan finds out I've told my friends, he'll never get back together with me.

'Period,' I mutter, heading towards the exit. 'I need chocolate.'

I can hear Summer and Paige whispering about me, but I haven't got time for their childish gossiping; I have serious stuff going on. Stuff they'd never understand.

'Hey.' Summer reaches out for me, and I slow down. 'We're besties, yeah? Talk to us.'

'It's nothing. I'll see you at lunchtime'

There's a fallen tree trunk we always sit at in the park – we call it 'the log'. When we were younger, we'd meet here in the mornings or hang out after school. Paige carved our initials into the wood once. SLP. I run my fingers over the markings worn smooth over the years.

'I saw your text, you know,' Summer says.

I sit on the log and take out the sandwiches Mum made me. 'Which one?'

'About Mr Ward. But then you deleted it.'

The bread turns to tasteless mush in my mouth. They can't know. What if they tell Ms Willis, the headteacher, or worse? What if they say something to my parents?

'I was wrong,' I say. 'He walked into the room and reminded me of Dylan for some reason. But of course it's not him.'

My friends sit on either side of me.

'So why did you lie in the next message and say you accidentally sent a text that was meant for your mum?' Summer continues. When that girl wants to make a point, she doesn't stop until she's made it.

I shrug and pick a daisy at my feet, twirling it between my finger and thumb. I should have kept the one Dylan gave me. 'I was embarrassed. I don't want you thinking I'm a nutter. I mean, can you imagine having sex with a *teacher*?'

They both laugh at how absurd that would be.

'Disgusting,' Paige says. 'And totally creepy.'

Summer nudges me, but this time in a friendly way. 'Anyway, you already showed us that photo of Dylan. Remember? With the curly hair and stubble. Mr Ward looks nothing like that.'

I shrug again and take another tasteless bite out of my sandwich. 'I know. Stupid. That's why I deleted the text.'

'Did Dylan call you after Saturday?'

I shake my head and they both hug me as if that's why I've been acting strange lately. It hurts to lie to them, but it hurts even more that they think I'm so stupid I wouldn't be able to recognise the only man I've ever had sex with.

'Mr Ward *is* hot though. In a teachery way,' Paige adds.

Summer hums in agreement. 'I mean, I wouldn't change sides for him, but I can see why our girl here likes him.'

'*I don't like Mr Ward,*' I screech.

Dylan's surname sounds stupid in my mouth, like we're playing some kinky role-playing game. Mr Ward makes him sound boring and sensible, but Dylan isn't like that. He's smart and funny and cute and said he was crazy about me. I blink away tears before my friends notice, but luckily Paige has moved on to her favourite subject: Jacob.

'We're going to try... you know,' she says, pointing to her lap.

So he hasn't even gone down on her yet? Poor Paige. No guy his age has any idea how to pleasure a woman. She's looking at me expectantly, like she wants me to share all my experience, but I don't want to. All I want to do is climb back into bed with Dylan and be that twenty-one-year-old uni student again who he was really into. The woman he'd probably be falling in love with by now if he hadn't found out the truth.

'I don't feel well,' I say, getting up and throwing my sandwich in the bin.

The girls call out after me, but I ignore them. I need to come up with a plan to make sure Dylan and I can be together again. Whatever happens, I'm going to make sure I get my way.

TWENTY-SEVEN
JULES

Work was awful again yesterday. Steve was fawning over Devon and Ameera as they worked on the new campaign, and no one noticed that I've done nothing but write a newsletter in three days. I could skip work for a week, and no one would even care. Maybe Steve is keeping me on out of pure guilt. Or maybe he feels threatened because he knows I could do a better job of running the place than he has.

I'm meeting Lynsey for a drink. Vino, the only nice bar in town, is quiet for a Friday night. Lynsey is running late, as usual, so I order a gin and tonic and find a table in the corner, where I get out my phone to text Leah.

Don't forget there's pizza in the freezer. I'm out with Lynsey but won't be home too late xx

I watch the ticks turn from grey to blue.

K

That's it. Just a K. Exactly how much time did she save omitting the O?

Leah's been acting off all week. It must be that boy she was upset about on Monday. I tried talking to her again, but she pushed me away. Even after all these years my children have a way of reminding me that I don't have a clue what I'm doing.

When I was Leah's age, I told my mother everything. I can still remember the smell of her embrace, Polo mints and lavender, as I curled up in her lap and babbled on about school and friends and boys. Sometimes she gave me advice, but most of the time she just listened and that was enough. Knowing she was there was enough. I miss her. I miss her so much. I can't wait for Reece to get back from Ibiza tomorrow.

It's not like Adam is any help, either. He's not even home most of the time. Apparently, tonight's work dinner is strictly business, no partners or clients. He called it 'boring stuff'. I looked in his underwear drawer this morning and the diamond bracelet was gone – he's either moved it to another hiding place or he's given it to the recipient. Someone who isn't me.

I take a long swig of my drink, holding my wrists against the cool glass. I wonder if that woman, Bea, is at the event tonight. I wonder what she's wearing this time. Perhaps, instead of long and red, her dress is short and black, the perfect frame for her perfect cleavage. Is she flirting with Adam right now? Is she placing her hand on his chest again, making him laugh so hard he throws his head back?

She can probably tell my handsome, successful husband is unhappy. It wouldn't be hard to snake her way through the cracks in our marriage and prise them open. I bet she's feeling way more confident about her chances now she's met me, his boring old wife. What kind of competition would I be? What man wouldn't prefer to have sex with a young, foreign beauty instead of his own haggard wife who he hasn't laid a hand on in over a year?

I drain the rest of my drink and push the glass away. This isn't healthy.

I look at my phone – it's later than I realised. No message from Lynsey. I text her partner John and ask if everything is OK, and he says she left ages ago. Maybe she's stuck in traffic. I'm ordering a second G&T when Lynsey enters the bar. She's out of breath like she's been running.

'Oh, there you are,' she says, hugging me in a sweaty embrace. She signals to the barman. 'I'll have what she's having but make it a double.'

We carry our drinks over to the table and she shrugs off her jacket, gulping most of her drink down and wiping her mouth with the back of her hand.

'Why does no one tell you toddlers are arseholes?'

'Literally everyone tells you that. It was my only topic of conversation for years.'

She laughs. 'I love my boys, you know I do, but little kids are these tiny devils who take you to hell and back then as they fall asleep say, "I wuv you," and bam, you're tricked into having a second one. That's where John and I went wrong, thinking we could have two. We should have stuck to one, so there was more of us than them.'

I pour some of my drink into her empty glass and she clinks it against mine.

'I take it bedtime didn't go well.'

'I had to read the same page of the same book thirty-seven times. Whoever invented waterboarding should have gone for the less messy torture option of getting a baby and a toddler to sleep simultaneously. You know what? They can have *my* kids. I'd happily rent them out to MI6.' She finishes the dregs of her drink and takes a deep breath. 'And how are you?'

'My husband is having an affair.'

We both burst out laughing. Each time we catch one another's eye we get louder and louder until a group of men at the bar give us a dirty look. It feels good to laugh this much, but I'm scared the tears in my eyes are going to turn into full-on sobs.

'Stop,' she says, waving her hand up and down. 'Stop. I'm going to piss myself. Jules, seriously, you really think Adam is cheating on you?'

I make a face. 'I'm probably being paranoid, but you should see this woman he's been working with. I met her on Tuesday when I went to his boring work dinner. She was gorgeous. Like a Bond girl.'

'So?'

'So she was flirting with him and he was enjoying it. And now he's out with work again.'

Lynsey's face goes all serious. 'Come on, Jules! You know he's not like that. He's not one of those swaggering, cocky prats who's all full of himself and would risk everything for an ego boost.'

'What if he's gone off me?'

She rolls her eyes. 'Leave off.'

'We don't have sex anymore.'

She doesn't look as surprised as I was hoping she would.

'Count yourself lucky. Must be nice not to be pawed at all the time. If the boys aren't trying to sit on me, John's rubbing up behind me. Every time I take anything out of the oven or unload the dishwasher, I have to crouch low to the ground or he's mauling me. I don't even like the cat sitting on my lap anymore. Urgh. Sorry. How long have things been weird between you both?'

I'm too embarrassed to tell her the truth.

'Three months?'

She waves her hand in the air as if blowing away my concerns like smoke.

'Adam's a good guy and it's normal, after so many years, for our men to take us for granted. It's when they start showering you with love and affection out of the blue that you should be worried. That's a guilty conscience.'

I give her a weak smile. So, being ignored means he loves me. That doesn't make sense either.

Lynsey grabs my hand. 'Jules, listen to me, you're smart and funny and loving, and you're the best mum I know. I'm sure everything is going to be fine.'

'But I want to be sexy again,' I say in a quiet voice.

'Well, I can't help you there,' she says, signalling at her crumpled shirt and her battered trainers. She always jokes about being a mess and not even having time for lipstick, but Lynsey has one of those faces that hasn't changed in twenty years. Adam has always called her 'effortlessly pretty' – whatever that means.

She rattles the ice in her empty glass and I notice something glisten at her wrist before slipping beneath her cuff. Lynsey never wears jewellery; she says the kids always pull on it and break it.

'What's that?' I ask.

She makes a face, placing her hands on her lap beneath the table. 'John bought me a bracelet for our anniversary last month. It's a bit ostentatious. I'll probably take it back.'

'Show me,' I say.

She gets up and smooths down her top.

'Let me get the next round. Same again?'

I'm left frowning at her back as she heads for the bar. Why won't she show me the bracelet?

TWENTY-EIGHT

JULES

I'm not going to mention the bracelet again. Lynsey probably doesn't want to show off about getting an expensive gift from her partner after I told her that Adam and I are having issues. Of course it isn't linked to Adam. Of course it's not *that* bracelet. For God's sake, she's known Adam as long as I have. He and John are good friends.

I'm being stupid again.

While Lynsey's busy at the bar, I glance at my phone. There are nine new comments on my Kandid photo and a message from Curious2. His first one since I confessed my sordid secret. My chest contracts as I click on his name, expecting his reply to be cruel or dismissive. It's not.

Tell me what you think about when you touch yourself

My stomach flips. OK. Not what I was expecting. I glance up at Lynsey, who rolls her eyes back at me. She's being ignored by the barman, who's chatting to a woman wearing a '21 Today' sash.

I'm a total hypocrite, imagining my husband buying gifts for other women while I sit in a bar contemplating sexting with a stranger. But I'm not really doing anything wrong – this man knows I love my husband, I keep telling him that. I'm simply sharing fantasies with someone who will never know who I am. I may as well be talking to an AI bot because I'm never going to meet this stranger.

The barman has finally seen Lynsey, so I quickly reply to Curious2. I don't tell him what I really think about when I touch myself; instead, I describe what I've been imagining Adam doing to Bea. I'm sure a psychiatrist would have something to say about turning my fears into fantasies, but at least this way I can trivialise my insanity.

> I imagine that I work at a fancy corporate firm. My colleague is ruggedly handsome, his fitted suit always straining at his toned chest. We're meant to be at a work dinner but instead I tell him I need his help with some numbers.

As I picture this, I imagine myself as Bea. I bet she has no back fat, no unruly bikini line, no streaks of grey in her hair.

> I'm wearing a short black dress, and as I bend over the desk to get my papers, his hand slips between my legs. I part them and he knows we're never going to make it to dinner.

Lynsey places our drinks on the table, and I startle.
'What's up?'

I make a face. 'Leah's texting me, asking what she can eat for dinner. Give me a second.'

Three little dots appear. Curious2 is replying.

> God, that's hot. What happens next?

> I'll tell you later.

Three little dots appear. Disappear. Appear. He's back again.

> Do you talk like this with other guys on Kandid? I've never done this before.

> No, I never reply to them. They're awful. You're the only one I've shared my secret with.

> Would you count this as cheating?

> Definitely not! I would never do any of this in real life. I love my husband, I'm just very frustrated and I don't know what to do about it.

> I'm here if you want to talk about your feelings. I mean it. I didn't contact you to be a creep.

I want to keep talking to him, tell him more, tell him everything, but Lynsey is pushing my drink towards me. I put my phone away.

'Adam loves you,' she says, as if we're still in mid-conversation. 'You know John and I didn't get married because of you.'

'What?' I blink.

Why? Has she always been attracted to my husband? Is that what she's about to tell me? I take a long gulp of my drink, wincing because she's got us doubles.

'Yeah. I said to John there was no way he and I would ever be as good as you and Adam are at being husband and wife, so there was no point.'

Oh.

'That's ridiculous.'

'I'm serious. Not everyone is cut out for married life.'

I think of my mother and how she never remarried. 'Why

would I look for love when I have all the love I need right here,' she used to say, holding me tight. The last two years of her life she didn't even know who I was.

'John would love to get married,' Lynsey continues. 'But I prefer to be with someone because we *want* to be together, which we do. Not because I made a promise I can't easily get out of.'

The drink is strong, and her voice is starting to sound far away. 'Do you think John would ever cheat on you?' I ask.

She looks amused. 'No way. He's too lazy, too disorganised, and he's a crap liar. You think he'd be smart enough to lead a secret double life? He can't even remember what day bin day is. Anyway, he'd be stupid to throw away what we have for a quick shag.'

'What about you?' I ask, finding all of this a lot less funny than she is. 'Would you ever cheat on him?'

I think of Curious2 and how he enjoyed my story. I turned him on, and it felt good to not have to be in the same room as a man to make him hard. I wonder if he's unhappily married too. Is it his wife's fault he's talking to me... or mine?

Lynsey sucks on her lemon, still pondering my question. 'If I ever felt like cheating, then I'd know John and I were on a road to nowhere,' she says. 'As soon as you start looking around and checking out other guys, your relationship is over anyway.'

I always imagined I could tell Lynsey anything, but she wouldn't understand this. And I don't need to hear her say that confessing about my private life on Kandid for male attention is a sign I should leave Adam, which I'd never do, or that I should meet up with this Curious2 guy. Which I also would never do.

Lynsey reaches out across the table and takes my hand. 'Listen, if you're thinking of leaving Adam, that's OK. Never stay in a relationship that doesn't make you happy.'

One minute she's saying Adam is perfect and the next she's encouraging me to leave him?

'No! We're fine. It's just a blip.'

She seems comforted by that and changes the subject to her friend Fiona, the one with the duck-obsessed ex. Much to Lynsey's amusement, she's already met someone online and it's serious.

I lean forward, another person's drama a welcome distraction from my own. 'How serious?'

'Very. She's completely obsessed with him. You know that Kandid app I told you about? She met him on there. She was sharing all the issues she had with her ex and this guy was really nice to her. She felt listened to, you know?'

I know.

'So they've met up?'

'Not yet. He's English but lives abroad in some remote village in Italy or Greece or something. I don't know. But she says they've spoken a lot. They've even talked about moving in together.'

I'm both sceptical and a bit jealous. He either really likes her or she's going to be the next double-page spread in *Take a Break* magazine.

'And she's not freaked out by all of this?'

'No. She's all in. Apparently, he's really smart and wealthy. He's even helped her make money on crypto with her divorce settlement. Sounds too good to be true, if you ask me, but she's happy and at least this one isn't obsessed with poultry. She's flying over to see him next month.'

Maybe Fiona's story isn't sad and pathetic after all. Maybe it's me who needs to stop being so cynical.

'She's brave to start again,' I say.

Lynsey drains her drink and shrugs. 'When you get to our age, you know what you want, and you don't muck about. I'm happy for her. He's rich, he adores her and he's got a house in the sun. Result. Let's hope the sex is good.' She makes a face. 'Sorry.'

I smile and swirl the ice around in my glass with my paper straw. I think of Curious2, and my stomach tightens. I guess it's not that difficult to get obsessed with someone you've never met before.

'Do you think if you and John broke up, you'd get into another serious relationship?' I ask Lynsey.

She looks up at the ceiling, taking her time to answer.

'No.'

'That's sweet.'

'I'd sleep around.'

I laugh, covering my mouth to stop me spraying my drink everywhere.

'It's true. I'd shag, shag and shag. I'd shag men and women, older and younger than me, threesomes and orgies. Just sex. All the kind of sex I haven't had a chance to have yet. No way would I get serious and live with someone again. For what? To have long conversations about the best energy provider, and arguments over what to watch on Netflix, and nights taking it in turns to cook dinner, and have to listen to him moan about work or look after him when he has man flu? No way. I'd buy a little bedsit with a nice view, fill it with weird objet d'art, and do what the hell I want. I'd go back to my photography, maybe take up pottery or yoga, and grow sweet peas on my balcony. And when I got horny, I'd call someone, and we'd have sex and then they'd piss off again.'

I can't stop laughing.

'I'm not joking,' she says. 'It sounds bloody great. Now stop talking dirty to me because I'm getting too excited by the idea of solitude and sixty-niners on tap. Let's order that nice chocolate cake they do here and tell ourselves how lucky we are to have it all.'

I tell myself today is a cheat day and order the caramel cheesecake. She has the chocolate cake, and as she tells me about her kids' latest antics, I think about what she said. I have it all. I literally have everything I have ever wanted, yet here I am suspecting my best friend and my husband of lying to me while hypocritically flirting with a stranger.

All my unfounded fears would stop if only I could talk to Adam... but I'm too scared. I'm scared that if he confesses to no longer loving me, I'd be expected to leave him – and I don't think I could.

I'd prefer to be like all those famous women who ignore the antics of their philandering husbands because they're focused on the bigger picture. No point cutting your nose off to spite your face when life is better as a couple. I prefer to live in denial and proud ignorance than be someone others feel sorry for.

If Adam left me, I wouldn't want frenzied sex with a million others like Lynsey says she would, because deep down I know I could never, ever love anyone as much as I love my husband. I just don't know how to get him to love me back.

TWENTY-NINE
JULES

Adam didn't come home last night. He texted to say his clients wanted to go on to a bar after dinner, which meant he'd miss the last train home so would stay in a hotel instead. He reasoned it was easier than a taxi and that way he wouldn't wake me up. He has a company credit card so I can't even check what hotel he stayed at.

Maybe it wasn't a hotel. Maybe he went straight back to Bea's house, or whatever other woman he met last night.

I get on my hands and knees and fish the box full of my mother's money out from under my bed, flicking my fingers through it, smelling the musty scent of time. No one knows about this cash. All those years my mother was squirrelling it away while slowly losing her mind, what she was really doing was giving me a way out. Nothing is stopping me from putting it all in a bag right now, jumping on a plane and never turning back.

But then what? Leave my children, my job and my friends behind because my husband no longer loves me? And what about all the lovely plans we had for when both kids leave home? I can't walk away from a shared past and a dream future.

Maybe I'm overreacting. Or if Adam *is* having a fling, maybe he needs to work through something and then he'll come back to me and we'll both pretend it never happened.

I can cope with that, can't I? It's worth it. My family is worth it.

'Mum! There's no cereal left!' Leah shouts from the kitchen.

I push the money back under the bed and head downstairs.

THIRTY
LEAH

Anything for you, Leah.

An entire week has passed since Dylan last kissed me. I can't stop thinking about how eager he'd been to please me when I went to his flat last Saturday, how he'd treated me with respect like I was an equal and not some stupid child he doesn't want near him. I don't understand why he's being like this. It's not as if I've changed; I'm still the same person. He's just scared, now he knows my real age, that he'll get in trouble. But I'd never let that happen to him. I'd protect him. Protect *us*.

I'm standing outside his flat. I've realised the only reason he can't talk to me is because we're at school, in public, but if we could have some time together, alone, he'd see that our connection is still there. The downstairs door hasn't been fixed yet, so I let myself in. At the top of the stairs, I stand before his front door, brace myself and knock.

Nothing.

I ring the doorbell.

Nothing.

Did he see me and is pretending he's not in?

Last Saturday he told me he'd been jogging, like he does

every morning. I look at my phone. It's nine forty-two. How long does a run last?

I grasp his key in my hand until it leaves red lines on my palm. I like the bite of the metal against my skin. What if this is his spare door key and I let myself in and get into his bed? I know he still wants me; I can tell by the way he can't stand to look at me at school.

I slip the key into the lock. It slides in. It turns! The door opens with a light creak, and I stand there, one foot in and one foot out. Do I wait for him inside like in the movies? That could be romantic and exciting. There's no way he'd turn me away. But what if he does? I would die.

I shut and lock the door again and head back downstairs. Once on the pavement I weigh up my options: wait for him here or talk to him at school on Monday? A figure is running towards me, earplugs in, hood up, head down. It's him. I scurry away before he sees me, a grin spreading across my face.

I've just had the best idea to get him to finally accept that we're meant to be together.

THIRTY-ONE
LEAH

I've been crying all weekend. Art is my last lesson on a Monday, and the thought of another ninety minutes staring at Dylan without being able to touch him is too much to bear.

I wish I could speak to Reece about this but instead of coming back home after his holiday on Saturday, he went to stay with some friends. 'Friends', yeah right. He's free to hook up with whoever he wants, and I have to keep my love a secret. I was crying so hard last night that at one point Mum came in to ask if I was OK and I had to lie to her and say it was period cramps. She tried to hug me again, but I pushed her away, scared it would only make me cry even more.

But I have a plan. I've finally worked out how to show Dylan that our love is worth fighting for, and I've been all morning impatiently waiting for lunchtime so I can put it into action.

'Coming to the park?' Summer is waving a packet of crisps at me. She's still in her PE kit, all sweaty and glowing. Paige is waiting for us at the front of the school. Jacob has his arm around her, and a few of his mates are hanging about, including the new boy, Santi. I know they're my age, but they all look so young to me now.

'I'm going to the library. I have some homework to do,' I say.

Summer screws up her face. 'It's the second week of school, Leah. How are you behind already?'

I shrug and she rolls her eyes and walks away. She's still angry I didn't meet up with them on Saturday. They all went to the cinema, the boys too, including Santi. She told me he was there like I should care, as if I don't have bigger things to worry about.

'Suit yourself,' Summer says, joining the rest of them.

Paige looks over her shoulder at me, as if Summer has said something about me, and they head to the park. I'm not eating lunch; I have to get to the art block and talk to Dylan before my lesson.

I chose my outfit carefully last night. I'm wearing a short summer dress with buttons down the front, thin stockings and high boots. But it's what I have on underneath that matters.

My mum was in the living room yesterday, doom-scrolling through her phone as usual, so I went to her bedroom to see if she had any more of those cute vintage dresses. Her wardrobe is so crammed full of stuff it's ridiculous – I've never seen her wear half of it. I still haven't fixed the strap on her black dress that I wore to Carnage, but it's in my room so I'll do it later.

I was searching through a drawer where she keeps her handbags and that's when I found a load of unopened packages. Every single one was sexy lingerie. So gross! Not even the classy kind, either, but the ones you get in Ann Summers with a picture of a French maid costume or whatever on the front. I nearly puked in my own mouth.

Why the hell would she have stuff like that? At least all the packs were unopened. I took the one that contained a black lacy corset with matching suspenders and tried it on in my room. It fit perfectly. It's not as if my mum could have got into it anyway!

And that's what I have on under this dress. The cheap lace has been itching so badly all day, but it will be worth it to see Dylan's face. No way will he be able to resist me in this.

I can see him through the glass of the art room door. He's setting something up; it looks like chicken wire and plaster of Paris. He has some of it on his face, a white streak against his tanned skin that's beginning to fade after the summer. He looks so sweet, the way he's concentrating on what he's making. I guess this is a demonstration of what we will have to do in class. I watch him for a while, the way he moves, his fingertips white and shiny.

Without making a sound I let myself into his room, lowering the blind of the glass window. The light click of the door makes him look up, his face changing into a million different expressions all at once.

I can't do what I need to do here. There's no lock on the door.

'Leah, what are you doing? Class isn't for another hour.'

I don't say a word as I head for the photo lab. It sounds fancy, but it's not really. It's a dark cupboard at the back of the art room where photography students can process their pictures. I open the door and step inside. Then I wait.

He follows. I knew he would.

The light is red, the air heavy with the scent of chemicals. It's warm too. I shut the door behind him and lean against it.

'No,' he says, but his voice is thick and strangled like that time I made him get on his knees.

I leave my blazer on but start to unbutton my dress. He swallows.

'Leah, please,' he says.

What's he saying please for? Does he want me to go on, or stop?

I don't ask, I just keep unbuttoning my dress until I'm standing there wearing nothing but the black corset and stockings, my dress disappearing beneath my blazer. Dylan looks like a demon in this light, his face tinged red and his eyes completely black. He's trying to back away from me, but he can't: the space is too small and I'm leaning against the door.

I take his hand and run it over my breasts that are spilling out of the top of the corset, down over my waist and between my legs. His fingers are cold and wet against my thighs, and I realise they still have plaster of Paris on them. He's literally leaving his mark on me.

'Don't be scared,' I say. 'No one will know.'

He's straining against his jeans; I can see the outline of his erection. I knew he still wanted me! I pull him closer, our lips inches away, and I can taste the coffee on his breath. He leans in, like he's going to kiss my neck, and a groan escapes my lips.

'Fuck you,' he whispers in my ear.

I freeze.

'Fuck you and your stupid fucking games, Leah.'

I don't understand.

'You still care about me, Dylan. You still want me,' I say, running my hand over his thigh. I know he does, I can feel how hard he is against my hip.

'Move.'

I wrap my arms around his waist and pull him into me, his knee pressing between my legs. I go to kiss him but his hand travels up to my face and squeezes it, his fingers grasping my cheeks and pushing my lips out like a fish. It hurts.

'Do your dress up,' he says slowly through clenched teeth.

I just stand there. He squeezes tighter.

'Do your dress up, Leah, and let me out.'

My fingers shake as I attempt to do up the buttons. They're tiny and keep slipping. I'm trying to speak but his grip on my face is too hard.

When I'm done, he lets me go and pushes me to the side, opening the door like he's stepping out of a sauna and into a cool breeze. Once in the bright light of the classroom, he throws his head up to the ceiling and rubs his face with two hands. He's getting plaster in his hair. I go to walk past him, but he grabs me by the wrist and pushes me into the corner of the room. My head hits the wall with an echoing *thunk*.

For a thrilling moment I think he's going to kiss me, but he doesn't. He puts a hand on either side of me on the wall, so I'm trapped, and his voice drops to a low growl.

'Don't you dare try that shit with me again. Do you understand? How many times do I have to tell you to leave me alone?'

I swallow down the lump in my throat, but it doesn't help.

'I thought you liked me,' I say. I'm crying now, I can't help it, huge tears roll down my sore cheeks.

His face twists from anger to something softer, something like guilt and sadness. He steps back. 'You're nothing but a kid.'

'Would you have wanted more if I was the woman you thought I was?'

'Maybe,' he says quietly. 'Probably. But you're not a woman, you're a crazy, psychotic child, desperate for attention.'

There's that word again. Crazy. But he liked me making him crazy.

'Dylan, I—'

'Don't you get it? I hate you, Leah. I can't even stand to look at you.'

I reach out for him, but he slams the wall beside my head, making me yelp.

'Get out!' he shouts.

I run past him and throw the classroom door open, slamming straight into Santi. I thought he was hanging out with Summer and the boys. Why is he always lurking in the corridor?

'Leah, are you...'

I don't hear what else he has to say because I'm running too fast.

.   .   .

Santi is waiting for me when I come out of the girls' toilets. How long has he been standing there? I had to adjust my dress as I'd buttoned it up wrong and I still had streaks of plaster coating the inside of my thighs. My face was streaked black and white with mascara and plaster of Paris, which took ages to wipe off too. I look close to normal now, even though my eyes are bloodshot and my cheeks red.

'Leah,' Santi says, jogging up to me. 'Are you OK?'

It's the most he's ever spoken to me.

'I'm fine.'

'What the hell did Mr Ward say to you?'

'Nothing. I wanted to talk to him about something, but he was busy.'

Santi's forehead creases but he doesn't say anything further.

'Want to go for a walk?' he asks. 'We still have twenty minutes of lunch.'

I follow him around the perimeter of the school until we find ourselves at the back of the field. A few girls are playing football, but no one is paying any attention to us. Santi sits on one of the benches and I join him.

My face hurts where Dylan squeezed it. I rub my cheeks, wondering if they're bruised. He hates me. Dylan hates me. He said he can't stand the sight of me. I start crying, heavy, ugly sobs, what's left of my mascara stinging my eyes.

'I can come with you if you need to report anything,' Santi says.

I shake my head and lean into him, and he puts his arm around me but in a nice way. I feel safe. I wrap my own arms around his neck, crying into his shoulder, and he tightens his hold. He doesn't ask me questions or tell me everything is going to be OK, because I know it's not, he just waits until I stop crying.

'Sorry. I made your collar all messy,' I say, trying to laugh but failing.

He smiles. He really does have a nice smile.

'I'm a good listener,' he says. 'You know, if you want to talk. But you don't have to if you don't want to.'

I nod and sniff, then I take his hand. His smile widens and he gives me a look as if to say, *For real?* I nod again and lean my head on his shoulder.

'I don't like him,' he says. 'Mr Ward. He's... I don't know. He picks on you a lot.'

'It's not like that.'

His brow creases but he stays silent for a long time.

'We better head back,' he says eventually.

I don't know how long we've been sitting here, his hand heavy in mine, but I feel a bit better.

'Can I sit next to you in class?' he asks.

Shit! I forgot I have art next. How am I going to sit through an hour and a half of looking at Dylan after what he said to me? I want to cry again.

'I must look a real mess,' I say.

'No. You're really pretty,' Santi replies. 'Sorry, I didn't mean...'

I kiss his cheek and he blushes, which gives me an idea.

'I'd feel safer if you held my hand,' I say.

Santi nods slowly, like he's my protector, threading my fingers through his. I only have to pretend I like Santi for a little while until I change Dylan's mind. Everyone knows men want what they can't have; let's see how much he really hates me when he sees me with someone else.

THIRTY-TWO

LEAH

'Oh my God, you bitch!' I screech.

I'm rushing to get breakfast before school and find Reece lying on the sofa in nothing but boxer shorts, with a blanket slung around his middle and a plate and fork smeared with congealed ketchup on the coffee table beside him. I pull the blanket off him, and he kicks out, his eyes still half-closed.

'When did you get in?' I ask him.

'Keep your voice down! Like three or four o'clock this morning,' he says, scrambling on to his feet and pulling back the blanket like it's a tug of war. I can smell his rum breath from here.

'You have a bedroom upstairs, you know.'

'I didn't want Mum to hear me. Last thing I needed was her playing twenty questions in the middle of the night. That woman never sleeps.'

Fair enough. I throw myself on the couch beside him and he slings his arm around my shoulder.

'I hear you have a boyfriend,' he whispers into my ear.

I push him away. 'Your breath stinks.'

He blows in my face, and I laugh.

'Who told you that?' I say.

'Mum. She texted me every day I was in Ibiza, sharing random stuff I never asked to know about. I guess she thought I'd reply if she gave me some juicy gossip.'

'How was your holiday?'

He tightens his hold around my neck. 'Tell me who this guy is first!' he growls in a mock-manly voice. My brother couldn't be tough if you paid him.

I struggle out of his hold and shrug. 'No one. Met some guy at Carnage but he turned out to be a dickhead. Mum caught me crying so is probably making up some drama in her head. It was nothing.'

He watches me fiddle with the ring he bought me, a golden L, as I think about Santi. We spent the whole of art class yesterday holding hands and I noticed Dylan's gaze slip to us more than once. He kept watching as we left the class-room, sipping his stupid fancy coffee like it didn't bother him. As we reached the door, Santi kissed my cheek and I turned my head so our lips touched. I swear I heard Dylan take a sharp breath.

Reece knows I'm not telling him the whole truth, but he doesn't say anything. I switch on the TV so he doesn't ask me any more questions. Some blonde woman in a bright pink blazer on the local news is interviewing someone about online fraud. Boring. I mute it.

'It's your birthday tomorrow,' Reece says.

'I know.'

'Excited?'

'No.'

'You should be. I came back for it.'

'If Mum's taking me to Al Fresco, I'll kill myself.'

Reece passes me the fork off the dirty plate beside him and I pretend to stab myself.

'What on earth are you— Oh, Reece!' Mum has entered the

room and as soon as she spots her golden boy, I'm forgotten. 'I thought you were staying with friends!'

Ha. I bet his latest hook-up threw him out.

Mum hugs him and I notice her holding her breath. No bad words for her little prince, though. If that were me, she'd be sending me straight to the shower.

'So tell me all about it!' she exclaims, like Reece has popped in for a cup of tea and a gossip, and not like he's so hungover he's hanging out of his arse. 'Look how brown you are. Are you rested? You look tired. Maybe you should have a quiet day today.'

Reece grunts a 'yeah' in reply and I turn the TV up.

'All you need is love,' the morning television presenter is saying. 'But what if it comes at a price? Janet Jones, from Liverpool, thought she'd found the perfect man online. Three months later she was homeless, estranged from friends and family, and conned out of her life savings. Sextortion is on the rise, with sexploitation gangs specifically targeting lonely over-forties.'

Reece makes a face at me, and I burst out laughing.

'Why do they always do that?' he cries. 'Sexploitation, sextortion, well sexcuse me, I think it's time they sexterminated the lonely boomers off these dating sites.'

'Maybe they're sexperimenting,' I say. 'They aren't as sexperienced as you.'

Mum shushes us and turns the TV up.

'It's not only dating sites where both men and women are being tricked in the name of love,' the voiceover says, showing footage of an old lady in her fifties staring out of the window.

God, this is so pitiful. I can't watch. I get up and start stuffing some fruit and snacks into my schoolbag, but Mum is totally riveted. 'Even social media and confession sites, such as Kandid, are becoming new hunting grounds for fake lovers to find their vulnerable prey.'

'Anyone sad enough to go on Kandid deserves all they get,' Reece shouts.

'It's not all old people,' I reply. 'I heard someone in my class was using it like a diary last year. Mainly because no one she knew would see it.'

'Urgh.' Reece clutches his head and gets up, throwing his blanket on the sofa. Mum immediately starts folding it up. 'Kandid is full of old men moaning about their neighbour's lawn not being trimmed, or sleazeballs having affairs. No wonder these extortionists find it so easy to trick dumb old people out of money.'

Reece staggers upstairs and Mum switches off the TV. She looks even more irritable than normal.

'We need to talk about tomorrow,' she says.

Oh my God, this woman is obsessed with birthday parties. Please, birthday gods, don't let her buy me a sprinkle cake.

'I'm going out with my friends on Saturday,' I reply, opening the front door. 'Maybe the cinema or something.'

'OK, good, but tomorrow night we're having your party at home.'

What? 'A party?'

'You know... a family dinner. You, me, your dad and Reece. Let's make the most of having him home before he goes back to uni next month.'

Oh yeah, because it's all about Reece.

'I'll get us sushi and a cake – that cheesecake you like from the fancy bakery near the post office. Invite your friends.'

'Fine.'

Mum goes back to plumping up the sofa cushions and I grab my door keys, stuffing them in my bag. I stop. There's a piece of bright yellow paper amongst my schoolbooks that I don't recognise.

I pull it out and unfold it. Someone has written on it in big black letters:

I'M WATCHING YOU, LEAH.
I KNOW ALL ABOUT YOU AND MR WARD!

What the hell is this?

My heart is thundering, my skin puckered in cold sweat. I turn over the paper. There's nothing written on the back. I look inside my schoolbag but there's no other note or anything suspicious. I read it again, squinting at the handwriting. It's written in thick, bold capital letters – anyone could have written this. What the hell is going on?

'What's that?' Mum asks from the other side of the room.

My hand is trembling so hard the paper is making a flapping noise like boat sails in the wind. I whip around. 'Just leave me alone!' I shout. 'You're always on my case.'

'I'm worried about you, Leah,' she says in that forced fake voice of hers. 'You've been a bit... distracted lately. You hardly mention Summer or Paige anymore and you've been dressing differently. Are you OK, sweetheart?'

I stuff the yellow paper back in my bag as she crosses the room.

'I'm fine,' I say, applying lipstick in the hallway mirror with a shaky hand.

She's standing between me and the door.

'You look pretty,' she says as I push past her and leave the house.

Someone knows about me and Dylan and they're warning me off him. Who knows I slept with my teacher, and what do they want from me?

THIRTY-THREE

JULES

Work's quiet. Steve is out of the office and I'm struggling to find anything to keep me occupied. Devon is at Ameera's desk and they're working on the new campaign. Every time I walk past them, they stop talking, but I can see the graphics on the screen. They have it all wrong. Why would they want to target teenagers with a brand that's out of their price range when women my age still associate Medusa with quality? Yet everything I see online or in the back of magazines advertising to my demographic looks like something an eighty-year-old would wear. This is exhausting.

I'm going to say something. I can't stand here watching my colleagues fail.

'Devon,' I say, standing behind him.

He doesn't hear me, so I repeat his name louder.

'Devon!'

He rearranges his features from irritated to accommodating and smiles down at me.

'What's up, Jules?'

Never mind. I'm wasting my breath.

'Would either of you like a cup of tea?'

He holds up their two Starbucks cups and I nod. Of course, they don't. I don't want tea either, but I go into the tiny kitchen anyway and switch the kettle on. My phone keeps showing me breaking news articles – murders, climbing inflation rates, political scandals – and I think back to the feature on the news this morning about how men prey on women via sites like Kandid. Surely it can't be that common. Who would be so desperate for attention they'd give a stranger they met online all their money?

Maybe Reece is right. Maybe anyone over the age of forty should stay off the internet altogether. Best we stick to our book clubs and knitting circles if we want to make new friends.

I stay in the kitchen pretending to make tea and keep scrolling through my phone. No new message from Curious2, nothing interesting on social media, no text from Adam or the kids. Even Lynsey hasn't replied to my latest WhatsApp.

I'm about to put down the phone when it beeps loudly. It's a text from Adam. I open it, expecting it to be another reminder to buy bread or loo roll, but it's not.

I love you

The three little words are followed by a red heart emoji.

I stare at it, like it's written in code. I can't remember the last time Adam said that to me, let alone in writing. I think back to what Lynsey said in the bar a few days ago: *It's when they start showering you with love and affection out of the blue that you should be worried. That's a guilty conscience.*

This is beyond out of the blue. The red heart shines from my phone screen like a bloody full stop. I think of Bea's red dress. The shade of her lipstick. The colour of lust and violence and regret. Waves of anger bubble in my chest then subside to deep exhaustion. What does this mean? Adam isn't the kind of man who likes grand gestures or public displays of affection. He's steady and stoic and all the things I wish I was more of.

All week I've been veering from wanting to burn down the whole world and make a drastic change to my life, to simply accepting my unhappiness, taking the easy road and plodding along peacefully. I can't decide if feeling so angry about everything makes me powerful or stupid. Maybe his text means nothing. Or maybe it's time I faced the truth.

I go to reply then stop myself. I can't. Even a heart emoji would be a lie, like papering over the cracks. I put my phone face down on the counter and swallow down the lump in my throat.

I can't keep pretending like everything in my life isn't falling apart – my job, my marriage, my children – when all I do is try to make them happy. Leah really upset me this morning, acting like I don't know what will make her happy on her birthday. Of course I do! Because what my petulant child doesn't know is that her gift from me and her dad is us paying for her and her two best friends to see their favourite band in concert tomorrow night, the ridiculously named Flying Donkeys.

The plan is for Paige and Summer to meet her at our house after school tomorrow, open her presents and get ready. We'll eat her favourite sushi and cake, then I'll drop them off at the train station for 6.30pm. I even bought her the tour t-shirt to wear. She's going to love it. She should do, it cost me a fortune, but it's worth it if it pulls her out of her miserable funk.

I take a deep breath and try to banish away thoughts of my husband kissing another woman, or stadium crushes and perverts, or my children taking drugs or getting hurt. I tell myself if I imagine it all, then none of it will happen; but it's all lies.

I have no control over the decisions the ones I love make.

The house is empty when I get back, so I eat an anaemic salad on my own in front of a re-run of *Seinfeld*. Leah texts to say she's gone for a McDonald's with her friends, God only knows where Reece is, and Adam is out at work drinks. Or so he says. I didn't reply to his text in the end. I meant to, then he told me he was out again tonight, and I couldn't bring myself to keep pretending we were a normal married couple.

I go to bed at ten o'clock, but an hour passes and I'm not tired. I click on the Kandid app and write to Curious2.

> What do you do for a living?

He replies right away.

> Finance. Need any investment advice? Seriously, I'm always happy to help.

Weird response. It makes me think of that sextortion report on the news. I don't answer and he continues typing.

> What do you do?

> Fashion

> Sounds glamorous. Do you enjoy it?

> I don't enjoy anything anymore.

> I know how you feel.

He still hasn't told me why he's on the app. I searched his username, but he hasn't left any posts of his own. Lurker. How can I tell if he's genuine or pretending to be someone he's not? Only one way to find out.

> Why are you on here?

Curiosity. You?

Same. People get less curious with age. It's not a good thing.

Exactly. When I saw your post, I had to reply. I was worried about you. It looked real, not like you posted it for attention like everyone else on here.

It has never occurred to me that he may be worried about *me* trying to somehow trap *him*. I wonder if men are easier to trick out of money by someone pretending to be young and beautiful than women are. I'm going to delve a little deeper.

Are you in a relationship?

Kind of. I'm with someone but I think it's over.

My stomach flips and I hate myself for feeling happy about this news.

Are you looking for another relationship?

Are you?

Of course I'm not! Yet... is this how new relationships begin? Is this how things started with Fiona and her new man? She obviously trusts him. Lynsey says Fiona has photos of him, but they haven't video called yet because the WiFi doesn't work in the village he lives in. Sounds a little suspicious to me.

I keep typing.

Send me a photo of your face.

Send me one of yours.

No. I can't do that.

I wonder what Curious2 pictures when he's messaging me. I think of that often, how he must imagine me based on nothing but a photo of my bum. Would he be disappointed that my eyes have crow's feet, and my mouth is puckered by thin lines that are only visible after a long day when my lipstick starts to bleed from my lips? Would he notice that the skin on my hands is loosening and the veins beginning to rise, or the way my hair is not as thick as it used to be and no longer shines? Would he care?

I think he would, but I wouldn't. I know that if I met him, I wouldn't care what he looked like because the only reason I speak to him is to be heard. When I message him, I don't think of anyone. I don't see a face or a body or even hear a voice, I feel a pair of arms around me and sense the weight of someone beside me who understands.

I still get messages from other men on the app, but I don't reply to them because talking to Curious2 feels different. *He's* different. We're the same: two lonely, scared, frustrated people who aren't brave enough to do anything about their miserable lives. Yet... it's probably better this way. He's local. Imagine if he turned out to be the old man down the road or one of Reece's friends!

> Have you told the woman you're with how you're feeling?

He replies right away.

> No, because I don't know how I feel anymore. I thought I did, but since talking to you everything has changed.

My tummy does another little flip. I don't want to ruin anyone's relationship, but I feel the same way. Talking to him has shifted something inside of me too.

How do you think she'd react if she knew we were talking on
here?

How do you think your husband would react if he knew you
were sharing sexual fantasies with a stranger?

React? I don't think Adam *would* react, and that's the problem. I want to tell this man that Adam is having an affair and
would probably be relieved to have the perfect excuse to leave
me. But putting it in writing makes it too real, like I'm wishing it
into being.

I genuinely don't think my husband would care that I was
talking to you. He hasn't cared about anything I've done for a
long time.

He's an idiot. Where's my photo? :)

I can't show him my face, but I have more photos of me in
the same sexy lingerie as the first photo. I send one of me in a
black lacy bra, cleavage spilling out, nipples visible beneath the
sheer fabric, and two more of me bending over. I'd felt so
empowered taking those pictures at the time, convinced Adam
would look at them in the office and be desperate to get home to
me. I'm flooded with shame at the memory of his indifferent
'nice' response.

I don't realise I'm holding my breath until a reply flashes up
on my screen.

These photos are incredible. YOU are incredible. You deserve
to hear that every day.

A shiver of pleasure runs down my spine. I'm incredible.

He saw those photos and he didn't think, *Nice.* He thought I was incredible. There are two more messages.

> You're so sexy.

> I haven't got a thing done all day because all I can think about is you.

OK, that's too much. We're going too far.

I don't reply; instead, I turn out the light and imagine Adam saying those words to me. I imagine wearing that outfit for my husband, the look on his face as he tells me he's been thinking about me all day, and the sex we have without me taking off my underwear. My thighs are damp, and my breath is heavy when I hear the key in the door, instantly feeling guilty. I listen to every familiar sound my husband is making downstairs: Adam locking the front door, putting down his heavy work bag, taking off his shoes, climbing the stairs.

'Did you have a nice time?' I ask as he quietly opens the bedroom door.

The light from the hall illuminates him enough for me to see him jump as he takes off his jacket. 'Oh, you're awake.'

He blinks as I switch on the light. His voice has a slight slur to it, his shirt unbuttoned enough for me to glimpse a few strands of chest hair. Did he unbutton it? Or did Bea do that?

I push my legs together, still aching from my desire to be touched. If this were any other marriage, I'd help him take off his work clothes with a knowing smile or a wink or some kind of code only we understood. He'd appreciate me waiting up for him; he'd probably be the one to suggest sex. Something quick, something hungry and urgent. But this is Adam, looking at me as if it's an inconvenience that I'm still awake. As if having to talk to me is an extension of his arduous workday.

'Whose leaving drinks was it?' I ask.

'Mike. He's one of the developers. You don't know him.'

Does Adam? Does Adam know this Mike enough to choose beers with him over a night alone with his wife? A woman who strangers think is sexy and beautiful, but her own husband can't even make eye contact with.

Adam looks guilty and I can't help thinking about his random 'I love you' text that I didn't reply to, and the missing bracelet, and all his nights out.

He keeps his boxers on as he shuffles to our en-suite bathroom. He doesn't normally get this drunk. I listen to him brush his teeth and do that annoying gargling thing he does with the mouthwash. He pulls on a t-shirt and gets into bed beside me.

'You OK?' he asks.

If he'd asked me this a few years ago, I would have rested my head upon his chest, told him about my day, listened to his stories, but somehow this feels like a confrontation. Like he's daring me to start an argument.

'I'm fine,' I mutter, turning off the light.

My inner thighs are still throbbing, and my face is damp where a single tear is working its way down my cheek. I'm thankful it's dark in our room and he's stopped asking me questions. He didn't even shower. He's lying next to me, smelling of beer and expensive perfume, and he hasn't even tried to hide it.

THIRTY-FOUR

JULES

'Happy birthday!'

I pull back Leah's curtains, sunlight flooding her bedroom and making her glow like an angel. She curls up in a ball and covers her eyes.

'Who the hell *does* that?'

I give her a kiss on the top of her head, choosing not to react. 'It's your birthday and I've made you pancakes!'

She groans. 'I'm sleeping!'

'Extra syrup.'

I leave her to get ready for school while I prepare her breakfast. I've bought her a few gifts to unwrap – clothes and a bag she wanted – but her main present is the concert tickets for her and her friends. If she's not blaring out that awful rap music, she's listening to Flying Donkeys. They're a rip-off of the Rolling Stones, but why would she know or care about that?

The gifts are from Adam too, of course they are, but he has no idea what I've bought. If it were down to him, he'd probably just give the kids a handful of cash and a quick hug. But I think our children deserve a bit of fuss on their birthdays. Memories of my own birthdays as a child flash through my mind. Even though my mother never had much money, she made a fuss of me right up until her dementia hit. The first time she forgot my birthday was the first day I felt like I was losing her. I will never let my children down. They will always know I'm thinking of them.

Leah flies into the kitchen in a haze of perfume, her thick hair bouncing around her shoulders like a hood. I can't remember the last time my hair bounced.

'Where's Dad?' she asks, picking at one of the raspberries on her plate.

'He had to leave for work early and didn't want to wake you. He'll be home for your special dinner, though.'

'Cool.'

'And your brother stayed out last night but texted to say he'd be back this afternoon too.'

Completely unbothered. I wonder if she'd be so unfazed if I wasn't here to wish her a happy birthday. She's eyeing up the pile of cards on the table and the two squidgy gifts. I know what she's thinking – Reece got more presents on his birthday. But the concert tickets were expensive and they're in one of the envelopes. I grin at her, gesturing that she sits down.

'Come on, eat up. We can do presents tonight when everyone is here.'

'I'm not really hungry,' she says, smiling at the messages she's getting on her phone. 'Summer says she and Paige have a surprise for me this afternoon.'

I know. A surprise I paid for.

'It's crap having to go to school on my birthday.'

'There's nothing stopping you from celebrating it on the weekend too.'

She ignores me and keeps scrolling through her phone.

'My friends are waiting for me.'

'What about your pancakes?'

She folds them into a quarter and stuffs them in her mouth, then grabs her schoolbag and heads for the door.

'Thanks!' she shouts through a mouthful of mush.

She's not drunk the fresh orange juice I squeezed, and she didn't even notice the 'Happy Birthday' banner above the door.

THIRTY-FIVE
JULES

I'm working from home today. I need to email Steve to let him know our monthly catch-up meeting will have to be via Zoom. He's never in the office lately so what difference will it make? It's not like the rest of the team appreciate my input.

I clear up the breakfast things and tidy up the living room. Adam asked me once why I bother putting a vase of flowers on the dining table, moving it when we eat, then putting it back afterwards, considering we have no visitors to appreciate the effort. He doesn't get it. He doesn't understand how flowers make me smile, even if I'm the only one who sees them. That sometimes life isn't about the big things but all the silly little things that make us feel special.

I place my laptop on the clean table and open it, but I don't have that fire inside of me that I used to have. I've always loved my job; I would stay awake at night excited about a new collection and sharing my ideas with Steve into the early hours of the morning. But Medusa doesn't feel mine anymore. Work, my children, my husband – they were the three things I lived for, yet they've turned to sand running through my fingers and I don't know how to make them stick. Am I *meant* to let them go? Is that what they're all expecting?

I'm trying not to feel hurt about my job or take it personally, but I can't help it. It *feels* personal. Steve and I had such big plans for the company. I was practically his business partner back in the day; now I'm no different to the old desks we need to replace. The only time Steve gets excited about me coming into work is when I'm carrying homemade cupcakes. He gave me a lot of space when Mum died – I needed it and I appreciate it – but now it feels the same as it did when I went on maternity leave and struggled to get back into journalism. I took my eye off the ball. Things moved on. People changed things while I had my back turned. I don't know how to squeeze myself back in.

I scan my work calendar, relieved to see I have no meetings today, only my monthly catch-up with the boss. Good. Today is going to be busy with Leah's birthday plans. I have to pop out later to pick up the cake and order sushi.

My phone beeps. The Kandid symbol flashes up and my stomach squeezes into a tight knot.

> The first thing I looked at when I woke up were those photos you sent me.

My body fills with a warm glow as I imagine this man, whoever he is, thinking about me, imagining what I look like, stroking the screen of his phone wishing it were my skin he was touching.

> Good morning to you, too.

> Are you having a nice day?

I consider telling him it's my daughter's birthday. I want to pick up the phone and hear his voice, tell him about the mundanities of my day, tell him my husband only cares about work and possibly another woman, and how much my kids hate me. But I can't. This man doesn't care, not really; we are one another's distraction from the clusterfuck of our lives right now.

Yeah, just a normal Wednesday.

I have a proposition for you.

Oh?

Not like that. It's a business opportunity.

That seems a little presumptuous. I hardly know you.

Yeah, you do J. I think we've both got to know one another pretty well lately.

He's right. I've told him more about how I feel than I've told Adam in a long time. Some days I've hardly got anything done at all, too busy telling him my dreams, my fears, funny stories about my past.

I told him about my mum dying and the sale of her flat and even how scared I am that my children are going to end up leaving me right alongside their father. He has done the same, telling me his fears and explaining how hard it is to be vulnerable in front of the woman he loves because he knows she needs him to always be the strong one. He's told me he's trying to connect to his partner but it's not working, and I told him she doesn't sound good enough for him.

I go to type back then stop. My stomach drops. He typed J. Why did he type a J? He doesn't know my name.

J?

What?

You wrote 'J'

Oh, typo

No. It wasn't a typo.

I glance out of the window, squinting as the shadows shift over the bushes in my garden. The fence surrounding our house is low. We don't even have a burglar alarm. I type fast, my fingers trembling.

I have to go

Have I upset you? Was it the business talk?

This is weird. This whole thing is getting too heavy. This isn't what I want. I don't know *what* I want. I hate myself, and I really hate that I can't get this stranger out of my head!

I want to call Lynsey, ask her what she thinks of this whole mess, but she hasn't answered my messages in days. Back in the bar she told me that when a woman starts thinking sexually about another man then her marriage is already over. Is that true? Or is she trying to tell me something herself?

I stare at the message Curious2 sent me and reply.

No, you haven't upset me. Well, maybe a little. I don't know. Talking to you makes me happy, you make me feel good about myself, and I don't like that. It shouldn't be you who does that.

It should be your husband, right?

Yes.

I click off the app and throw my phone into my bag. I can't deal with this right now. I need to focus on my job and Leah's birthday later.

Another thirty minutes go by, and all I've done is flick through Facebook. How am I expected to work when no one in the office gives a shit about me and all I can think about is Curious2 and whether my marriage is worth saving?

I call Lynsey and she answers on the third ring.

'Oh, hi,' she says. There's a scrabbling sound at the other end, like she's covering the mouthpiece.

'Everything all right?' I ask.

She gives a light laugh. 'Yes, of course. I just got the kids down for their nap. Sorry I've been shit at replying to your messages.'

'Oh, don't worry about it.'

'Wait, it's Leah's birthday today, isn't it? Crap, I forgot to post her card.'

I'd noticed. First time in seventeen years Lynsey hasn't sent her goddaughter a card.

'Give her some money from me. Twenty. No, fifty. I'll pay you back.'

Fifty? That's more generous than normal.

'Is everything OK, Lynsey?' I ask.

'Yeah. Um, someone's at the door. I have to go. Chat soon, OK?'

She hangs up before I have a chance to say anything. That was weird. Then it dawns on me. Her boys go to nursery on a Wednesday. Why was she so desperate to get me off the phone, and why would she say her boys were asleep? She's normally home alone all day today.

I think about the last time we met up, how she was late, how she hid her new bracelet, how Adam left for work early this morning and said he'd be in meetings all day.

No. I'm being stupid. I'm going to drive myself mad

thinking this way. Lynsey's my best friend and Adam wouldn't do that. He wouldn't.

I go back to my laptop, write some ideas down for next season's newsletter campaign, then give up and wander into the kitchen for food. I smother four digestive biscuits with chocolate spread and check my phone. Nothing. No message from Adam, my friend, my boss, my secret man or my kids. Not even a thank you from Leah for the birthday fuss that only I made for her this morning.

Being invisible can only last for so long. Eventually people will notice you – even if you have to burn down the whole damn world to make them see.

THIRTY-SIX

LEAH

I keep thinking about that yellow note I found in my bag, telling myself it's nothing. But it's not nothing – it's proof that someone knows about Dylan and me. And that someone can destroy my life. I tore it up into tiny pieces before I left for school this morning and threw it in my bedroom bin. I was sick of staring at it, driving myself mad with worry, but now I wish I'd kept it to see if I recognise the handwriting.

God, this is so not fair. I should be thinking about my birthday today, the gifts people have bought me and the fuss I'll be getting tonight, yet instead I'm fixated on who could have seen me and Dylan together. The only person I can think of is Santi, but he's too nice. And he likes me. He wouldn't try and scare me, would he? I run my finger under my eyes to tidy up my make-up and put on a brave face. It's probably nothing. This is my special day and I'm not going to let anyone spoil it!

Paige and Summer are literally hopping up and down outside the school gates when they see me. Paige is holding a chocolate cupcake with a candy heart in the centre.

'Happy birthday!' she shouts, making sure everyone around us can hear.

I pretend to look embarrassed, but I secretly like it.

'Thanks,' I say, as Summer hugs me.

'We'll give you your present at your house after school,' Paige says.

'What?'

Summer whacks Paige on the arm and Paige's eyes widen.

'She means we might come over later,' Summer says.

Mum told me to invite my friends tonight but of course I didn't, because why would I subject them to that? They're acting kind of weird, though. Why do they want to crash my lame family birthday takeaway?

'But aren't we going shopping on Saturday and to see that new Zendaya movie? You can give me my gift then, it's no big deal.'

Paige and Summer give each other a coded look. 'We can't wait that long. You're going to love what we have for you,' Paige says. Then she nudges me and nods in the direction of the bike shed. 'Talking of love.'

Santi is walking towards us. He doesn't take his eyes off me the whole time. The boy is totally obsessed with me. He's even asked to see photos of my family, saying how much he'd love to meet my brother and hang out with us. It's a bit much but I'm secretly pleased because I need him to be really intense so that Dylan gets jealous. But then, what if Santi's the jealous type too and the note is him warning me off Dylan? Or worse. What if he's worked out I'm only using him?

It wasn't meant to go further than holding his hand in art class but then yesterday, when I saw Dylan walking towards us in the corridor at the end of the day, I kissed Santi properly. With tongue. He's actually a good kisser. Before our lips touched, he did that thing they do in the movies where he tucked my hair behind my ear then put his hands on either side of my face as he kissed me. It was perfect and I know Dylan saw it all.

Paige and Summer know about the kiss, and they've been going on about it non-stop, which is also part of my master plan. One more week of this and Dylan will be begging me to take him back. I think about the note again and consider warning him, then decide not to. It's only going to encourage him to keep away from me.

'Hey,' Santi says, sliding his arms around my neck and kissing me slowly in front of my friends. A few girls in the year below us stop and stare and, even though I'm pretending, I still feel like I'm cheating on Dylan.

'Did you know it's her birthday?' Paige says, handing me the cupcake she's holding.

'What?!' he cries, keeping his arm around me. 'Why didn't you tell me, Leah? I would have made a big deal of it.'

What wouldn't he make a big deal of? I take a bite of the cupcake, the icing smearing over my lips. Santi leans over and kisses me until we're both covered in icing. I burst out laughing. I don't think Dylan has ever made me laugh. Santi wipes some icing off my cheek, and I notice the side of his hand is stained black with ink.

'What's that?' I ask, holding up his hand.

He pulls his hand away. 'Art homework for that dickhead, Mr Ward.'

'You really hate him, eh?' I ask.

He makes a face I can't quite work out and pulls me closer to him. 'Yeah, and you should, too.'

THIRTY-SEVEN

JULES

I've done all of Leah's birthday errands. I treated myself to a sickly caramel thing at the overpriced coffee shop on the high street and I now have thirty minutes to pretend I've done some work before Steve and I have our monthly meeting. I wonder what we'll talk about. He probably wants me to take over the PR comms for the new campaign, because there's no way Ameera and the others will have any idea what they're doing.

I push open the front door as Reece is pulling it open.

'Oh good, you're home. Help me set up your sister's birthday.'

'I was just on my way out.'

I shut the door with my foot and push him back playfully. He doesn't object. Leah would never let me do that.

'Have a cup of tea first. Come on, you've either been asleep or with friends since you got back from Ibiza. I want to hear all about your birthday and what you got up to.'

I place the cake in the fridge and put the kettle on. He glances at his phone, his mouth set in a straight line.

'Five minutes. Seriously, Mum, I have someone I need to see.'

'You'll be back for Leah's party though, won't you?'

'I thought it was more of an early dinner thing.'

'Yes, sushi will be here at five thirty. Have some tea.' I switch the kettle on. 'So, was Ibiza wonderful?'

'Yeah, it was fun.'

'You look well. What about your friends?'

His cheeks go pink and I squeal.

'Did you meet someone special?'

Reece and I used to have so much fun gossiping about the boys he liked when he was younger. I know he talks to Leah about stuff like that, but I'm no longer part of their fun. When did that change? I make his tea and pass it to him.

'No gossip.'

Boring Mum, not in the inner circle anymore. He sips at his tea in short bursts – it's still too hot to drink – then pours the rest down the sink.

'I'm running late. I've got a couple of people I need to meet, but I'll be back for five.'

He grabs his backpack and slings it over his shoulder as my laptop starts to ring. I blow Reece a kiss, but he doesn't see me, he's already out the door.

'Steve!' I say, plastering a smile on my face and tilting the laptop on the kitchen table so he can't see the mess behind me. 'How's it going?'

'I was expecting you in the office today.'

I grimace. 'I know, but I've had terrible headaches all week and I figured I'd get more done at home. I was just talking to Reece about his holiday. How long has it been since you saw my kids? Honestly, you wouldn't recognise them. Reece is a man now. And can you believe Leah is seventeen today?'

The look on Steve's face tells me there's nothing he wants to talk about less than my children. I glance at the time on the top right of my Mac. I really must start decorating for Leah's party before she gets home, and before the sushi arrives.

'Everything OK?' I ask.

He looks far from OK.

'I have some news. I announced it to the team over lunch. Shame you weren't here.'

My chest tightens. 'Good news?'

'Yes and no. Listen, Jules, we've known one another a very long time, right?'

I nod. This doesn't feel like good news.

'I didn't want to have this chat over Zoom – but it is what it is.' He takes a deep breath. 'I've sold forty-nine per cent of the business to Starz.'

It takes a while for me to process what he's saying. Starz is an American teen brand which sells ugly overpriced sunglasses and gaudy handbags that young influencers flog on TikTok and YouTube. I know this because Leah raves about their stuff and I always refuse to buy it.

'But that's not our market,' I stutter.

'It's *exactly* our market, Julia. Youth is everything and Starz will be taking Medusa across the pond.'

Why didn't he mention any of this to me? I thought we were friends. Colleagues. Partners!

'And you're keeping the remaining fifty-one per cent?' I ask.

Steve swallows. 'For now, but I've been thinking this through for a long time and... I think the time has come for me to put my future first. My family.'

Nonsense! He doesn't give a shit about his family. Why doesn't he tell the truth, that he's going to hand the entire business to someone else because he wants to be rich and carefree and drive a Porsche around Marbella while he's still young enough to not look completely ridiculous.

'So there's a chance you'll walk away from Medusa? Steve, Starz don't understand our brand at all. Not the vision we built. They'll change everything. And what does that mean for the team? How did they take it?'

Steve has the gall to smile. 'They're over the moon. It means we'll be merging with Starz's offices in New York. Great opportunities for staff to go over there and the brand will be integrated into Starz's future campaigns. They work with Lil Bass. You probably don't know who she is.'

'Yes, I do.'

'Well, imagine her wearing our next collection!'

Must I?

'So if you stay, the UK office will remain too, right?'

Silence. So that's how it is.

'I don't know yet. Probably. Depends on who buys the remaining shares.'

'So where does that leave me?' I say it so quietly I'm not sure he's even heard me.

'It's not the end of the world, Julia. There are lots of options. There's the opportunity to work remotely, or take the very generous redundancy package, or even move to New York. Although...'

He knows I'm not going to move to New York.

'Of course, we don't want to lose you...'

We? Who's 'we'?

'But let's be honest, your heart hasn't been in it for a while now.'

That's not true! This has nothing to do with my heart, but all to do with my age. He says it like I've been treading water for years, waiting for the opportunity to be paid off, when the truth is I've been slowly pushed out by all the younger, hungrier children Steve insists on hiring. The ones who are happy to earn a pittance as they still live with their parents and 'experience' is a currency they can afford to be paid in. I bet Ameera and Devon will jump at the chance to move to New York, because they can, because their lives haven't properly started yet.

And mine? I guess mine is over. Never mind that I have the most experience, that I have built the company from the ground up, that my kids are fully grown and I won't be taking time off to raise my family or tend to any more ailing parents. I'm free to dedicate everything to my job now just as my job decides they need to make room for younger blood.

'I thought you'd be happy to finally get to slow down,' he says. He actually believes his own bollocks. He thinks I'm like Cynthia, wanting to go from being a mother to biding my time until I can be a grandmother. As if caring for others is my only worth. No one is telling Adam to slow down. No one thinks it's a treat for men to get to stop before they want to.

'Why do you think I want to slow down, Steve?' I ask.

I can tell by the expression on his face that I haven't been successful in hiding the steel in my voice.

'You've had a lot on lately. Give yourself a break.'

'And do nothing for the next thirty years?' I shout.

He recoils, genuinely shocked by my reaction. He's probably wondering why I'm making life hard for myself. He probably thinks he's doing me a huge favour. Fifty is only two years away. The world expects women like me to look forward to having less to worry about, doing less, being less. Maybe I can take up macramé?

I can feel my overpriced caramel coffee monstrosity climbing up my throat.

'Sleep on it. Let's have a chat when you're back in the office tomorrow,' Steve says. 'These things are always easier to discuss face to face. I'll look after you.'

I don't want you to look after me! I want to scream. *I want to be able to look after myself!*

I give him a shaky smile and agree that everything is going to be fine. My life is falling apart, but God forbid I upset anyone's feelings. As long as everyone's happy, who cares if I am?

I'm so sick of making the right decision for the sake of others. What if I made a bad decision for a change?

THIRTY-EIGHT

LEAH

Santi hasn't left my side all day today and it's beginning to irritate me, but I can't say anything because I need him to be extra attentive. Art is our next subject and Dylan is watching. We're sitting at the back, as usual, and Santi is stroking my waist with his left hand. With the other he's kissing the palm of my hand, telling me for the thousandth time that I should have told him it was my birthday because he would have planned something special for us.

It takes all of six minutes for Dylan to snap.

'Santi, focus on your work and not your girlfriend, please.'

The look Dylan is giving me is full of disgust. Is he angry because Santi isn't listening, or because Dylan wants me for himself? I can't stop thinking about the note I found in my bag. I want Dylan to be jealous of Santi, not the other way around. Santi's the only one who has seen me get upset around Dylan. If he suspects something, he could ruin everything. I edge away from him, but he sidles closer to me.

'Chill, Mr Ward. It's Leah's birthday!' Mel at the front of the class shouts out. I don't know Mel very well, but he's Jacob's friend which means he's now Santi's friend, too. Abdul, another one in their gang, joins in. 'Yeah, sir. Santi's just giving his girl some sugar.'

The class erupts into laughter, and I feel my cheeks prickle and sting. Dylan narrows his eyes, his jaw set hard. Is it working? I hold his gaze, trying to gauge what he's feeling, imagining what he's thinking. Does he wish he were my boyfriend? That he could take me out tonight, spoil me on my birthday, worship me how he did on that one perfect day together?

'Back to work,' Dylan says, turning to the whiteboard. 'Mel. Abdul. See me after class.'

The time goes fast and before I know it the bell signals the end of the lesson and the end of the school day. I'm waiting for Dylan to tell me he needs to talk to me after class too – maybe he'll wish me a happy birthday and apologise for what he said last time we were alone; maybe seeing me with someone else will have reminded him of what he's lost. But Dylan doesn't say anything. Even when I slow down, Santi's hand in mine pulling me towards the door, he refuses to make eye contact with me.

'Have a nice evening, everyone,' Dylan calls out.

'You doing anything nice tonight, sir?' a new girl I've never spoken to asks him as she pulls her bag on to her shoulder. Lick-ass.

I listen as I pretend to do up my laces, Santi and Summer hovering by the door waiting for me.

'I have a date,' Dylan replies with a sly grin directed at me.

He has a *date*?

No. He's lying to make me jealous. He can't be over me that easily.

A few of the students make an 'oooh' sound but I can hardly hear them because there's ringing in my ears and my legs feel numb. Santi's saying something to me about us going on a proper date, but I can't hear him. I've gone deaf. I can't see straight.

At the school gate Santi turns to me and kisses me softly on the lips.

'I'll call you later,' he says before heading to the bike shed. 'Let me know when you want to meet up. Invite your friends if you want.'

I don't reply. He's getting on my nerves now and my plan didn't even work. I can't believe Dylan has a date.

'You OK?' Summer asks.

I can see Paige is already at the bus stop, waiting for us.

'Yeah. Go on without me.'

'Don't forget we're coming to yours later.'

'OK. Whatever,' I say. Their birthday present is the least of my concerns right now. 'I need to talk to Santi about something.'

I do need to talk to him, actually. I need to finish things. Summer raises her eyebrows, implying we're about to have some major make-out session, and I make a face, playing along as if I'm really into my new boyfriend. But it's not him I want to talk to right now – it's Dylan.

Summer heads to the bus stop, then without my friends or Santi seeing me, I wait in the shadows of the art block. It takes forty minutes until Dylan finally exits. I know he walks home from school because I know where he lives and it's only ten minutes away. Will he be going home first and getting changed, or meeting this mystery woman somewhere? Or maybe he was lying, trying to sound more interesting than he really is, and he'll be home alone all night instead.

I picture him answering the door to me in his pyjamas, his hair all messy like he's been watching TV in bed. I imagine him giving me a lazy smile when he realises it's me, rubbing the back of his neck, telling me to come in seeing as it's my birthday. I imagine this all the way to his house as I keep twenty steps behind him, slowing down behind parked cars so he doesn't notice me following. I even turn the volume off on my phone so nothing can give me away.

Dylan goes straight home and I'm about to follow him all the way to the front of his building when I notice a woman. Because that's what she is. Not a girl like me or a uni student, but a proper woman. And she's old. I presumed he liked girls his own age or a bit younger – girls like me who are tall with long brown hair and who like the same things he does – but she looks like she's in her mid-forties, old enough to be his mum. Maybe she is.

Dylan leans against the wall as she walks up to him, giving her the same smile I imagined him giving me. She looks behind her then leans against him. When she kisses him, she holds on to his hair with two bunched fists, her full body flush against his. Not his mum, then.

I can't stop watching. I wish I could get closer; I want to hear her voice and what he's saying to her. His hands go around her waist and he's kissing her back in a way that he never kissed me, like she's strong and dangerous, like he wants her to eat him whole. She laughs, deep and throaty, pulling him away from his building towards the direction of The Anchor pub down the road. They fall against the wall on the way, kissing hot and intense like they can't wait to rip one another's clothes off. He's never done that with me. He treated me like I might break, not like he wanted me to do the breaking.

I stand there, eyes filling with tears, the realisation finally hitting me that Dylan doesn't love me – he hates me, just as he said he did. It's completely and utterly over between us. They round the corner, and a sudden rush travels through me as I remember I still have his door key. I can enter his flat and wait for him. No, they will probably come back together. But I could go in there and take a look around, see if she's really his girlfriend or if she's some random date he met online.

I run across the road and bound up the stairs to his building two at a time, pushing open the main door that never locks. At the top of the building, my heart hammering in my chest and my breaths painful and sharp, I let myself into his flat.

It's quiet inside and it smells of fresh paint and ground coffee, all the canvases casting eerie shadows on the wall. His bed is unmade. I sit on it, running my hand over the side where I lay eleven days ago. Sex with him had turned my body to liquid, making me heady with desire. I would have done anything for him. I did. I wonder if he's changed the sheets since.

Next to his bed is a weird tube that looks like an orange and blue glue stick. I pick it up and read the writing on it. It has arrows at the bottom that say 'NEEDLE END'. Is it drugs? I peer closer and read the words at the top: 'EpiPen adrenaline'. Isn't that for people with allergies?

I don't like how little I know about him. I want to learn more. I want to learn everything.

I put it back and pick up a glass bottle, spraying myself with some of his aftershave. It brings back memories of how his neck smelled when I kissed behind his ears. I hate that I still want him, regardless of how cruel he's been.

I think about the yellow note and go through his meticulously organised paperwork, seeing if he got one too. But all his letters are white, and boring. Should I ask him whether he got a note, too? No, because if he didn't, he'll freak out and keep away from me even more than he is already.

His wardrobe door is open, and I look through it. OK, this is a lot of band t-shirts. Some I've heard of, like Kiss, the Beatles and AC/DC, and some I haven't. I pick one up – it has the outline of a woman's face on it. Blondie. Don't know her. I try the top on over my dress and look in the mirror. It's cute. I keep it on and look around the rest of his flat. Everything is so neat and tidy. I want to wreck the place and let him know he can't get away with being so mean to me. But I can't because he can't know I have his key. Maybe I should put it back now or drop it behind the radiator, so he thinks he misplaced it.

Then I think of him with that woman and the blood in my veins burns like molten iron. Is that what he really wanted all along? An older woman who is experienced, who isn't stupid and young and scared like me. Maybe he was humouring me all the time he thought I was twenty-one, pretending I was hot but deep down thinking I was sad and desperate.

I hate him. I hate him so much! I stay in his flat for ages, staring out of his window watching the silhouette of the trees claw at the greying sky. I wonder if anyone can see me in his flat from outside. Whoever knows my history with Dylan might be watching me right now, collecting evidence, planning my destruction. It could be anyone.

It's not until I see the faint stamp of the moon that I realise how late it is. I try to check the time, but my phone is dead. I look at the clock on his microwave. Shit! Hopefully my friends changed their mind about coming to my house tonight, but Mum is definitely going to go ballistic that I'm late for my own stupid birthday tea.

THIRTY-NINE

I miss one bus and the next one is ten minutes late. By the time I get home I expect to see everyone in front of the TV, but instead the front door is yanked open, and Mum starts screaming at me.

'Where have you been?'

Paige and Summer are there, standing next to the dinner table with sushi and a cheesecake on it. The sushi looks hard, and the cheesecake has gone dry. I glance at the kitchen clock – it's nearly eight thirty.

'My phone died,' I mumble, frowning at my friends. What are they still doing here? And why do they look so pissed off?

'Your father is driving up and down the neighbourhood looking for you. We thought something had happened. Summer said you were with a boy.'

'I was,' I say, widening my eyes at her as if to say, *What the fuck?*

'You're such a liar!' Summer shouts. She's leaning forward on the table, her nails pushing into the wood. 'I rang Santi at five o'clock and he said he hadn't spoken to you since we left school this afternoon. He's been really worried about you. We all have. And now we've missed the Donkeys.'

What the hell is she talking about? That's when I notice Paige sobbing, like proper crying, her little fairy face all red and blotchy. They've both changed their clothes and are wearing Flying Donkeys t-shirts. Paige throws something at me: three slips of paper that float to the floor like leaves. I pick them up. They're tickets to a gig in London for this evening. I don't get it.

'That was your surprise,' Summer says. 'Your mum paid for the three of us to go to the Flying Donkeys tonight. It started ten minutes ago so it's too late. Even if we leave now, by the time the next train comes and we get there, it will be over.' She slow claps. 'Well done, Leah.'

'I didn't know,' I say. 'I'm sorry, but I didn't know.'

'You're so fucking selfish,' Paige says between sobs. I've never heard her swear before.

Reece is on the couch. He looks up and I expect him to say something funny, tell everyone to calm down, but he looks at me like I'm a piece of shit. That hurts more than anything.

'I don't know what you're playing at, Leah, but your mum's right. You've changed,' Summer says, her voice like ice.

'I had no idea you'd planned a surprise!' I shout back.

'It's not only that, Leah,' she retaliates. 'You've been acting weird lately. We're meant to be your best friends, but you keep secrets from us, lie to us, you even dress differently now.'

I made an effort for my birthday today with a tight black dress and my high, lace-up boots. It's a bit over-the-top for school, I know, but I thought I looked cute. I know Dylan was checking out my legs.

'Yeah, since when have you been a fan of Blondie?' Paige says.

I forgot I was still wearing Dylan's t-shirt. I pull it down. It's longer than my dress.

Paige gives me a look of disgust. 'Let's go,' she says, pulling Summer by the arm.

My friends leave without even a hug or a goodbye. With a

sharp sigh, Mum picks up the sushi and cake and drops it all in the bin, giving me a shake of her head like she's so angry she can't even talk. I'm starving, but I don't say anything. I can't believe everyone is acting like this, as if I'm not under enough pressure as it is with Dylan and that freaky note. How was I supposed to know my parents got tickets for a gig for me and my friends tonight?

'So? Where were you?' Reece asks once Mum is out of the room. 'And where the hell did you get that top?'

I can't deal with him and his golden boy judgement right now. He acts like he's so bloody perfect around her when he's the one selling drugs and sleeping around.

'Fuck you,' I say, giving him the finger.

'Don't speak to your brother like that!' Mum shouts, storming in from the kitchen. I've never seen her look this mad before. Always the same – choosing Reece over me. Then Dad walks through the front door.

'Oh, thank goodness you're safe,' he says. 'Happy birthday, sweetheart. It's scary when we don't know where you are at night.'

'You'd know all about that,' Mum snarls.

'OK, Jules. Let's all calm down. Leah's fine.'

'Calm down?' My mum is screaming now, and she's holding something up above her head – a scrunched-up piece of black fabric and something lacy. 'You want to explain what the hell these were doing in your room and why they're both ripped?'

Oh, crap. That's her dress and the underwear I took from her wardrobe.

FORTY

JULES

'What were you doing in my room?' Leah screams at me.

Adam stands there, useless as usual, and Reece continues to scroll through his phone. Maybe if her father got involved more often, our daughter wouldn't be so secretive and sneaky.

'*Your* room?' I shout. 'What were you doing in *my* wardrobe stealing *my* dress and brand-new underwear?'

Reece mumbles something that sounds like 'nasty' but I ignore him and continue telling Leah off.

'I was putting a wash load on and picked up a bundle of clothes from the floor of your room – which is a pigsty, by the way – and found these.' I wave my clothes in her face.

The black underwear was from a very expensive online shop, back when I thought some satin and lace might bring my sex life back. I didn't realise until I received it that it was too small, and I'd never got around to sending it back. As for my dress, that dress, the one I met her father in. When did she wear it and what did she do in it? The straps are ripped, and the hem is all muddy.

I found my clothes in her room at the same time her friends arrived, so I decided I would talk to Leah calmly about it tomorrow. Let her enjoy her birthday with her friends first. But after the disappearing stunt she just pulled, I don't know what to think anymore. Who was she with? And why is she wearing sexy underwear?

'You don't understand!' Leah screams. She's still holding her schoolbag, her face red and pinched like she's been outside for hours. She has a faint bruise on either side of her cheeks.

'So tell me,' I say, folding my arms. 'I'm all ears. What was so important tonight that you let your family and friends down, on your own birthday, and worried us all sick?'

It must be serious if her best friends don't even know what she's been up to. They're good girls, Summer and Paige. They were as worried as we were. Even the boy they mentioned, Santi, even he was really worried. Leah pushes past me up the stairs and slams the door of her bedroom shut. I chase after her, wrenching it open. I never allowed our children to have locks on their doors for safety reasons, and the way she's acting now, I'm relieved.

'I can't believe you're treating me like this on my birthday!' she wails, tears streaming down her face. She pulls her schoolbooks out of her bag and a piece of yellow paper flies out. She looks at it, confused, then screams and scrunches it into a ball before throwing it back in along with a bottle of water and a power pack for her phone. What the hell is going on?

Adam joins me at the bedroom door.

'Come on, Leah, love. Let's talk about this,' he says.

I know she won't, though. This is how she gets when she's in a rage, thinking the world is against her.

Despite that knowledge, I lower my voice and try to speak calmly, like the 'parenting teens' podcasts tell you to do. 'Leah, please. We're worried. You can tell us anything.'

She gives a snort of a laugh and rolls her eyes.

'You two want to talk to *me* about good communication? Yeah, right.'

Well, clearly 'talk calmly' doesn't work. 'You're not leaving until I get some answers!'

'Get out of my way!' she shouts. She's trying to push past me, but I'm blocking her exit.

'Leah! I'm serious. Tell us what's going on.'

Leah shoves me and I pull her schoolbag out of her hand, throwing it to the floor. Adam gives me a look that he's been giving me more and more lately. Disappointment, exasperation, a profound sadness that he really expects more from me than this.

'Enough,' he says quietly, manoeuvring me out of the way.

Leah snatches up her bag, pushes past us and runs down the stairs.

'Where are you going?' I shout, chasing after her.

'I can't breathe in this house! You all treat me like a child.'

Leah races out of the house and I go to follow, but Adam stops me.

'Let her go,' he says. 'Let her cool down.'

'But she might do something stupid.'

'She won't. She's angry and sad and humiliated. Let's talk to her when she calms down and comes back.'

'But what if she doesn't come back? What if something happens to her?'

Why isn't he worried? Why doesn't he do something?

I'm crying huge, heaving tears of fear and guilt. I can't stop thinking of all the terrible things Leah might be caught up in, how we've failed her, and how many of my own secrets I'm keeping, but Adam doesn't say another word to me. He simply shuts the front door behind our daughter and heads for the bedroom.

'Where are you going?' I scream at his retreating back.

'I can't do this anymore,' he shouts out.

Does he mean me? Our marriage? I run after him, but he slams our bedroom door in my face and locks it.

FORTY-ONE

JULES

What if it's drugs? Maybe that's what she was stuffing in her bag when she left. Maybe she had coke wrapped up in that bright yellow paper. Reece has gone to his room so it's just me now, pacing the house and checking my phone every five minutes. How can Adam lock himself in our room, knowing I'm frantic and his daughter is running around at night alone? And what about her brother? Does he know something?

I knock on Reece's bedroom door, and he opens it, giving me the same look as his father did. Why is everyone acting as if *I'm* the crazy one?

'Do you know what this is about?' I ask him.

He shakes his head slowly.

'I think she's on drugs.'

Reece laughs then rubs his face back into a serious expression. 'Believe me, I'd know if she was on drugs. She's being a spoiled little princess, as usual. Probably got some ridiculous crush on someone again, like she had with that Nathan kid.'

'Not funny.'

That entire situation was terrifying. Leah's headteacher said if it happened again, she would get expelled. Surely my daughter learned her lesson.

'It's not a boy. Her friends said they called her boyfriend and—'

'Mum, chill. Seriously. I know you wasted all that money on the gig, but at least she's not hurt, and nothing happened to her. I'll talk to her when she comes back. OK?'

I place a hand on my son's cheek. My handsome, caring, clever boy. 'Thank you.'

Although 'chill' is the last thing I'm able to do right now.

I go into Leah's room, and I look around. Mothers can sense when things are more worrying than they seem; we have an inexplicable connection to our babies that even science can't explain. Something is happening here, something serious. And regardless of what her father says, I'm not going to stand by and watch her make any more bad decisions. There have to be some clues somewhere.

Leah's room is disgusting. I've refused to clean it since she was thirteen, not that she lets me in here very often, but this is next-level vile. From where I'm standing, I can see three mugs, a half-eaten bowl of cereal, and what looks like a screwed-up case from the cupcakes I made her friends weeks ago. Half the contents of her wardrobe are on her bed and the other half are on the floor, where I left them after finding my dress. I don't know where to start looking, so I put her clothes away one by one, searching in every pocket as I go. Then I move on to the countless handbags she has, no idea why I bought her another one for her birthday, but all I find are old receipts, some sticky sweets and hair bands.

I look under her bed, instantly wishing I hadn't as it's nothing but mounds of dust, then rifle through her bedside table. There's no alcohol, not even a cigarette. Nothing. Maybe she has something hidden in her schoolbag, but I can't check because she's taken it with her. *Dammit!*

Her room stinks of burned paper and I open the window. The letters! I fall to my knees and dive under her desk. Inside her metal bin I find a million bright yellow squares of paper ripped into tiny confetti and the remnants of burned letters. I squint at the curled-up pieces that crumble like dead moth's wings between my fingers. I can only make out a few words: 'is a bitch', 'our love can't be defined', 'the way you touched'. What does this mean? Who has she been writing to?

This is impossible. I sit on her bed then fall back on it, using her cuddly Garfield toy as a cushion. I remember buying her that cat for her sixth birthday; it reminded me of one I had as a child. She used to keep her pyjamas in it, and I once found a stash of chocolate she'd kept in there for months which had melted and seeped through the fabric. She'd cried when Garfield had to go in the washing machine.

My heart quickens as I push down on the toy, the palm of my hand hitting on something hard with sharp corners. I inch the zip back, my breath catching in my throat as I push my hand inside, where I can feel something solid. I pull out a wooden box, my heart beating so hard I can feel it in my mouth, images of pornography and heroin syringes filling my head. I open the lid but all I find inside is a lighter, a wad of letters – some of them with corners singed and blackened – along with a crumpled sandwich bag, a hard ball of masticated gum, plus a tiny football charm and a keyring shaped like a marijuana leaf. Hardly horrifying contraband.

With a mounting sense of relief, I throw the gum in the bin and go to do the same with the plastic bag, but then I peer closer. There's something inside. I reach in, my fingertips brushing against something tacky and plastic that feels like a hardened deflated balloon. I pull it out and with a small yelp realise what it is, dropping the used condom to the carpet, where it lands like a dead squid, pale and gelatinous.

Why the hell does Leah have a used condom hidden in her room? Why? Why would anyone do that?

My hands tremble as I sit on the floor and scatter the letters on the carpet. I know her thoughts are private – it was the first thing the therapist told me when she explained the thinking behind burning the letters – but this is different. This is about saving my little girl.

The first letter, conveniently dated like it's homework, tells me nothing. It's just a few sketches and complaints about how I don't stop moaning about the smell of burning so she'll burn these letters later. The next letter is a slightly singed drawing of a boy playing the guitar, with poetic writing around the edges. She's such a good artist. Half of it has been burned but it must be important because she clearly rescued it from the cinders. Who is this boy? Below the sketch she goes into detail about how she's going to lose her virginity at Carnage Festival and wear my dress. She *what*?

My skin starts to prickle, the back of my neck sweating yet the rest of me freezing cold. So that's why she was so upset the other day, because she lost her virginity to a boy who dumped her. I don't know what to do with that information. Should I tell Adam? I take a deep breath and try to be logical. She's seventeen now. That's not illegal, and at least she used protection. I know she did because *I'm sitting right next to it*!

But who did she sleep with? I need to know it was consensual and that he didn't hurt her. Was it that Santi boy Summer was talking to this afternoon? Was he the one who made her cry? Maybe it's in the rest of the letters. I kneel and spread them out, picking one up and then another, her blue, loopy handwriting blurring, words running into one another the faster I read. They don't seem to be in any particular order. The next one is dated yesterday.

I need you, Dylan. You told me not to tell anyone, but I have so many feelings bottled up. How am I meant to process this? Our secret is making me feel ill, and I think someone knows. Someone is warning me away from you, but it won't work – I won't let them come between us. I even considered going on that boomer app, Kandid, so I can get this out of me. It hurts, you prick. You're killing me.

Who's Dylan? What secret? Why don't her friends know anything about this? The next letter is dated the first of September. Her first day of sixth form.

I can't believe you're my new teacher. You are my one true love, the one fate brought me to meet at Carnage, and the one who I gave myself to – and now you're also Mr Ward, my art teacher? I feel both terrified and blessed. It's like the universe wants us to spend every day together. I know you don't see it like this yet, but you will. We need to give it time. I'm not going to lose you, Dylan. Nothing and no one will come between us.

Teacher? I don't understand. The next letter is screwed up. With shaking fingers, I smooth it down, picking out each word hidden in the creases.

I'll never forget the look on your face when you saw me in class on our first day. You went so pale, whiter than this page. I hope one day you will forgive me for lying about my age when we first met. If I'd told you the truth, you'd never have made love to me. If you'd known I was going to be one of your students, you'd never have even spoken to me. But look at what we became. I'm nearly seventeen, you're twenty-five, what's eight years?

I feel the ground move beneath me, the room is rocking, the

letters multiply and shift as I struggle to focus on the one in my clammy hand.

> *I know you say I must keep away, but I can't. What we have, it's real. It's true. It's love. You can't fight that – and I'm not going to let you!*

Everything makes sense now, while nothing makes sense at all. Images and words and memories solidify, shifting, slotting together. I gather all the pages together, run to the bathroom and vomit into the sink.

FORTY-TWO

LEAH

I can't believe I'm spending my seventeenth birthday sitting on a swing drinking warm vodka from the same plastic water bottle I took to Carnage Festival.

I've been staring at the new note I found in my schoolbag for the last fifteen minutes and I can't stop crying. The big black capital letters are blurring with my tears and the vodka, making it harder to read as every minute passes. Black against yellow, like a giant evil wasp out to get me. It's the same writing as last time, except this time the message is more frightening.

I'M WARNING YOU, LEAH.
LEAVE MR WARD ALONE OR YOU'RE GOING TO
GET HURT.

What do they mean by 'get hurt'? Do they mean my feelings or is this a threat? And why would anyone want to hurt *me*? I've not done anything wrong! I look around me. Are they still watching me? The park is quiet and still, but the lights aren't very bright – anyone could be hiding in the shadows, in the trees, behind the climbing frame.

A sob escapes my lips and I clamp my hand over my mouth. I should go home, I'm not safe, but I can't move. I'm too heavy, too tired, too angry to go back and face them all again.

I wipe my eyes with the back of my hand and take another sip of vodka, wincing as it burns the back of my throat. Half the bottle is already finished.

Maybe his new girlfriend or an ex is warning me off him. No, it has to be someone at school because the notes are always in my schoolbag, plus who else would call Dylan Mr Ward? Santi is the only one I can think of who would suspect anything or have a reason to keep me and Dylan apart, but I can't imagine him threatening me. He isn't a bad guy.

I stuff the paper in my bag at my feet and rest my head on the metal chain of the swing. I don't feel very well.

Santi has tried to call me three times this evening. What did Summer say to him? I bet he hates me too. Everyone hates me – no one even stopped me leaving the house. All my mum does is shout at me and all my dad does is try and calm her down. They're an embarrassment. When I'm married, I'm going to make sure I choose someone I actually like. Even Reece didn't back me up. Traitor!

The tips of my boots trail against the asphalt as I push myself back and forth on the swing. I'm only at the end of my road, not that anyone's come looking for me. It's cold. I should have grabbed a coat.

I glance at my phone – no one besides Santi has called. Well, I'm not going back home now. Screw them. All of them.

I have twenty-four per cent battery now thanks to the power pack I grabbed from my room. I try calling Paige again, but it goes to voicemail. So does Summer's. It's nine fifteen – it's not like either of them is asleep. Is that it? So they're not my friends anymore?

And the worst thing is, as if my life isn't completely ruined, I can't stop thinking about Dylan and that old bitch he was with. I'm still wearing his Blondie t-shirt over my dress. I rub the fabric between my fingers, bringing it up to my nose. It doesn't smell of him. It doesn't smell of anything.

Is he still with her? Did she stay the night? She was so elegant and put together and rich-looking. I bet she wouldn't sit in a park crying over Dylan if he dumped her; she probably owns a villa in Italy and goes on yachting holidays. What if he told her about me and they're lying in his bed together right now, naked, laughing about the kid in his class that has a crush on him.

I start crying again, the vodka burning my throat as I keep sipping. It tastes like petrol, but I don't care. I don't want to feel sad anymore, or scared, or lonely. I don't want to remember this birthday at all. My phone rings and I answer it without looking at the name, thinking it will be Mum or one of my friends. It's Santi.

'Leah. Are you all right?'

Hearing his voice makes me start crying again.

'What's happened? Are you hurt?'

Why would he say that?

Leave Mr Ward alone or you're going to get hurt.

'Paige and Summer aren't talking to me,' I sob. 'And I had an argument with my family.'

I hiccup. Can he tell I'm drunk?

'Where are you?'

'The park on my road. The one on Apple Orchard Lane.'

'I'll be there as fast as I can.'

'What? No. Don't come.'

I try to tell him not to bother, but he's already hung up. Santi lives outside of town. He cycles to school. I don't know how quickly he can get here. I go back to swinging and drinking and crying, staring at my phone, waiting for my friends to text me back, but all is silent. It's dark now, the wind is picking up. A few leaves scrape along the ground and the swing creaks. My hands are like ice, and the smell of autumn is already in the air.

There's a shape in the distance, the silhouette of someone standing by the tree. Dylan? What if it's the person who put those notes in my schoolbag? I blink and they're gone. I really need to go home but my body has grown even heavier and my hands are so cold they're like claws grasping at the thick metal chain of the swing.

Five minutes pass, then ten, then a loud clatter makes me jump off the swing, but it's only Santi throwing his bike to the ground. He sees me and runs, literally runs, towards me. He doesn't say anything when he reaches me, he just wraps his arms around me and holds me tight.

'We were so worried about you,' he says into my hair. 'You disappeared. What happened?'

How do I know I can trust him? I push him off me.

'What?' he cries.

'I'm scared.'

He looks around him like he's ready to fight the darkness itself. 'Who hurt you?'

No one... yet. But they want to.

'I'm OK,' I say. 'I've just had a really bad birthday. Everyone has been so mean to me and...' I hiccup. He puts his arm around me, and this time I lean into him, my legs wobbling, grateful for the literal support. 'You'd never hurt me, would you?' I say.

He's looking down at me, his eyes so dark it's like they're swallowing me whole. Of course it's not him leaving me those notes. Santi wouldn't scare me like that.

'Is this about Mr Ward?' he says.

What does he think he knows? I shake my head but it's obvious he doesn't believe me. I can't tell him about the threatening notes now – he'll report them to the headteacher, and all hell will break loose. This is something I have to deal with alone.

Santi leads me to a bench, where we sit down, the wood cold and grainy against my bare legs. I look over his shoulder at the mass of shadows behind him. I think we're alone, but it doesn't feel like we are. Whoever has been watching me might be watching me now.

'Where were you this evening?' Santi asks again slowly.

Another hiccup escapes and I rub at my face again.

'I lost track of time. I went to the shops, my phone died, then I missed the bus. I don't know why everyone is making such a big deal of it.' The lie comes easily but I'm slurring, making Santi pull back and search my face. He wipes the tears away from my cheeks, the way he did when Dylan made me cry on Monday. Two days ago. Just two days ago, I thought Dylan and I could have got back together, and in that time he's already found someone else. I start to cry heavy sobs again and Santi pulls me to him.

I'm cold and frightened, and I don't know who to trust anymore. Everyone has let me down, everyone but this sweet boy who I've been treating so badly.

I really thought that Dylan would love me if only I tried harder. I thought if he could see what he was missing, he'd remember what we had, what was worth fighting for, but he never really cared about me to begin with. My breath is coming in ragged starts, my chest so tight I'm shaking every time I try to fill my lungs.

'I'm sorry,' I say to Santi because I am. I shouldn't have used him like I did.

I pull back and look at his face. The way he's staring at me, so intense and tender, I want to feel that power again. I want to be wanted again. I go to kiss him, but he turns away.

'Don't you want me?' I say, tears streaming down my cheeks. I couldn't bear it if he rejected me too.

'Of course. I'm crazy about you,' he says.

There's that word again, the one Dylan used. Crazy. Is that

what I do to men, make them crazy? Or do they have to be crazy to get involved with me? Maybe I'm the one who's crazy.

'It's just that... you're drunk, Leah.'

'Only a bit. But it's OK. We can kiss.'

'I don't know...'

I pull him to me, and he lets me kiss him, and this time it's even better than before, because this time I want it. For real. This time I'm not kissing him because I want Dylan to see. I want to be with a boy I can trust who thinks I'm special. A boy I'm allowed to go out with. His arms are around me, his lips soft. I grasp the back of his head and pull him closer. I'm no longer cold. He stirs against me, and I realise I want more. I want to feel like I did with Dylan: I lead, they follow. Like magic.

I pull Dylan's Blondie t-shirt up and yank my dress up to my waist without our lips breaking contact, sitting astride Santi, one leg on either side of him. I can kiss him harder from this angle, and I can grind down on his lap where I can feel him straining for me against the cotton of my underwear.

It's easy, so easy, this power I have.

He breaks away, panting.

'What are you doing?' he says.

The streetlights of the park are a dull amber, but I can still see his face, his eyes wide with surprise, his mouth pink from where we've kissed so hard. Why has he stopped?

'Come on,' I say, reaching between my legs and his, rubbing him.

Dylan loved it when I did that. He wanted me to tell him what I liked, to take, take, take. The power courses through me, making my head spin. Being wanted, being desired, it's stronger than vodka. I want to see Santi beg for me, hear him groan at my touch, be unable to control himself. I'm in command; I can feel it like electricity at the tips of my fingers. I can do that to any guy I want. They answer to me.

Santi's growing harder beneath the denim of his jeans, so I

pull down the zipper and he makes a low moaning noise as I kiss his neck.

'Take me,' I whisper.

Dylan was my first, but Santi can still be my first in other ways. I've never had sex outside or in the sitting position with me on top.

He pulls my hand away and gently places me back on the bench beside him.

'Not like this,' he says.

'What?'

He shuffles uncomfortably as he zips up his jeans. His face is set stern, like I've done something wrong.

'Leah, I like you. I really like you.'

I go to kiss him again, my stomach hot from the vodka and the words he's saying. He turns his face away.

'I like you... which is why, if we do this, I want to do it properly. I haven't even taken you on a date yet. We don't have to rush. If we go further, it should be in a room, in private, somewhere nicer than this.'

'I don't care,' I say.

'You should.'

He may as well have slapped me across the face. I can feel the heat on my chest blooming with shame. I go to unscrew the lid from my almost empty vodka bottle, but Santi pushes it down.

'Leah, tell me what's going on. I know that shithead Ward did something or said something to you. You can trust me.'

Can I? Can I really?

'You're being a dick!' I shout. 'You should be thankful I want to have sex with you. I could have anyone, you know, and here you are calling me easy?'

'I didn't say that.'

I climb back on top of him. 'Come on, then.'

'No.'

Why can't he leave things alone? I don't want to talk or think about Dylan anymore. I want to forget. I want to have sex and be consumed by it all and drown in the moment.

'Fine! Then it's over,' I say, getting to my feet. I pull down my dress and t-shirt and gulp down the last of my vodka. It's beginning to taste of plastic.

Santi's face crumbles in the pale yellow streetlight.

'I know you've been using me all this time, Leah. I'm not stupid,' he shouts. 'Tell me the truth.'

I push him away and he stumbles backward.

'You can't deal with the truth!' I scream, everything sway-ing, my legs going soft beneath me. 'None of you can. This is all his fault and I'm the one paying the price.'

'Who?' he's shouting. 'Mr Ward? It is, isn't it? It's him!'

I can no longer focus on Santi's sweet little face. His stupid, childlike, trusting face. He picks up his bike and gets on.

'I'm going to kill him,' he says quietly. 'Whatever that creep did to you, I'm going to kill him.'

I tell him to stop, stumbling forward, trying to stop him cycling off, but I miss and fall face first on to the wet grass. Santi disappears into the dark as the shadows watch on and I puke all over the swing.

FORTY-THREE
JULES

I've read all the letters. Twice. I can't breathe. All the information I've gathered is whizzing around my head like a merry-go-round and it won't stop.

Leah has had sex with a man who's twenty-five years old and he's her teacher and she lied about her age and they smoked weed at a music festival and he believed that my sixteen-year-old daughter was twenty-one and he had sex with her in a tent my baby had sex with a grown man in a tent at a music festival and she was drinking and there were drugs and he touched her and she liked it and now he's her teacher and she wants more and she thinks it's love and he's twenty-five and her teacher he's her teacher her teacher her teacher and what do I do?

I don't know what to do. I can't make it make sense. I can't make it stop.

I vomit again.

I'm the adult, the parent. There has to be a solution, but it's not that simple. If I tell the headteacher, she'll expel Leah; she's already on her last warning. She tricked her teacher – he's trying to keep her at arm's length, and technically he didn't do anything wrong. Did he? Unless I lie and say he groomed her, but that's not true. She's chasing after him! She has his used condom, which I could show Ms Willis along with the letters, but Leah will defend him. I can't risk her getting in trouble or muddying her name any further. Even if he loses his job, she will get thrown out too and the only other sixth form college nearby is awful. All of this will ruin her chances of university and she's a bright girl. I won't allow her to ruin her future over yet another bad decision.

I need to tell Adam. I can't tell Adam. This will kill him, or he'll go after this man, and everything will be worse.

I don't know what to do.

FORTY-FOUR
JULES

I don't do anything. I take the used gum out of the wastepaper basket and place it back in the box. I then add the football trinket and keyring, and with bile still coating the inside of my mouth, I pick up the crumpled condom filled with the semen of my teenage daughter's teacher, and I place it back inside the bag and add that too. Then I take a photo of every letter and put them inside the box, which I zip back up inside the bright orange cat. It's the only way. I don't know where Leah is right now, who she's with or what she's doing, but I do know she will write it down. And when she does, I will read it and I will know what to do next.

It's ten o'clock and the house is silent. Adam has unlocked our bedroom door but no one has washed up, and all the lights are still on downstairs. I leave the mess and slide into bed beside my husband, who's listening to his podcast, eyes closed, hands clasped and resting on his chest. He looks like the sarcophagus of a heroic saint.

So still. So at peace.

My Adam.

So unruffled. So good.

Neither of us knows where our daughter is right now, yet only one of us cares enough that she's been vomiting. He plucks an earbud out of one ear and turns to me.

'Want to talk about whatever the hell tonight was about?'

I shake my head and pull the covers up to my neck. I haven't brushed my teeth, but I can't get up now, my legs no longer work. It's not like I'm getting kissed. He cocks his head to one side and pulls the other earbud out of his ear at the sound of a key turning in the lock downstairs.

'You talk to her,' I say, picking up my book and staring at the blurry sentences swimming over the page. Twenty-six little letters make up everything that matters. Everything my daughter wrote, everything I want to say, is made up of just twenty-six little letters.

Adam closes the bedroom door quietly behind him and I lie there staring at my sea of letters, muffled voices floating beneath the door. When he returns, he smiles and pops his earbuds back in.

'Well?' I ask, slamming the book closed.

'She's sorry. She said she didn't know about the concert and she's really sad she missed out.'

Where has she been, Adam? Has she been having wild sex in an alleyway with her teacher, Adam? Was she drinking and taking drugs and hanging around empty streets alone, Adam?

'Anything else?'

He shrugs. 'She sounds very tired. She said she wants to sleep.'

He places a hand on my shoulder and gives me a weak smile. My phone buzzes on the bedside table. I want it to be Curious2. I need to be someone different right now, but it's not him; it's Steve sending me a meeting request for tomorrow.

Oh, yes. I might be out of a job soon.

FORTY-FIVE
JULES

Leah and Reece are still in bed when I leave the house this morning. I know Leah starts school later on a Thursday, so I don't bother waking her up. I've hardly slept a wink all night, my stomach aching and body buzzing like it's full of live wires hissing and spitting under my skin. I haven't even had a chance to think about my job or yesterday's meeting with Steve. I don't know what any of it means in terms of my career, which is why I have to go in today.

I breathe in for four and out for eight as I drive to work but it does nothing to calm me or eradicate the images of my daughter sitting in class today, being taught by a man whose penis has been inside her.

Leah and her secrets. She lies to me, her father, her best friends, an innocent boy who appears to be totally smitten with her. I don't know who she is anymore. I want to kill this Dylan man, but I can't do anything until I know more, like where the hell she was last night. If he does anything further with her, now she's his student and he knows her real age, I can get him fired. I just need to wait.

I breathe in for four, breathe out for eight. In for four, out for eight. It's useless. No one tells you giving birth is the least painful part of being a mother.

'Julia!'

Steve is waiting for me at the entrance to the office building. Our company has been based in the same building since we first opened twelve years ago. We share the second floor with a solicitor and a chiropractor, and the shop downstairs has been a printer, a parcel delivery company and now a car rental company. The only thing that hasn't changed over the years is Medusa – until now.

My boss falls into step beside me as we enter the building. 'You look tired.'

Ah, what every woman wants to hear.

'Kids, you know. They don't let you sleep as babies and then they become teenagers and you're still up all night.'

He chuckles and I'm relieved he doesn't ask anything else. He waits for me to hang my jacket up and place my handbag at my desk, then he offers me a coffee, opening his office door and waving me in.

'After you,' he says.

He shuts the door behind us. I stay standing.

'I'm not enjoying this either,' he says.

I believe him. He looks grey – skin, hair, stubble, all monochrome like a dead man.

'Have I lost my job, Steve?'

He drops down into the padded seat behind his desk and it lets out an exhausted puff of air.

'No.' He rubs his face. 'Sit down, Julia. Please.'

I breathe out. I didn't realise I was holding my breath. I keep doing that. Surely breathing shouldn't be this difficult.

Steve is looking at me like he's studying a rock sample and I want to cry, yet I'm too overwhelmed to cry. I want to talk to

Curious2 about my mess of a life. Not my husband or best friend or my boss who is right in front of me, I want to talk to someone I have never met. God, this is ridiculous. I need a therapist not a crush on an internet stranger.

'Julia.'

I look up.

'I'm still not sure what the future looks like for Medusa. I won't sell my shares until I find the right person, so for now your job is safe... if you still want it. You can work from home, for now, although remember that, well, things may change if I hand over control.'

'Or?'

'Or what?'

Steve leans forward. I don't elaborate.

'Oh. Right. Yes.' He rubs his face again. 'If you choose to walk away, there's a redundancy package. It's generous.'

I stay silent because I'm empty. I'm done. He probably thinks me losing my job is the worst thing to happen to me when it's actually my husband and children I'm worried about losing right now.

'Look, Julia. Neither of us is getting any younger.'

He's really full of compliments today. Both our hands are resting on his desk, the tips of his fingers less than an inch from mine. They move, like he wants to take my hand, but he doesn't. What does Steve see when he looks at me? What am I to him, now I'm no longer one of the pretty ornaments to decorate his office with?

'I'm worried about you,' he says. 'You've not been yourself lately.'

He means I haven't been what he needs me to be. Although my mother dying has been very convenient when it comes to phasing me out. Sunday is the first anniversary of her death. I don't expect Steve to remember; I know Adam and the kids haven't. Everyone knows grief isn't meant to last longer than the time between death and the funeral. After that it makes people uncomfortable.

'You've just told me that you've sold half the company,' I say calmly. 'A company that I helped build and worked with you on for twelve years – and you didn't even have the courtesy to tell me first. How do you expect me to be acting?'

He runs both his hands through his hair like his team lost the FA Cup.

'Julia. Please. Don't make this harder for me. Do you think it's easy for me to hand over half my company to competitors and consider walking away from the rest?'

I do, actually.

'Leave behind everything I've worked so hard for?'

What *we've* worked so hard for. He talked about selling shares to employees a couple of years after starting the business, but then decided to retain full control. I should have pushed harder. We could have been partners.

'I didn't want to be a sell-out,' he says. 'But maybe it's for the best. I'm fifty-two and... How old are you now? Forty-eight? We've done our time, Julia. We're allowed to relax a little.'

A wave of exhaustion hits me, and I sit back in my chair. Maybe he's right. Maybe it's time I focused on my family. Lord knows Leah needs me more than ever right now. If I stay on at Medusa, I'll be working harder than I have in a long time for something I no longer believe in, plus I'll be working late to match US hours and spending even less time with Adam and the kids. They all need me. I'm hurt and I'm shocked, but maybe it's my ego imagining myself sitting where my boss is now.

'What would you do?' I ask him. 'If you were me?'

'I'd take the money. You should do what you want with what's left of your life.'

'I'm not dying, Steve.'

He takes my hand and grasps it tightly.

'But doesn't life feel like a slow death sometimes?'

I think of his wife, the beautiful young woman he doesn't love, and his children he hardly knows, and his company that's made him very rich, and I wonder whether death comes in many forms.

'You're right,' I say, pulling my hand away. 'I need to start living my life again.'

My boss beams a big smile at me, his teeth much whiter than they deserve to be.

'Atta girl!' he says, squeezing my hand again. 'There's life in the old dog yet. Time to have some fun. We all get less curious as we get older and that's not a good thing.'

He stands up, but I can't.

'What do you mean?'

'Oh, nothing.' He laughs quietly to himself. 'Just something I read online.'

FORTY-SIX
JULES

Ameera is at her desk picking at her salad, Kimberley is doing her make-up and Devon has a protein shake. The Medusa offices aren't big or fancy, there's no chill-out lounge and the crappy kitchen doesn't even have a door, so we're all forced to eat at our desks. I'm pouring hot water over a stale camomile teabag, thinking about Steve's 'curious' comment, when my colleagues beckon me over.

'Come and have lunch with us,' Ameera says.

I look at what they classify as 'lunch' and picture the large Tupperware box of pasta waiting for me at my desk.

'It's fine. I've already eaten,' I say.

'I'm so psyched about the Starz partnership and the New York relocation,' Devon says.

I stretch my mouth into a tight smile and nod.

'Will you be moving out there, too?' Ameera asks.

'I don't know yet.'

Lies often mean less talking.

'Oh, yeah, meant to tell you,' Devon adds. 'We're all going out on Saturday night for Ameera's twenty-fifth birthday. You should join us.'

I try and look interested. My twenty-fifth birthday was so long ago I can't even remember how I celebrated.

I take a sip of the tea. It scalds my mouth and has no flavour. 'Are you going into central London?' I ask because it seems like the right thing to say.

'Nah, staying local. I'll text you the deets.'

I won't miss this when I leave, the fake niceties of pretending the people you work with are your friends. They know that I know that they don't really want me to turn up on their night out, yet we'll all keep pretending they mean it for the sake of politeness.

'It's OK. I have plans Saturday but thank you.'

There. Saved everyone the embarrassment.

I don't do anything for the rest of the day except think about what to do with the Leah and teacher situation, until it's already time to go home. At least my job situation is easier to solve than my home life. I stride into Steve's office and tell him I'm taking the next week off as holiday while I decide what to do. I can't think about work until I sort out this teacher horror. He looks relieved, mumbling something about sending me the redundancy agreement to look over so I can make an informed decision.

It's killing me that Medusa is going in the wrong direction, but if I walk away, then I no longer have to worry about it. Ameera can do her TikTok videos, and Devon can plan his viral campaigns with pop stars, and I'll simply take my redundancy money and... I don't know what.

Fifteen minutes later, I'm sitting in my car too scared to go inside my own house because I don't know how to be Leah's mother anymore. I need to read her letters again; it's the only way I'll know where she was last night, but at the same time I'm terrified of what I'm going to find.

I'm running out of options. I either talk to Adam or the school or the teacher himself. I can't speak to Leah first. No way. She likes this man too much and she might do something awful, like run away with him. I don't even know who she is anymore. It's like my daughter has been replaced by someone else, a teenage changeling, an alien squatting in my home. Everything that comes out of her mouth is a lie and I don't know how to get her to trust me enough to tell me the truth.

OK. Ten more minutes while I collect myself. I go on Kandid and read back through the last conversation with Curi-ous2. It was only yesterday morning, but it feels like a lifetime ago. Before I know what I'm doing, I'm typing.

I miss talking to you.

Three dots appear. He's back.

You're looking beautiful today.

Why would he say that? He doesn't know what I look like... does he? I swivel around in my car. The street is quiet – there's no one hiding behind bushes or in any of the parked cars. What's he playing at? He's still typing.

I don't know that for a fact, of course, but to me you are always beautiful.

My stomach flips and I hate myself. I don't have time for this nonsense when my daughter is in danger. I put my phone in my handbag and get out of the car. Reece isn't home, and Leah is already in her room. I knock, but she doesn't answer. The house smells like a bonfire again. Shit! Has she been writing new letters and burning them? I need to know what happened last night.

'How was school?' I shout through the door. 'Were Paige and Summer still angry with you?'

Still no answer. I turn the door handle, once again thankful I banned bedroom door locks.

'Get out!' Leah screams. Her window is wide open, but the bedroom is still grey with thick smoke. She's in her pyjamas, sitting on her bed and looking guilty.

Her Garfield toy has moved, but her schoolbag is still outside her bedroom door where she dumped it last night.

'Did you go to school today?' I ask.

She shoots me a dark look. I'm not going to argue anymore – I need to be smarter than that, change tactic.

'Why don't you take a bath? You can use that L'Rélle bubble bath Lynsey bought me for my birthday.'

She looks up. 'The lavender one? That's the one Lil Bass was talking about on Instagram the other day.'

She rushes past me, no thank you or hug, and slams the bathroom door behind her. I wait for the lock to turn then shut her bedroom door. Her bin is full of burned paper.

Shit. Now what?

FORTY-SEVEN

LEAH

I accidentally poured half the bottle of Mum's fancy bath stuff into the tub. I shouldn't have because it's really expensive and she hadn't opened it yet, but also because the bubbles have formed a giant mountain and I can't even see the water under it all. I top up the bottle with water – she won't notice – and step into the foam.

My hair stinks like I've been sitting in front of a barbeque and my fingers are all black. I thought the air would have cleared by the time Mum got back from work, but everything in my room stinks now. I should have burned my letters on the patio or gone to Dad's allotment like Reece is always doing. Dad says Reece likes to grow flowers over there, but I bet he's experimenting with some new strain of weed or something. He gets away with everything, the git!

I didn't go to school today. I woke up with my head feeling like it was going to crack open and I couldn't face the idea of being in the same building as my friends who hate me and whoever has been sending me those creepy notes. At least if I stay at home, they can't spy on me or send me more threats. Then, as if I didn't feel shit enough already, I re-read every letter I've written over the last few weeks, including one I wrote to Santi when I got home drunk last night. I hardly remember him being at the park, but according to what I wrote, we nearly did more than kiss. I totally planned to finish things with him, then tried to have sex with him. I'm so embarrassed. I'm not writing letters anymore. It's a stupid idea. I've burned them all now.

Everything was going so well until Dylan became my teacher. My birthday present was ruined, my friends hate me, Santi thinks I'm trash, someone is out to get me, and now Dylan has some rich, older girlfriend who he likes more than me. Even my own parents and brother hate me.

If I had somewhere to go, I'd run away, but I can't even do that right.

I slip down into the water, close my eyes and fully submerge myself so only the tip of my nose is exposed. I wish I could stay like this forever.

At least Mum is feeling bad about her outburst yesterday and let me use her nice bubble bath. I'm bunking off school tomorrow, too. I'm scared. I'm scared someone wants to hurt me and I'm scared my friends will never speak to me again.

I don't know how I'm going to get out of this mess, but I do know one thing – Dylan is totally going to pay for this.

FORTY-EIGHT

JULES

'What's for dinner?' Reece shouts from the sofa.

He got home an hour ago, followed by his father. Except for Leah telling me to get out of her room, this is the first thing anyone has said to me all evening. I put a cheap joint of meat in the slow cooker before I left for work. It's shrivelled and dry, but it will be fine with some gravy.

'We're having lamb.'

Leah left her dirty bathwater in the tub and three wet towels on the floor, but at least she only used a bit of my bubble bath. She's wearing the same Blondie t-shirt she had on last night, wet hair leaving a dark patch on her back, and she's painting her nails while watching some superhero movie on the TV. Adam has watched all the Marvel films with the kids since they were little. It's their thing. When they were younger, he'd take them to the cinema to see the newest release and they'd come home shouting catchphrases or laughing about scenes I'd never seen. I used to think it was a lovely bonding experience. He was always so busy at work and this way the kids had something they would always associate with their dad. Now I wish I'd joined them.

Leah has burned every single one of her letters and her boots were covered in mud and grass. Was she with this Dylan last night? Or sitting in the park on her own? How can I protect her when I don't know where she is and who she's with? The kids both had tracking apps on their phones when they started secondary school, but as soon as Reece turned sixteen, he got rid of his and Leah followed suit. She said it was an invasion of her privacy and I had double standards as I'd allowed her brother to come and go as he pleased at her age. Adam had convinced me to trust her. I shouldn't have listened to him. I also found her empty Evian bottle amongst the ashes in the bin, and it smelled of vodka. Looking at her, you wouldn't know she was hungover, or suffering at all, really.

The living room looks full, even though there's only the three of them. They take up so much space with their bodies, their voices, the way they move.

I watch them. My family.

Reece slurping at a Coke and burping, legs splayed, the sound of his father chewing peanuts and gesticulating as he explains something in earnest about something I don't understand, and even Leah with so many emotions that permeate every inch of the house, thick and pungent as the acrid smoke. She doesn't care that her father and brother, who are both much bigger than her, are squashed on one sofa while she's spread out on the other. Various bottles of nail polish are lined up on the coffee table, tissues and cotton wool littering the carpet, the smell of acetone mixing with lamb and lavender bath products. My daughter, who was never taught that women are meant to make themselves small and quiet, to keep out of the way. Her generation doesn't mind filling a room. Maybe the future will be full of people vying for space, like a forest of saplings fighting for the last ray of light.

'Nice that we get to eat as a family before I leave,' Adam calls out from the sofa.

I wrench my gaze away from Leah. What's he talking about? 'Leave?'

He makes a face, as if his silly wife is so forgetful.

'The tech conference in Birmingham. I leave early tomorrow.'

Birmingham?

'It's on all weekend, remember? I'm a keynote speaker.'

'When are you back?' I stammer.

'The team and I are back Tuesday.'

By 'team' he means Bea. He's with Bea all weekend.

'Dinner is ready,' I say, doing my best impression of a Stepford wife.

The TV is turned off and the three of them head over to the dining area. I plate the lamb on to a serving platter and add it to the steaming potatoes and vegetables on the table, all in their individual white bowls like what the good mums do in the movies.

'And don't forget the parent–teacher evening on Friday next week,' Leah says, sitting down.

'You'll only have been back at school three weeks by then,' her brother replies, stuffing a roast potato in his mouth. 'What are they going to say? Most teachers probably can't even remember your name yet.'

I'm holding the carving knife. The mention of the word 'teacher' makes me grip the handle so hard I have to pass it to Adam, who slices the lamb with a benign smile. He keeps smiling at me lately. Why does he keep smiling? What is he hiding? The meat isn't crumbly and moist. It's meant to be crumbly and moist.

Adam turns his smile to Leah and gives her the biggest slice. 'I'm looking forward to meeting your teachers, sweetheart. I'm sure you're doing very well.'

She doesn't even flinch. Her own father mentions meeting the teacher she's had sex with, and my daughter's face doesn't even move. I want to lock Leah up in a tall tower and behead every single man at her school. Instead, I place the serving spoons on the table and sit down. This time I don't count my blessings like I did at Al Fresco. I can't lie to myself anymore.

'You're back at uni in a couple of weeks, right?' Adam asks Reece. 'Did you secure that room you wanted?'

He grins and nods. 'Yep. Final year and then I'm free!'

Look at him. My boy. My perfect boy who can't wait to leave me. Every single one of these people can't wait to get away from me.

'The lamb's nice, darling,' Adam says, chewing with purpose.

'Yeah, nice,' Reece says.

Leah nods.

Everyone in my family is a fucking liar.

FORTY-NINE

JULES

I always have Fridays off, but this one feels different. I'm on holiday and considering severance pay. Is this gardening leave? Maybe it is. Steve has sent me the termination agreement to look over, should I choose to take it, but I can't bring myself to open the attachment. I'll look at it later. I should be happy. I have time and the headspace now to deal with all the cracks in my marriage and whatever the hell I'm going to do about Leah. I have more money, too. If I agree to take it, the pay-off is a lot – a year's wages – plus we have the money from the sale of my mother's flat that I still need to do something with, and the money under the bed. We have money. A lot of money.

I wish I could call my mum. I'm not sure she'd have any advice for me, but at least she'd tell me everything was going to be OK and I'd believe her. I certainly don't believe myself when I say it.

I check my phone for the third time this morning. I've been awake since Adam left at five and it's nearly eight thirty. I messaged him an hour ago, asking if he had a minute to talk, but he hasn't replied yet. I can see he's seen it. He'll be arriving at his hotel soon even though his keynote speech isn't until the afternoon. He hardly said two words to me this morning. Isn't he concerned that I'm trying to get hold of him so early in the morning?

I'm being selfish. I can't tell him about my job and Leah over the phone while he's at a work event. I need to stop being a coward and tell him to his face. It can wait until he's back on Tuesday. I'll have everything sorted by then.

I climb out of bed, pull on my dressing gown and stumble to the kitchen. Leah is already in there eating a muffin without a plate, crumbs scattering over her pyjamas and on to the floor.

'Why aren't you dressed?' I ask.

She gives me a long look. 'Why aren't *you*?'

My hands itch with the urge to slap that muffin out of her hand.

'You need to go to school,' I say. 'They'll call me.'

'No, they won't. They didn't yesterday.' She's right, they didn't. 'I signed into the school system with your details and told them I have gastro issues. I'll go back Monday.'

'You're not ill.'

'I am. Headache,' she says, looking me straight in the eye. How does she do that? Liar, liar, everything's on fire.

It's probably for the best. I don't want her in the same room as that teacher. Whether she deceived him or not, the idea of him anywhere near her makes my skin crawl.

'Is everything OK?' I ask. 'Your friends? Lessons? You can talk to me about anything, sweetheart.'

For a fleeting moment something small, something young, flickers behind her glassy eyes. I reach out for her, and I think she's going to hug me, give in and tell me everything, but she doesn't. Instead, she pushes the last lump of muffin into her mouth, gives me a withering look and walks away. My instinct is to run after her, shake the truth out of her, but if I scare her away, she might leave for good. As long as we're under the same roof, I know she's safe. That's enough for now.

Also, if she's not at school, that means I can find out who this art teacher of hers is without her catching me. I'm going to confront him today, and if this piece of shit knows what's good for him, he'll be scared. Especially when I tell him about the disgusting, congealed evidence of his predatory actions. The thought of it makes my mouth fill with acid again, but I have to do this. Leah is still my baby, and I will kill and die for her.

She mentioned Kandid in one of her letters, saying she needed somewhere to share her secret. I searched for her on the app for an hour last night, but I didn't find any post that could have been her. I filtered via local area, looking for keywords such as 'teacher' and 'Carnage Festival' and 'virginity', but I found nothing. Good. I don't want her on that app.

I pour myself a coffee, lean against the kitchen counter and go to take a sip when my phone buzzes. I've changed my mind about wanting to talk to Adam now. I'll only worry him, then he'll rush home and get involved and that will make things worse. But both relief and annoyance flood through me when I realise it's not Adam, it's a Kandid notification. I click on it and my stomach lurches.

Good morning, beautiful

I take a sip of my coffee, the warm liquid making my stomach ache further. He called me beautiful yesterday as well. He doesn't know what I look like – does he?

You don't know I'm beautiful.

Yes, I do. We talk every day. You're exquisite.

This is ridiculous. This is also exactly what I need to hear right now. I put down my coffee and type with both thumbs.

What are you doing today?

Nothing. Work. You?

Boring house stuff.

Wish I was there.

Where? In my house?

Now you've made me sound creepy.

I laugh out loud. It's strange to hear it, the sharp bark of amusement I wasn't expecting to erupt out of me. It always surprises me how much I like this man. How much I enjoy spending time with someone who has no face, no name, no corporeal form. Maybe we'd all be happy with a perfectly programmed robot instead of trying to make other humans meet our needs.

He's typing more.

I can't stop thinking about you. It's distracting.

Tell me what you think about.

Dot. Dot. Dot. I wait. My phone beeps – it's a message from Adam.

What do you want to talk about?

Nothing urgent. Only wanted to wish you luck with your talk.

He replies with a thumbs-up emoji – the one that says, *I*

acknowledge you, but I don't wish to speak with you further. You bore me.

Curious2 is still typing. I wait. His reply appears.

> I keep thinking how you deserve better than what you have. I want to be the one who makes you smile every day. We should talk. I can help you.

Help me with what? I wait, but there's no more. I go to respond when my phone vibrates. It's Adam again.

Can you buy me some muesli for when I'm back on Tuesday, please?

An alert pops up with a ping. An email from Steve checking I received the termination agreement. Curious2 is typing. Then he stops. Nothing. Leah has turned the volume of her Lil Bass music up to ear-bleeding levels, making the walls vibrate and my head pound. I stare at the phone in my hand. I should be getting ready. I need to confront this bastard teacher.

Lil Bass's words punctuate the air like bullets.

You fucked with me
You messed with me
You never knew what was best for me

Mr Ward. Adam. Curious2. Steve. All of them blowing up my phone, my life. I don't know any of them. Not really. Not anymore. They need to go. These men need to get out of my life.

You're gonna pay
I'll get my way
You ain't gonna live another day

FIFTY

JULES

I'm standing at the school gates of St Margarette's, staring up at the large, imposing building. This is the best school in the area; my kids were both lucky to get in here. Whatever I say or do today, I can't mess up Leah's chances of completing her A levels and going to uni.

I'm going to tell this creep that either he resigns, or I'll tell the headteacher everything.

I breathe in for four, breathe out for eight, then give up and wipe my hands on my jeans. I can do this. It's not fear or nerves I'm feeling... It's rage. Pure, hot, white, burning rage. I plump up my hair, smooth down my shirt and march into reception.

'I need to speak to Mr Ward,' I say as firmly as I can.

It's lunchtime. I came here at this time on purpose so he wouldn't have to be pulled out of any lessons. The receptionist is a battle axe. I've dealt with her before. She's been at this school since before Reece started year seven. She's probably been here since the school was built. She adjusts her glasses, her lips pursed tightly.

'Do you have an appointment?'

Of course I don't. I didn't want to call ahead. I wanted to surprise him, shock him, make him squirm.

'It's an emergency.'

A large crease appears between her eyes.

'Ms Willis isn't in today, but if it's an emergency, I can try and locate the deputy head. Mr Travis is—'

'I need to talk to Mr Ward. Now!'

My voice is shaking, and my hands are starting to go numb. The old bat couldn't care less. I wonder how many parents storm into the school demanding to talk to teachers. God, I'd hate to work here. But this is different. I'm sure the other teachers aren't sleeping with their students. I don't care if he's tried to do the right thing so far, I know men and I know given the opportunity he'll sleep with my daughter again. And if not her, then some other naïve girl. He has to go.

'Mr Ward is at lunch,' she says. 'Perhaps when he's out of the staff room, I can let him know...'

Staff room. I know where that is. Without another word, I march down the corridor lined with students sitting on the floor talking, some reading, a few walking about eating sandwiches or scrolling through their phones. I make sure my hair covers my face, worried one of Leah's friends will see me and message her, but then I remember that no sixth-former hangs around the school at lunchtime.

The staff room door is shut. I open it with a bang.

'Is Mr Ward in here?' I shout out.

Over a dozen faces turn to look at me. I recognise them all, but none are men in their early twenties.

'Can I help you? You're Leah's mother, aren't you?' one of the women asks. She's one of Leah's former English teachers.

My breaths are coming fast now, and I feel light-headed. All I've had all day is a coffee. I should have eaten before I came here but I was too anxious. There's a kitchenette in the corner, where a group of younger people are talking. Are they teachers?

Three have their backs to me. Is one of them Mr Ward? I don't have my glasses on. I've just stepped into the room when I feel a hand close around my arm.

'This is a restricted space,' a deep voice says. I look up. It's the caretaker. He must be well into his seventies, but he's strong. 'Come along, now. Eileen did tell you that you needed to make an appointment.'

A number of children have gathered in the hallway outside the staff room, where the teachers are now looking at one another awkwardly, the silence thick and expectant. So much for feeling powerful and righteous. I shuffle my way back to the school entrance and stand at the front desk where Eileen, I presume, is shaking her head at me.

'I checked Mr Ward's diary – he's free to see you at twelve fifteen on Monday. Name?'

I tell her everything she needs to know then walk back to my car. By Monday, I'll have everything I need to ensure this piece of shit leaves the school and doesn't go near my daughter again.

The day passes in a blur; I can't focus on anything. I'm still shaking from my school visit, and I don't have the energy to look at all the emails Steve has sent me. By early evening all I've done is tried and failed to read a book and checked my phone over fifty times – no new messages from anyone.

I call Lynsey's mobile but it goes to voicemail, so I try her home phone. John answers, accompanied by squeals and splashing sounds.

'This was probably the worst time to call, right?' I shout over the sounds of bath time. 'I'm trying to get hold of Lynsey.'

'Oh, Jules. Hi. Take the soap out of your mouth. She's gone away.'

'What?'

It's hard to hear anything over the cries of the two boys and the thumping bass of Leah's music reverberating through my walls. She hasn't left her bedroom all day. If she'd heard about my outburst at her school, she'd have said something by now. So at least I have that to be thankful for.

'Lynsey has gone to stay with a friend for a couple of nights,' John says.

What friend? *I'm* her friend!

'Is she OK?'

'Don't suck the sponge. Wait. Sorry. She's been struggling, Jules. Did she not tell you?'

'What happened?'

'I bought her a gift for our anniversary, and she broke down crying. Apparently, she doesn't care about presents, all she needs is a break. So I took a few days off work and she's gone to stay with a friend.'

Why didn't Lynsey tell me she was having such a hard time? Something doesn't add up. I was planning on telling her about Leah, but this is clearly not the right time.

'Jules, I have to go,' John is saying. The boys have started screaming, forcing me to hold the phone away from my ear. 'Text her. I'm sure she'd love to talk to you.'

Would she really like to talk to me? Suspicions start to creep in and cloud my mind again. What if she's not at a friend's house? What if my husband isn't really in Birmingham? What if John and I are both being lied to?

He hangs up and I text Lynsey. I ask her if she's OK and if she's free to meet tomorrow night at Vino. She replies immediately with a thumbs-up and says she'll see me there; she has something to tell me. I close my eyes and imagine being told by my best friend that she's sleeping with my husband in the middle of a crowded bar on a Saturday night. No. That's not it. She's having a hard time with the kids, and she needs a break, and I'm her friend. I should be thinking about Lynsey's mental health, not accusing her of the worst thing a friend could do. Tomorrow I'll focus on her for a change.

In the living room, Reece is eating a Chinese takeaway. Crap, I'm such a terrible mother. I totally forgot about dinner.

'I ordered you that cashew chicken you like. Leah took her food to her room.'

Such a good boy. I sit down next to him. He's watching a nature programme.

'Did you know Plato used to get high on mushrooms?' Reece says, slurping up his chow mein. 'It was more of a fungus, actually. Back then they would mix it with barley to make a kind of fermented drink that gave them a trip that was a bit like LSD.'

I'm not sure what he wants me to say in response, so I tell him that no, I didn't know that. Who *does* know that? Reece is enraptured by the documentary, so I keep listening to his facts. This is one of the things I love so much about my son. Some would call it obsession, or hyperfocus, but I've always seen it as simply passion. He loves pottering around at his father's allotment and learning about strange plants. And he never does small talk – all his conversations are big and deep. I wish I could be this interested in something. Anything.

'It's so strange how society has deemed drugs bad, even weed and mushrooms, which are totally natural,' he says, pointing at the screen, where a surrealist painting is being shown. Bosch, I think. 'When some of the best ideas, art, music and writing have come from people being fucked out of their heads.'

I want to tell him not to swear, but I also don't want him to stop talking. I pick at my chicken, watching slow-motion footage of a mushroom growing, sneaking glances at how animated Reece looks.

'You know Yeats was a pothead and Picasso smoked opium for a few years. It's so cool how nature creates all this shit that can make us either brilliant... or dead. Two sides of the same coin. Look at that dude.' He points at the TV again. 'Pope Clement the seventh, died eating a poisonous mushroom. *Amanita phalloides*. I guess someone has to make a mistake so the rest of us can avoid them.'

He laughs and shovels another mouthful of noodles into his

mouth while I sit transfixed, listening but not really listening. Staring at the screen but not really watching. I don't care about death cap mushrooms or these so-called genius men, but I don't want to move either because my son and I are alone watching TV, and all is still, and all is good again. Peace. For a moment I can pretend my life isn't falling apart. I can learn some useless facts about plants and fungi while my brilliant boy slurps his noodles beside me. This is the part of being a mother I love the most.

I curl my legs up and rest my head on his shoulder. Reece shrugs me off and gets up.

'Where are you going?' I ask.

He sits on the other couch. 'Giving you some space.'

And all is cold and empty again.

FIFTY-TWO

JULES

It's quarter to eight and I'm sitting at our usual table in Vino. Lynsey is fifteen minutes late and not answering her mobile phone, and Adam has hardly messaged me either since he left for Birmingham, except for a few funny memes. We're not a funny-meme-sharing kind of couple. This forced attentiveness on his part is putting me on edge. What the hell is he hiding?

Lynsey said she had something to tell me and is now bailing on me? Something weird is going on. I push down the lump in my throat with the rest of my Pinot Grigio and stare out of the bar window. The sun is starting to set, the pavement full of smokers and people pretending autumn isn't around the corner. I made an effort tonight, thinking it would take my mind off everything. I splashed out and had my hair and nails done this morning. I shaved and trimmed and plucked. My make-up looks great and I'm wearing a new leopard-print dress that stops two inches above the knee. It's a subtle print and I have good legs, the only part of me that has stayed the same. It was a bit of a mindless impulse buy as this is probably the last week I can get away with not wearing tights.

I order another glass of wine and scroll through my phone

while I wait. Curious2 hasn't messaged me either, not since yesterday morning after saying he could help me. I replied with '???' but nothing. This is ridiculous. I don't need to spend time with others to have a nice evening. Nothing is stopping me from enjoying one more glass of wine then going out on my own somewhere. Like the cinema. Loads of people go to the cinema alone.

Empowered by my decision, I pay the barman for my drink and scroll through my phone. Lynsey is calling. My stomach churns. Surely she's not going to destroy my life over the phone.

'Jules! Thank God you answered. I was just about to leave Fiona's house to meet you when something awful happened. She's in a real state.'

Lynsey's been staying with Fiona! I'm flooded with relief then instantly feel guilty.

'I thought she was in Greece with her new rich lover,' I say.

Lynsey is out of breath, like she can't talk fast enough. 'That's why I'm calling. It was fake. All of it. He wasn't real.'

'What do you mean, not real?'

'It was a con!' she hisses, like she's trying to shout but doesn't want her friend to hear her. 'He stole from her. She gave him her savings, Jules. Twenty-three grand! He'd been investing money in crypto for her – she'd been seeing returns on a few hundred here and there so totally trusted him. He was sending her gifts and photos of his villa. He was so convincing, she thought he was the one. Then she gave him the money and he disappeared. The whole thing was a trap.'

The wine coating my tongue has turned sour. She met this man on Kandid, and she believed everything he told her.

'He'd been watching her, Jules! He knew everything about her: her address, what she looked like, how much money she had. The police think he's local, but it's impossible to trace him. He could be anyone.'

I look around. Everyone in this bar is younger than me.

There are lots of groups of women, mostly in their twenties, a few mixed groups, a lot of couples who look like they're on their first date, and a group of men in the corner. Two are on their phone. The more attractive of the two looks up from his screen and, upon seeing me staring at him, straightens up. I look away.

'Is that why he wouldn't meet up in person?'

'Exactly! She said he kept offering to help her. He was so nice and kind, not creepy like the others online. Honestly, why she would go on a bloody confessions app and be so vulnerable in the first place, I don't know. His profile has disappeared now, although I bet he has dozens of other aliases. Twenty-three grand,' she breathes. 'Wait, she's calling for me. I better go.'

I hang up and stare at the Kandid logo on my screen. I should leave the app. I could delete my account in two seconds, and it would be like none of this ever happened. One less thing to worry about. Except, what if Curious2 *is* real? If so, he needs me as much as I need him. Plus, I need to stay on the app in case Leah goes on it.

The man whose eye I caught earlier is still looking over at me. Lynsey said Fiona's man had been watching her. He could be here. Curious2 could be genuine, but he could also be any one of the men in this bar and I'd never know. He may even be someone who already knows me.

'Jules!'

I jump and swing around, nearly toppling off my high stool.

'Devon?'

'I'm so glad you came! We're over there,' he says, pointing at an alcove hidden behind the bar. Ameera, Kimberley and a few others from work wave back. I had totally forgotten about Ameera's birthday.

The last thing I need after Lynsey's shocking revelation is the excruciating pain of enduring work colleagues young enough to be my kids pretending to be my friends. But I have no choice. I can't exactly insist that I'm perfectly fine sitting alone in the corner staring at my phone and drinking myself into a stupor. I struggle off the stool and follow Devon.

'Happy birthday, Ameera!' I say, giving her a half-hearted hug. 'I bought you a little something but forgot it. I'll bring it to work when I'm back in the office.'

It's a lie, but she's too drunk to notice. She's pointing to a half-finished bottle of tequila in the middle of the table and some shot glasses. Jesus Christ.

'Come on, you have to have at least one!' Devon cries.

There's lime and salt, too. This is not what I signed up for tonight. So much for my solo cinema trip. I smile, like all of this is hilarious, and take a sip from my shot glass. The tequila burns and they all cheer. How embarrassing. Getting drunk with them is nothing but an extension of the polite small talk we do at work.

My phone buzzes in my hand. Adam is calling me. Thankful for a reason to walk away, I excuse myself and wander to the entrance of the bar, where it's quieter. A group of guys are drinking pints outside. The nice-looking man I noticed before is there, still watching as I lean against the wall with my hand cupped around the mouthpiece of my phone so Adam can hear me.

'How's it going?' I ask him.

It's quiet at his end. Of course, it is. My husband is alone, working hard, making money for his family, and I'm the stupid, paranoid idiot in a bar making life unnecessarily more complicated for myself than it needs to be.

'The speech went really well. We've finished dinner so I'm going to head off to my room now. How are you?'

Maybe he does care about me. Maybe I'm reading too much into his nice messages and he simply loves his wife.

'I'm having a quick drink with Lynsey,' I reply, because I can't exactly say I'm downing tequila shots with kids half my age.

'That's nice. All OK at home?'

'Yep. I got your message about the muesli.'

'Good, good. Right, well, see you Tuesday, then.'

Is that it? Is that all we can manage?

'Jules.' He pauses. I recognise that tone – that's the bad news voice. My stomach twists. 'We need to talk.'

My initial instincts were right. I don't want to talk, because I know what he's going to say, and I don't want to hear it. He's waiting for me to answer, but anything I say will be wrong. Someone is calling his name in the background. A woman.

'Adam, you promised me one more drink.'

'I'd better go,' my husband says.

'Who's that?'

'See you Tuesday,' he says and hangs up.

I stare at my phone screen for what feels like forever, streaks of red and white from the passing cars flashing on its surface. It's over. He doesn't need to wait until Tuesday, he's already said it. I swallow and it hurts, like razor blades being scraped down my oesophagus. Who was that woman? Was it Bea, or someone I know nothing about? I dab at my eyes. Is she wearing the bracelet he bought her? I blink three times. Does he love her?

The night has dimmed to a dull grey, the air punctuated by the bright glow of the cigarettes and lighters of the drinkers nearby. The group of men with pints has thinned, but the handsome one who looked at me earlier is still staring. He's dressed like Reece, like all young men look today – loose t-shirt, fitted jeans and no jacket even though the evening air has a bite to it. He's exactly the type of guy I would have slept with in my twenties: silent, self-assured, dangerous. I wonder what he sees when he looks at me. He's probably wondering the same thing I am. What the hell is an old woman like me doing here?

Or maybe he's not. Maybe I'm another Fiona – scared,

nely, easily manipulated by a little flattery – and he's figuring
ut how to con another desperate old woman.

I go back to my colleagues who barely know me and the free
equila, my mind full of images of my husband and his mistress.
pour myself another shot and sit down with a thud. I need to
ave or find someone my own age to talk to.

'Is Steve here?' I ask.

Everyone laughs. Devon passes me a slice of lime.

'Why would we invite the boss?' Kimberley says with a
iggle. 'He's, like, double our age.'

I thought she liked him. She always acts like he's the best
hing ever. At one point I thought she was sleeping with him,
ntil I found out she lives with her girlfriend.

'Well, you invited *me*,' I say.

Ameera rubs my arm. 'But you're cool, Jules.'

Pretty little liar.

'I'm old.'

Ameera makes a *pfft* noise. Jesus, she's so drunk. I study her,
he faded lipstick and droopy eyes, the way her backbone has
urned to jelly, so her neck can no longer hold her head up. And
yet she's still so beautiful. Delicate. Ethereal. Is anyone out to
con *her* tonight? No, when you're young and pretty, it's you who
gets to have what you want. The rest of us are left to throw our
money at anyone who's bold enough to tell us what we yearn to
hear.

I think back to what Lynsey said to me on my fortieth birthday. 'Congrats, now you're sixty per cent less likely to get raped.
Roll on sixty-five, then you're practically in the clear.'

We'd both been drunk and laughed like drains, even though
there was nothing remotely funny about what she was saying.
That's your choice as a woman growing older – unwanted
sexual attention, exploitation or invisibility.

I push a bottle of water over to Ameera and knock back my
shot of tequila. My mouth fills with saliva, but it gives me the

courage I need to stay a little longer. I swallow it down with the dregs of my wine.

'It's true, Jules,' Kimberley says. The girl beside her is all sharp angles and soft eyes, her arm draped around Kimberley's shoulder. 'We all want to be like you when we grow up.'

The others grin and I don't know whether to laugh or cry.

'No, you don't. There's nothing remotely "cool"' – I make bunny ears in the air – 'about me. Honestly. My life is very boring.'

'You're not being boring right now,' Devon says, filling my empty wine glass up with Prosecco.

He's right. I'm not. If my life is about to implode, I may as well go out with a bang...

FIFTY-THREE

JULES

I'm on a dance floor! I'm not sure how I ended up here, but I know it's a Rihanna song I'm dancing to because Leah plays it all the time. My boots only have a slight heel, but my thighs are already aching, my toes numb. My face is numb, too. I've moved on to drinking water, but it's not working fast enough to clear the tequila from my system. Nothing like getting a hangover before you even get home.

'You have some great moves,' Kimberley says, grasping my hip bones so we're moving to the music together. Her girlfriend does the same behind her, laughing in her ear, kissing her neck. I laugh too and push my hair off my damp forehead. OK. This is fun. I'd forgotten what fun felt like.

Vino officially closes at eleven o'clock, but upstairs they have Checkers, Hertfordshire's cheesiest nightclub. If you can call it that. It costs five pounds to get in and Devon wouldn't take no for an answer when I told him it was past my bedtime and I needed to call a cab.

'Come on! We're having fun. Come upstairs for a dance.'

He bought me a ticket and I followed them all in. That was twenty minutes ago. Maybe an hour. Who cares? Ameera,

Devon and Kimberley keep calling me Cool Jules and saying they wished their mum was as fun as I am. It's not the compliment they think it is.

'Wish you could come to New York with us,' they say. 'Wish you could be our boss.'

They're drunk, they probably don't mean it, but I lap it up like a starving cat being handed a shallow dish of milk.

The bar is still open downstairs, but it's mostly empty. Everyone that was down there is now up here dancing ironically, apparently, to pop music in a vile nightclub which they pretend they only go to because it's funny, not because it's their only option for miles around.

Men are watching me. Some are old and drunker than I am. Men who think because they still feel like they're twenty-one, that twenty-one-year-olds will want to take them home. Men like that never look at women like me, women their own age. There are other men though, younger ones, and I feel their gaze move over me like a silk scarf being draped over bare skin. I shiver and think about Curious2. He's younger than me. He told me once, even though I've never told him my age. Is he the kind of man to stare at a woman on the dance floor? What would he do if he saw me right now?

I'm shoulder to shoulder with people writhing and swaying, their slick arms rubbing against mine, their hair in my face and their laughter in my ears. The music moves through me and it's like I'm not here. I'm not anywhere. It's just me and the moment. What would my children say if they could see me now? What about my husband?

We need to talk.

I don't want to think about that. Not yet. All I want is to be here, right now, suspended in time like I'm someone else for one night only.

A man turns away from the bar and heads towards me, his broad shoulders silhouetted against the bright flashes of disco lights. He's holding his drink and smiling at me. He's young, but not too young. Does he want to dance with me? I imagine him circling my waist with his large hands, his chest pressing against my back, his breath tickling my collarbone. I smile back as he nears me, reaching out for him, letting him know I'm up for a dance.

'Show me your moves, then,' I shout over the music.

'You what?'

I hook my thumbs into the waistband of his jeans. 'I said show me what you've got.'

He laughs and leans closer. I can smell the bourbon on his breath.

'Go home, love. You're embarrassing yourself.'

He walks away before I have a chance to reply. Which is good, because I don't know what to say. I just stand there, swaying, like a rocking horse no one wants to ride anymore. One of those decrepit, antique things people only keep in their homes because they feel bad throwing it away, even though it's turning into an eyesore. Rotten. Dangerous. A little bit scary.

The man has joined his friends at their table. He says something and points at me. They all laugh and shake their heads. Oh. I see. I'm *that* woman. My head is pounding and my throat tight. I need to get out of here. I want to go home. What the hell was I thinking dancing in a nightclub? I inch my way to the exit, my hand sliding along the walls sweaty with the condensation from too many hot bodies.

I'm nearly at the bottom of the rickety stairs, my hands slippery on the handrail, when I miss the last step and stumble. Someone catches me.

'I'm fine,' I mutter, my voice thick with tears of shame.

I look up. It's the young guy from before, the one who was outside with the smokers. I don't need to see the pity or concern in his eyes; I've had enough humiliation for one night. I mumble a thank you and head for the exit, but he chases after me.

'Hey, are you OK?'

'Fine.'

I'm not fine. I lean against the wall outside. I try to focus on him, but everything is spinning. He really is very attractive. He's probably going to say something excruciating like, 'My mum has that handbag.'

'You're shaking. Do you want some water?'

Vino is practically empty, and he leads me to a table. It's nice to be able to hear him away from the awful music upstairs.

'I'm Robert,' he says.

He has neat hair, very light stubble, and small, rounded lips – I think they call it a cupid's bow.

'I'm Jules.'

Robert rushes to the bar and returns with an unopened bottle of water.

'I've been watching you all night,' he says. 'Sorry, that sounds weird. I mean, I was trying to make sense of it. You know, the people you were out with.'

'Why? Because they're young and I'm old?'

He laughs. 'No. Because they looked boring and you're exquisite.'

Exquisite. Where have I heard that before? Robert scratches the back of his neck, making his t-shirt ride up.

'I feel stupid,' I say, blinking back tears.

'Why?'

I play with my wedding ring, twisting it round and round my finger. He glances at my hand but doesn't say anything. He has three rings on one hand, heavy ones like a musician would wear. I can't tell if one is a wedding ring.

'I'm too old for this place,' I say.

'No. You're too *classy* for this place.'

I laugh. He has kind eyes and a nice smile. I sip at my water, collecting myself, the edges of the room beginning to settle into place again.

'Where are your friends?' I ask.

'Upstairs. Not my scene. I was on my way home.'

I wonder what Adam is doing right now? It's gone midnight. Is he asleep, or does some woman have her long, tanned legs wrapped around him, around my husband, the man who got bored of me? And what about Curious2? All that time I've spent talking to a stranger online when there are real-life men in the real world who are friendly and kind and probably not trying to con me out of my life savings.

'Do you ever get curious?' I ask Robert.

His face screws up in confusion, or perhaps concentration.

'Curious?' He makes a humming sound, sending it straight into the pit of my stomach. 'Yeah, I guess I'm curious about a lot of things. I'm very curious right now. You?'

My wedding band is so loose it spins freely around my finger, clinking against my engagement ring. Adam proposed with a tiny diamond that he always said he'd replace with something bigger when we had more money. Maybe for my thirtieth. Then, for my fortieth. We have money now, but I told him I don't care about diamonds. It sounded romantic at the time. It doesn't matter now, anyway.

'I'm always curious,' I say. 'Sometimes I wish I wasn't.'

Robert is slim but toned, and for a fleeting moment I imagine what his body looks like beneath his t-shirt. I bet his chest hardly has any hair on it, and his stomach is taut and perhaps even rippling with muscle beneath his skin.

He checks the time on his phone.

'Sorry, I'm keeping you,' I say, going to stand.

He places a hand over mine. 'Stay. I don't have anywhere to be.'

I sit slowly back down. His hand is still on mine, his finger playing with my rings.

'Are you happy?' he asks.

'Not really.'

'They're very loose,' he says. He spins my rings round and round. 'You're going to lose them.'

I'm not looking at my hand; I'm looking at him because he's looking at me. No one has looked at me like that for a long time. He slips my rings off my finger, and I let him. He hands them to me, and I drop them into my handbag. When I look back up, his pupils have grown to black, and his jaw is set hard. What am I doing? What the hell am I doing?

I take a shaky breath and stand. 'I need to get home. I'm going to the toilet, then I'll call a cab.'

He nods and I edge my way to the back of the bar towards a small corridor, where there are two doors, both simply marked 'toilet'. Outside is a sink and mirror. I lean against the unit and stare at my reflection. My hair is thick and wild, mascara smudged beneath my eyes, but I'm glowing. I apply some lipstick and run my wrists under the cold tap. My hand feels naked and wrong without my rings, but I don't put them back on. I need to get used to not wearing them. I have three days left until my husband leaves me.

I comb my fingers through my hair and flinch as the figure of a man materialises behind me in the mirror.

It's Robert.

FIFTY-FOUR

JULES

'I wanted to check you're OK,' he says to my reflection in the mirror.

I hold his gaze. All is silent this far away from the bar; there's no one around.

'I'm fine.'

'Good.'

He doesn't move, and neither do I. He steps forward and stands behind me, gently moving my sweaty hair away from my face, the tips of his fingers brushing my neck.

'I lied about the reason I was looking at you earlier,' Robert says.

I go to say something, but it comes out as a sigh.

'I kept looking at you not only because you're attractive, but because you looked sad.'

Our eyes are locked in the mirror, his stare drilling into mine. He places a hand on either side of me, trapping me between him and the sink. His mouth is so close to my ear I can feel his stubble on my cheek.

'Are you sad, Jules?'

I can't answer. My throat is blocked with years of words, of pain, of mounting frustration. This doesn't feel like seduction, it feels like kindness. I lean back against him and close my eyes at the feel of his warm chest against my back, his hands touching mine. He kisses the damp skin above my collarbone and a sound like a cat's mew escapes my lips. I open my eyes, shame flooding my face, but he likes it. He's pressing harder against me, kissing me deeper, moving his lips towards mine. Images of Bea and Adam flash against my closed eyelids. Is this what he does to her in the office? On their client dinners? In the hotel room right now?

We need to talk.

I turn until I'm facing Robert and slowly, very slowly, he parts my lips with his own. His kiss is soft and warm and gentle and urgent. Our chests pressing against one another, his hands lost in my hair, he pushes us towards one of the toilets and the door gives way until he has me pinned against the cold tiles. And I let him. Because it's too late now. I want this and I'm too far gone.

He locks the door and places his phone on the cistern beside him as I drop my handbag to the floor.

'Do you want me to stop, Jules?' he asks.

I shake my head.

'Talk to me.'

'No, don't stop,' I say. 'I want this. I want you, Robert. Please. Don't stop.'

I can't see anything, the room is mist, all I can do is feel. His mouth is hot against my neck, my chest. He slips down my dress and pulls my bra to one side. I gasp as his mouth closes in around my breast, licking, sucking, greedy, his hand climbing up my thighs. Every inch of me is burning. I don't recognise the sounds I'm making, groans and sobs and something altogether desperate.

A single tear rolls down my cheek; it's been so long since anyone has made me feel this way. The only hands that have caressed my skin have been my own. The only lips that have travelled over my body have been those of characters in my fantasies. My body is screaming for this. I need it. I push his hand between my legs, begging for more, telling him how much I want it.

'Are you sure, Jules?' he asks, his breath hot against my lips. 'What about your husband?'

'Fuck him.'

Robert laughs, and I'm ashamed by how much it turns me on. He likes it. This. The danger. He likes that we're doing something forbidden. His finger hooks beneath my underwear and inches it down. Slowly, really slowly. I'm wound so tight, it's not going to take much for me to completely unravel.

He laughs lightly against my mouth as he cups me between my thighs, noting with just one caress how much I want him. His lips twitch with pleasure as I buck against his hand, his eyes locked on mine as groans of pleasure escape my throat. With every stroke I grip him to me tighter, clasping the back of his head, pressing him closer to me. His fingers move deftly, exploring me slowly at first then faster and faster until my legs feel like they're going to give way completely. In no time at all I'm climaxing with an anguished cry, trembling in his arms as he holds me, shuddering against him, my damp cheeks pressing into the crook of his neck.

He lets me go and I'm undone. I fall to the cold bathroom tiles, chest heaving and tears pouring down my cheeks, my lips clamped between my teeth to stop a wail from erupting out of me.

He crouches down and wipes the tears from my face with his thumb, tilting his head to one side as if trying to read the chaos clawing at my mind.

'I'm sorry,' I say, taking a shaky breath. 'I need to go.'

He nods but doesn't say another word as he helps me up and places his phone in his pocket. I grab my bag off the floor as he unlocks the toilet door and I clamber out of the tiny room.

What have I done? What have I done? What have I done?

I need to call a cab. I straighten my dress and rummage inside my bag; at the bottom my rings shine under the fluorescent light of the toilet. I pick them up, look at them and put them back on. I'm complete again.

I pull out my mobile and Robert takes my hand, angling it so he can see the photo on my lock screen. It's a selfie of me and Leah that we took in Spain a few months ago.

'She has your eyes.'

I snatch my hand away and keep blinking, but the tears won't clear. This man, this handsome man who has reminded me of everything that's missing from my life, is now nothing but a hazy blur. He may as well not be real.

'I shouldn't have done that,' I say with a croak, avoiding my reflection in the mirror as I head back to the bar.

'Jules,' he calls out. I turn. 'Don't worry about it. We all make mistakes in the heat of the moment.'

But this wasn't a mistake, this was a decision. A decision I *enjoyed*. And now I have to live with the consequences. Whatever Adam has to tell me on Tuesday, he won't be the only one making a confession.

FIFTY-FIVE

JULES

My head is pounding, my mouth tastes of week-old cat litter, and a rock of guilt is crushing my chest. I don't want to open my eyes. I don't want to deal with today because I don't want last night to have been real. I push my face into the pillow and let out a muffled cry. I'm a disgrace!

My phone is on the bedside table. I reach for it, knocking my empty bottle of water and glasses to the floor, their clatter sending shooting pains to my head. The clock on my phone says nine forty-eight, but it's the date that catches my eye. And finally, with a violence that takes me by surprise, the dam holding back a year's worth of tears gives way.

Today is the first anniversary of my mother's death and I have never needed her more than I do right now. She was always there, and then she was but she wasn't, and now she never will be. When she died, it was like falling to the bottom of a very deep well. As I sat by her bedside, her paper-skin hand in mine, I feared every one of her laboured breaths would be her last. I'd hold my own breath with each of hers, exhaling with her, until eventually only one of us was breathing. I didn't think life could get any worse than that day. I was wrong.

My phone buzzes. It's not Adam; it's someone on one of my many WhatsApp groups asking when parent–teacher evening is. I close my eyes, my head pounding to the beat of my heavy heart. My mother wanted to be cremated and we planted a tree on the cemetery with a plaque on it. I don't want to stand beneath that tree alone today, but I guess I have no choice. I wonder how much more I will have to do alone once Adam leaves me.

I open the Kandid app and click on my inbox. Curious2 never did tell me how he wanted to help me.

> It's the first anniversary of my mother's death today. No one has remembered.

He replies right away.

> I'm so sorry. I promise I'm going to make it right soon. I'm here for you. Always will be.

What does he mean by that? I haven't got the energy to answer – even lifting up my phone makes me want to vomit. I have no right to feel sorry for myself after what I did.

I rub at my sore eyes, puffy and swollen, images of last night flashing behind my lids like blurry stills of an old movie. The touch of skin on skin. The smell of that man. What was he called? Robert, I think. I can feel it now, the pressure of his hand between my legs, the way every part of me was reaching out for him, begging to take all this pain away. I hate who I've become. I hate that it happened. But most of all I hate that I still want more.

Curious2 says he's going to make it all right soon. Make *what* right? I should be scared – Fiona's life has been ruined by a stranger online – yet all I keep thinking is that I want this man to save me.

Last night I was given a taste of something dark and wrong, and I liked it. But it was a one-off, never again. I've already crossed the line; I'm not going to add to my mistakes.

Before I change my mind, I unsubscribe from Kandid and push my phone under the pillow, racking sobs bruising my chest and tears soaking the cotton. It's over. Everything is over.

Adam is calling me, but I ignore him. It's too late to save my marriage, but I *will* save my daughter. Even if it's the last thing I ever do.

FIFTY-SIX

JULES

Every inch of me stings under the hot stream of water. I rub at my swollen eyes and turn my face up to the shower head, gasping for air and getting nothing but soap suds and steam. Rubbing shampoo into my scalp, I hum the song about washing the man out of my hair. But which man? If I'd been a better wife, mother, employee, none of this would have happened.

The water drums against the glass shower pane.

Do better. Do better. Do better.

I step out of my bedroom, hair in a towel and robe tied tightly. Reece is in the hall loitering.

'What?' I snap.

He raises both hands up in surrender. 'Whoa. Was only seeing if you're OK.'

'I'm fine,' I say, letting out a long breath. 'Just a bit sad.'

He's staring at my mottled face, my red eyes, my puffy lips.

'You came home late last night,' he says.

I laugh. 'What's this? Are you my mum now?'

We both realise what I've said. 'I miss her, too,' Reece mumbles.

I forget it wasn't only my mother we lost; Reece also lost a grandmother. A woman who adored him, who would take him on long country walks. She loved nature. It was my mother who gave Adam the idea of getting an allotment, told him a man had to provide for his family in more ways than one. She knew all about men who couldn't provide.

I let out a sob and Reece gives me a long hug.

'Love you, Mum,' he mumbles into my shoulder. 'I hate to see you so upset.'

I can't reply though because I know if I open my mouth, I'll start crying again. My beautiful boy trying to comfort me, completely unaware I've driven his father away.

I need water. I head downstairs and Reece follows.

'What's going on?' Leah asks, coming out of the kitchen with a piece of cheese in her hand. Who walks about eating a lump of cheese?

'Don't you want some bread with that?' I ask, adjusting my robe. 'Or a cracker?'

She gives me a look like I'm mad. 'Why's your face all blotchy?'

Reece thumps her arm.

'Oi, knobhead,' she shouts.

Her brother widens his eyes, but Leah still doesn't get it. 'What?'

'Today's Grannie's anniversary.'

She pops the last of the cheese in her mouth. 'Oh, right. Sorry.'

I look at the kitchen clock behind her. It's already three o'clock.

'What are your plans today?' I ask.

They shrug, both of them now absent-mindedly looking at

their phones. I can go to the cemetery any day; it's the living I need to focus on right now.

'Want to watch a movie?'

Leah mumbles something about homework and Reece says he has to see someone about something. Always someone about something. I turn to head back to my room as Leah calls out to me.

'Dad rang,' she says. 'Said he couldn't get hold of you. I forgot to tell him the flowers arrived about an hour ago.'

Flowers? I go back down the hall to the living room, where a large bunch of sunflowers sits proudly in the middle of the dining room table.

I look at the label.

I'M HERE FOR YOU x

No name. In all the years we've been together, Adam has rarely bought me flowers, and there's no way he'd send me anything without addressing it to me and signing his name. Sunflowers always make me think of my mother and our last family holiday together to the South of France. I stroke the delicate sunflower petals, as thin and soft as the skin of my mother's hands on her last day, and smile at the memory of her disappearing each morning with the kids into a field of yellow.

'Did your dad send them?' I ask Leah.

She shrugs. 'He didn't mention anything. He sounded in a rush.'

My heart is beating. Who, apart from Adam and the kids, knows sunflowers are my favourite flower? I think I wrote that I love sunflowers on my Kandid bio. I want to check but I can't, I deleted the app, but I'm sure I mentioned sunflowers. Curious2 said he was going to make everything right and he somehow knows where I live. A man I've never met now thinks he's my saviour and he knows where I live.

FIFTY-SEVEN

LEAH

I lost my virginity to Dylan Ward three weeks ago yesterday and now I wish he were dead. He's ruined my life and I'm going to make him pay. I've also decided I'm not going to let those stupid notes scare me anymore. If someone is out to get me, then bring it on because I'm dragging Dylan down with me.

I've washed his Blondie t-shirt and I'm wearing it to school today. It's mine now. I want him to see me in it and realise I'm going to destroy his life.

'Hi,' I say, jogging up to Paige outside of school.

She has her hair in two plaits and is wearing her Flying Donkeys top. A hard ball forms in my guts. I wonder if she's been wearing it every day since my birthday, waiting for me to see her in it, trying to make a point in her usual passive-aggressive way. She doesn't answer as I fall into step beside her.

'Hello!' I shout.

She makes a sound but doesn't stop walking.

'Hey,' I say, reaching for her arm. She slows down. 'How many times do I have to tell you and Summer that I'm sorry? I didn't know about the concert. I don't even know why you're so angry with me. *I* missed out on my birthday present, not you.'

Paige breathes out heavily through her nose like a little pony.

'It's not that, Leah. You lied to us. Summer and I were really worried about you, and you still won't tell us where you were.'

I chew on the skin inside my mouth. I keep doing that. There are already little bumps sticking out, but I nibble on them anyway.

'You wouldn't understand.'

Paige throws her hands up in the air. 'See? You can't even trust us now. And God knows what is going on with you and Santi, but he's really upset.'

My stomach, my chest, my throat ache. All of me aches.

'I was drunk, and I said some mean things.'

'Why? Why the hell were you drinking on your own in the park, Leah?' she spits out.

I take a step back and raise my voice. I don't see why they get to be the only ones hurt in all of this. 'Because you and Summer never answered your phones!'

She huffs and swings back around, her long braids whipping me in the face as she heads for the school entrance. I turn the other way towards the art block, where I find Dylan setting up his class.

'Ah, Leah,' he says when he sees me. 'I haven't seen you in class lately.'

He's smiling. Why the hell is he smiling?

'I know you have a new girlfriend,' I blurt out. 'I didn't know you were into grandmas.'

'Grow up,' he mutters under his breath.

I fold my arms. 'You're not going to get away with this.'

He smiles widely, like he thinks I'm being ridiculous, then his smile turns to a frown when he sees what I'm wearing.

'Where did you get that t-shirt?'

He pulls my arms apart and opens up my blazer. I smile. That's rattled him.

'Answer me! Where did you get that top, Leah? It's vintage. An original.'

'Are you scared?'

He scoffs again. 'Of you? No.'

'You should be. I got this without any issues,' I say, stroking the Blondie top. 'Imagine what else I can do.'

His eye is twitching. I'm getting to him. He leans forward so close I can smell the coffee on his breath. 'Fuck you.'

'You already did, and now everyone is going to hear about it.'

His eyes narrow as he takes me in, like he's contemplating whether to say what's on his mind. I wonder what he sees when he looks at me. I wonder if it's me he thinks about just before he falls asleep.

'Have you been getting any notes?' he asks. 'You know, threatening notes on yellow paper?'

My chest constricts and I try to steady my breathing. 'Have you?'

He nods. 'This is serious, Leah. Whoever it is knows about us and is warning me to stay away from you.' He peers over my shoulder. 'They said they'd hurt you if I didn't.'

Hurt *me*? Why me? Dylan is still staring at me intently, studying me, trying to read the expression on my face.

'Who's scared now?' he says with a sneer. 'Best you do what the notes say and leave me alone,' he adds before turning away.

Why isn't he more worried about this? I grab his arm and pull him back. His eyebrows shoot up in surprise.

'Show me the notes you got,' I say.

He laughs.

'Show me!' I cry, running over to his desk. I pull open the drawers and rummage through books and pens. He's still laughing.

'Go away, Leah.'

His backpack is under the desk. I crouch down as he runs over but I'm too fast.

'Get out of there!' he shouts as my hand closes over three sheets of yellow paper and a thick black marker pen. I turn the sheets over. They're blank on both sides.

'Wait. It was you?'

He straightens up and gives me a lopsided smile. I want to claw at his face with my nails. It was him all along. The sick prick wanted to frighten me! I'm trying so hard to keep my tears at bay but it's not working. I wipe at my face with the backs of my hands, but his expression doesn't change. He's actually enjoying watching me suffer.

'Oh no, busted,' he says in a deadpan voice. 'I should have known it would take more than a few threatening letters to keep you away. Psycho girlies like you need something stronger... like a straitjacket.'

'I'm telling,' I say, my teary words sounding ridiculously immature as they strain at my throat. 'I'm going to tell Ms Willis everything!'

Dylan doesn't move an inch.

'You think anyone will believe you? I know all about your bunny-boiler reputation, Leah. Anything you say will simply be the word of an infatuated teenage girl against her professional, respected and very exasperated teacher. I've already spoken to Ms Willis about your crush on me. She told me all about you and some poor boy called Nathan.'

I clench my back teeth and keep blinking. He's wrong, because I'm not lying, and I have a way to prove it. Dylan has no power over me – not if I don't let him.

'I have evidence,' I hiss.

He blinks slowly and shrugs, like I'm boring and he has better things to do. 'Like what? A blurry photo that doesn't even look like me?'

'Your DNA.'

He straightens up. Ha, not so smug anymore, arsehole!

'What do you mean, DNA?'

I step forward. I'm not as tall as him but I make sure to meet him eye to eye. Our noses are practically touching, and when I speak, I hope my breath is hot on his face.

'I have your sperm, Dylan. Your cum. The condom from the first time we had sex. You think Ms Willis will think that's an infatuated teenage girl thing? Where would I have got it from if I'm not telling the truth?'

His chest shudders as he takes a deep breath. He's trying to look calm, but I know he's not. I can see by the way his eyes are practically shivering in their sockets.

'You went through my bin? When?'

I shake my head. 'The festival.'

'You took the condom from the tent? Who the hell does that?' He runs both hands through his hair. 'You're a freak, Leah.'

I don't care what he thinks of me anymore. I have the upper hand and it feels good, like electricity under my skin. I lower my voice, so he has to step even closer.

'*And* I can describe the inside of your home: the layout of your living room, your artwork on the walls, the brand of coffee machine you have, the sound your bed makes when we're screwing on it. How will you get out of that one... *sir*?'

He swallows, his mouth opening and shutting like a landed fish. With every breath he takes, his chest shudders even more.

'Now look who's scared,' I say with a wink.

I open the classroom door and walk down the hallway. I can feel him watching me.

'You're going to pay for this!' I shout over my shoulder.

I thought the corridor was empty but it's not. Santi is there with a bunch of boys in our year. I should talk to him, apologise about Wednesday. I catch his eye, but he gives me a strange look and turns away.

FIFTY-EIGHT

JULES

Leah's school doesn't have a large car park, so I park at the back out of sight. I'm early. The appointment is during lunch, but I've been nervous all morning and couldn't wait around any longer. I reapply my lipstick and smooth down my hair. I took hours to get ready. I don't know what to expect when I confront this Dylan man, but I do know I want to feel strong, which means not looking as old and exhausted as I feel.

My phone buzzes but it's more WhatsApp group chat triviality. I hate that my first thought was of Curious2, and my stomach still flipped, but he's gone. He can't reach me anymore because I'm no longer on the app. I push away thoughts of him knowing my address and focus on sorting out my daughter's drama today and my marriage tomorrow.

The lunch bell sounds, and I stay in the car as a swarm of sixth-formers exit the school and head for the high street. Leah is there but she's not with Summer or Paige. Have they not made up yet?

I watch her as if she's not my daughter. The swish of her long hair, her clothes pulling and straining over her body, the way she walks like she always knows where she's going. My baby isn't a child anymore. Most teenagers cross the bridge from childhood to adulthood without even realising they've already arrived. But Leah knows. I can see it in her face. She doesn't want to be anyone's baby anymore.

I wait until it's all quiet and I'm not likely to be spotted by Leah's friends, then head for the art block. Through the glass of the classroom door, I can see there's already someone inside. I can't make out all of him, only a fragment of a Ramones t-shirt and baggy jeans. He's young, but not young enough to be excused for the vile things he's done.

Taking a deep breath, I turn the door handle, step inside and sit at the desk before the teacher.

'You must be Leah's mum,' he says with a grin. 'Nice to see you again.'

Fuck.

FIFTY-NINE

JULES

'What kind of sick joke is this?' I shout, jumping to my feet. 'Where's Mr Ward?'

The young man laughs. I liked his smile on Saturday night – now I want to wipe it off his face with the classroom chair.

'*I'm* Mr Ward. Please. Sit down.'

I lower myself back down and place my hands on my lap to stop them from shaking. I'd planned a speech; I knew exactly what I was going to say. I was going to stay calm and in control, tell the awful teacher about the letters and condom, threaten him with police action if he didn't resign from his job immediately. It doesn't matter that she's the one who pursued him, that he didn't technically break any laws, he shouldn't remain teaching at this school having done what he did. I still want to say all of that, except no words are coming out of my mouth.

This can't be Dylan. This is Robert, the man I nearly had sex with.

'You look different,' he says. He leans closer, his fingers intertwined. 'More... mumsy.'

My lips part but all I can manage is, 'Why?'

'Why what, Jules? Why are you in bars cheating on your husband? Why is your teen daughter a psychotic stalker? Why are you wasting your time right now?'

'I have evidence,' I croak.

He scrunches his lips together. Lips that kissed mine two days ago. The same lips that kissed my daughter. I push the back of my hand against my mouth and swallow down the rising bile.

'Yeah, Leah told me all about the evidence. You really have a messed-up kid there, Jules. Like mother, like daughter.'

The adrenaline of surprise is turning into something else now, something simmering, something hot. My hand shoots out as I go to slap his face, but he grabs my wrist mid-air.

'I wouldn't do that if I were you.'

I get to my feet, ripping my hand away from his. 'You're a disgusting predator and I'm going straight to the police!' I scream.

His eyes shoot to the closed door.

'You know I'm nothing of the sort,' he says quietly. 'Sit down.'

'Fuck you! Who the fuck abuses young girls then preys on drunk women in bars?'

Robert, Dylan, whatever the hell he calls himself, shakes his head slowly from side to side.

'She's the liar, and you know it.' He's so calm, so sure of himself. 'If you know the whole story, then you'll also know I told her to keep away from me. She's followed me, harassed me and stolen from me.'

'Did you know I was her mother on Saturday?'

He laughs softly. 'Of course I did. I'd already seen your photo on her phone, but I would have guessed anyway. She looks exactly like you. A mini, dark-haired version.'

'And you've been following me?'

'No. That was simply luck. When I saw you at the bar on Saturday, I thought *you* were following *me*, but when I realised you had no idea who I was, I took my chances. It was too easy, Jules. You were far too easy.'

I drop back into my chair like I've been punched.

'You lied about your name.'

'No, I didn't. Dylan is a nickname.'

'So why me?' I say under my breath. 'What kind of sick pervert gets a thrill from doing that? Isn't one of us enough?'

He takes his phone out of his pocket and holds it up to me. It's a video. It's not very clear but I recognise my leopard-print dress, my hair, my voice. He presses play. It's us, in the toilet cubicle. It's a grainy video of me being brought to orgasm.

'Are you sure, Jules?' Dylan is asking me in the video. 'What about your husband?'

'Fuck him,' I reply.

Dylan watches me as I watch his screen, his mouth twitching into a smile as I blink back tears.

'This is my favourite part,' he whispers, moving his phone closer to me. 'That little whimper there, like a kitten. Leah makes exactly the same noise, you know.'

I lunge across the table at him, but he's faster than me. He pushes his chair back, then in one swift motion he has my face in his hand, squeezing my cheeks together.

'Maybe more of a tiger than a kitten,' he says, his lips inches from mine. 'I would have done more, you know. You asked me if I was curious, and I was. I reckon you'd have been a way better lay than the other mothers I've been with.'

I pull away from his grasp and slap him as hard as I can. 'Others?'

He just laughs. 'Let's call it a side hustle. You think teaching pays?'

Is this what he does? He seduces older women, married

women, mothers at the schools he's worked at, then blackmails them? I think of Fiona. I think of the news report about women my age being extorted, threatened, blackmailed.

'What do you want?'

'I want you to bring the evidence to me tomorrow and I won't show anyone the video.' He writes something on a Post-it note and sticks it to my chest. 'Come to my flat. I promise I won't seduce you again. You've served your purpose.'

I pluck the pink paper square off my top and push it into my jeans pocket.

'Don't mess with me, Jules. I have your telephone number, and that of every parent in this school. Including your husband's. This video could go viral in a minute.'

'All I have to do is bring you the condom?'

He nods.

'And then you'll leave me and my daughter alone?'

He leans back against his desk and folds his arms. 'With pleasure. I'm not the bad guy here. I was high when I first met Leah, then a few days later I was horny. Nothing wrong in either of those things when you think you're sleeping with an adult. Believe me, I wouldn't have gone anywhere near her if I'd known her real age. If anything, *she* hunted *me*.'

'But you hunt others,' I say quietly.

'I've never forced any woman to do anything she didn't want. It's not my fault you desperate mums don't want to pay the price for your mistakes.'

'You make me sick,' I spit.

'Like you're so innocent? I asked you. I explicitly *asked* you if you wanted it. It's in the video. And you begged me, Jules. I didn't do anything you didn't want. *You* took a risk, not me. I simply saw an opportunity to protect myself and I made the most of it.'

I get to my feet even though my legs don't feel like they can carry me. I don't say another word as I hook my handbag over my shoulder.

Dylan calls out to me as I head for the door.

'Oh no, Jules, you didn't think I was actually attracted to you, did you?'

SIXTY

JULES

y some kind of miracle, I manage to drive home without
etting into an accident and I head straight to Leah's room,
ulling everything out of her Garfield toy. I don't know who I'm
ngrier with: Dylan, my daughter or myself.

Me. It's all my fault. I've not been there for my daughter
nd now I've made everything worse.

No more letters – she must have burned them all in the end
– but the rest is still there. I slump against her bed, falling to the
arpet with her giant Garfield clutched to my chest. I failed her.
 had the best mother in the world, and I didn't learn a thing. I
ake a deep breath, take the disgusting bag and its contents to
ny bedroom, and stuff it under my bed beside the shoebox of
noney. Every night, I sleep on a bed of lies. When did my life
ecome such a mess?

My phone buzzes and I glance at it. There are now three
mails from Steve, and another text from Adam.

*I'll be back 10am tomorrow. Please be home, we need to talk.
It's urgent.*

This is it. The beginning of the end. If I'm honest with myself, I've been waiting for this moment for months. I thought I would be inconsolable when the day finally came, but I'm not – it's all rather anticlimactic. I'm empty. Hollow. A part of me relieved that the wait is finally over.

My phone buzzes again. It's a text from an unknown number. Dylan. He wasn't lying about having every parent's telephone number.

> *Be at my house tomorrow 9pm with what I asked for or this little beauty gets shared far and wide.*

He's attached a video clip. I don't press play. Instead, I stare at the message for such a long time my hand starts to cramp. It's time to do the right thing, no matter who it hurts in the process. He can't ruin my life any more than I already have. I reply, pressing each key as if every jab was a punch.

> *I've changed my mind. I'm telling my husband, my daughter and the police. I suggest you start running.*

SIXTY-ONE
LEAH

I have a free period this morning. We all do on Tuesdays. A lot of our classmates come to school later, but if it's not raining, my friends and I sit on the field to chat or do the homework we didn't do on the weekend. I find Paige and Summer sitting at the picnic table where we always meet. They both look up, look at one another, then carry on writing.

'I'm sorry I've been lying to you,' I say, sitting next to Summer. She shuffles away from me. I pull at my long ponytail, smoothing it over my shoulder.

'Have you come to tell the truth? Or more lies?' Paige says.

She slams her pen down and they both shut their textbooks. 'Go on, then!' Summer shouts at me. 'Stop messing us about and spit it out.'

I'm still playing with my hair. I don't know how to say it. Where to start.

'OK. The reason I was late for my birthday is because... Remember the guy I slept with at Carnage? Dylan? The one I thought Mr Ward looked like?'

Summer rolls her eyes. 'Is this about that stupid text you sent?'

'We told you not to get obsessed with anyone else,' Paige pipes up. 'Look what happened with Nathan.'

I knew they wouldn't understand.

'That's not what happened. Look, I lied. I mean, I told the truth in the text, but lied that I'd sent it by mistake. Mr Ward *is* Dylan.'

Summer makes a face at Paige, but I keep going. '*It's true.* He totally freaked out when he realised my real age. He's been so mean.' My eyes fill up with tears and I let one roll down my cheek. It works, they're both listening now. 'I thought on my birthday, once I was seventeen, he'd be less creeped out about us, so I went to talk to him at his flat. That's when I saw him with another woman, an older one, and why I got home late and missed the concert.'

I pull the cuffs of my blazer over my hands and dab at my eyes with it. I love my friends so much. I should never have put a stupid guy before our friendship. Paige glances at Summer, who's frowning at me, like she's trying to read the truth on my face.

'So you're saying Mr Ward is definitely the guy you had sex with at the festival?'

I nod really fast. 'And on the Saturday before school started. He's had a haircut and shaved since then, but it's him. I promise.'

'Show me that photo again,' Summer says.

'I don't have it anymore. He deleted it off my phone.'

She kisses her teeth.

'It's the truth! You were there, in art class, the first day. Don't you remember the way he was with me?'

I don't think she does, because neither of them appears convinced.

'Let's ask him,' Summer says, pointing at the art block.

Dylan is outside the building talking to Ms Willis, the head. He's laughing at something she's saying then they part ways, Ms

Willis heading back to the main building and Dylan to his classroom.

Summer runs up to him, Paige and I struggling to keep up with her. What the hell is she going to say? *Hi, sir, did you have sex with Leah?*

I'm hissing, 'Don't, you'll make things worse,' through my teeth as I run behind her but she's making the same face she does when she's about to win a race. There's no way to stop her when she gets like this.

Dylan has his head bent low against the wind, his shoulders hunched. He's wearing a white cable-knit sweater and looks really cute, even though I hate his guts. His face falls when he sees me, but he recovers quickly.

'Good morning, girls. Can I help you?'

'What's your first name, sir?' Summer asks, walking beside him. Just like that. Like everyone is allowed to walk around asking teachers what their name is. Dylan keeps walking, but a little slower, and I hold my breath. My friends aren't seeing what I'm seeing. They haven't noticed the way his skin has paled by two shades, his Adam's apple bobbing in his throat, the way his brow has furrowed a little.

'Robert,' he says. 'My name is Robert Ward.'

Robert? Why is he lying?

Summer gives me a dirty look and stops walking as Dylan continues out of sight through the double doors. The three of us remain standing outside the building, my friends looking at one another like they knew they were right all along. They believe him. Of course, they believe him.

'He's lying,' I say, my voice tinny and high. I don't sound convincing at all.

'I've got to get to the gym,' Summer mutters, walking away. Paige follows her. I run to keep up.

'You have to believe me. His friends call him Dylan. It's really him. He's been threatening me, saying I can't tell anyone.'

With a sigh, they both stop again, and Paige takes out her mobile phone. She types in the school website address and holds it up to me. It's a photo of Dylan alongside headshots of the entire faculty. The photo doesn't even look like him; he looks old and serious. Even I wouldn't believe that the hot guy who made love to me and said he was crazy about me, the same person I shared a spliff with at a music festival, is the grey-suited man staring back at me through her phone screen.

Under the photo of him is his name. Robert Ward.

'Maybe Dylan is a nickname,' I cry out. 'All of my brother's friends have nicknames, it's a boy thing. Ask Santi! He knows how horrible Dylan has been to me. Ask him!'

'You're a liar,' Paige says. 'You lie to everyone. Jacob told me Santi told him you were only with him to try and make Mr Ward jealous. What the hell, Leah? I can't believe you'd treat your friends like this all because you're crushing on a *teacher*.'

Summer is nodding beside her, but they have it all twisted! The bell rings and they rush off to class before I have a chance to defend myself. I run back to the art block, barging into the classroom before anyone else gets there. Dylan looks up with a start, something hard coating his gaze.

He rolls his eyes at me. 'You really can't keep away, can you?'

'Why are you pretending your real name is Robert?' I shout.

'Enough, Leah.'

'Why are you lying?' I pound at his chest with my fists, and he grabs hold of my wrists, his thumbs pressing into my flesh.

'I'm not lying. My friends call me Dylan. It's a joke, because I play the guitar. You know, Bob Dylan? Bob. Robert. Anyway, Robert is my first name.'

'It doesn't suit you.'

He sighs and lets me go.

'Get out.'

'I am going to destroy you,' I say slowly under my breath.

Year nine students are filing in, but I don't care. 'I'm going to tell my parents everything.'

He smiles. Why does he find all of this so amusing? With a glance over his shoulder, he leans in close and whispers, 'I doubt your father will be as shocked by your revelation as he will be by mine. Tell your mother I look forward to seeing her soon.'

SIXTY-TWO

JULES

I woke up too early this morning, and the last four hours waiting for Adam to come home have felt like an eternity. I've still not looked at my job termination agreement and I've ignored three calls from Steve. I've cleaned the house from top to bottom, cried twice, called Lynsey three times but she didn't pick up, and taken a long bath.

Then I spent an hour getting ready doing my hair, my make-up, painting my nails and putting on nice underwear. I'm wearing the flowery dress Adam bought me two years ago and said I looked 'pretty' in. I know it's stupid to make such an effort when I'm about to admit to adultery, but it's better than wearing my baggy pyjamas with a hole in the knee while my husband tells me all the different reasons why he no longer loves me.

I don't want to be a divorcee. I don't want this. He hasn't wanted me for a long time, and now I'm giving him the perfect reason to leave me for good. I don't know how to be honest with Adam and still keep him.

Getting divorced in your forties isn't unusual – if anything, it's a rite of passage. Lots of my friends have left their husbands. Much like me, they'd made their careers smaller to fit around the children they wanted to be there for, and then, once the kids had grown up, realised there was nothing left to stay for. The difference was they weren't financially independent; so many of them stayed with men they no longer loved. It was a matter of which pain was greater – being with them or starting their lives again from zero. That's not my problem, though. I have money. My issue is that I don't want to live without Adam, and I don't want my life to change.

Actually, I *do* want my life to change. I want it to be a better version of the one I have that *includes* my husband. I want the life everyone thinks I already have.

I've put the laundry away and changed the bedsheets; everything is clean and neat. I've even arranged the cushions nicely on the bed. Why do I have so many cushions that no one but my husband sees? How many minutes do I waste every day arranging damn cushions? I throw them at the wall, one by one, then pick them all up again and place them back nicely on the bed. I'm arranging the final one when I hear the key in the door.

'Jules?' Adam calls out.

'Upstairs.'

I listen to the familiar tread of my husband's feet on the stairs, wondering how many more times I will get to hear it before everything changes.

'You look nice,' he says as he steps into the bedroom. 'Where you off to?'

He's wearing a suit without a tie, the top button of his collar undone. His hair is getting long. I wonder if he needs me to make him an appointment, then I realise with a start I may never get to do that for him again. Maybe this other woman likes him with longer hair. Maybe Adam will never speak to me again after today.

'I'm not going anywhere. You said you wanted to talk.'

He peels his shirt off and I marvel at how toned his arms still are, how strong his shoulders have remained after all these years. Those were the arms that held me when we first kissed as the world entered a new millennium, the same arms that rocked our newborn babies and enveloped me when my mother died. Will I ever feel them around me again?

'Is everything OK?' I ask.

'No. Not really.'

My hands are sweating. I want to wipe them on my dress, but I don't want him to see. 'Whatever you're about to say, let me say something first.'

I'm sitting on the bed. He's still standing, waiting. A bead of sweat collects at his collarbone and I watch it travel beneath his shirt. I don't like that he's nervous, too.

'I've done a terrible thing,' I say.

There. It's out now. I can't go back. I watch his face, but there's no reaction. Adam isn't the kind of man who flies off the handle: he likes to gather all the evidence, weigh it up, analyse it, make it make sense. He needs more information.

'I didn't mean it to happen, and I've walked away from it now, but I got close to another man. We didn't have sex, it was more of a—'

'I know.'

My stomach drops. Everything stops: my breathing, the world, everything. All I can hear is water rushing in my ears like I'm going to be swept out to sea. How does he know about Dylan? Has Dylan sent the video already?

'I know about the app,' Adam says.

App? I don't understand. I nearly say it, I nearly say Dylan's name, but Adam is talking fast and thank God he is because I suddenly realise what he's saying.

'You know about Kandid?' My voice is croaky. It doesn't even sound like me.

He nods. 'And I know about Curious2.'

'How?'

'Because it was me.'

The rushing water in my ears gets louder and I have to steady myself against one of our many cushions until everything comes back into focus.

'What was you?' I manage to stutter.

If he's been checking my phone, then he must have done that before the weekend, before he went away for work. How long has he known about me talking to another man?

'It's me,' he says again. 'I'm the guy you've been talking to. Curious2. That's me.'

Adam sits beside me, the sag in the bed making me wobble. He places a hand on my arm. I'm shaking.

'You thought you were getting close to a stranger online, but you weren't. You were talking to me.'

He shows me his phone, taps on the orange K logo. Opens it. Our conversation pops up and he scrolls to the start and the very first message he sent to me. It says 'Account no longer exists' beneath my old username.

'I don't understand.'

The water in my head is more of a buzz now. I screw up my eyes, focusing on my husband's words.

'How? I don't...'

'A few weeks ago, when we were watching that documentary about Cleopatra, you were on your phone and then ran off crying. I thought you'd received some bad news, so I looked at your phone. Just a quick glance. I would never do that normally, but I was worried. Except it wasn't bad news. You'd posted that photo and people were commenting.'

That was nearly four weeks ago. I rack my brain, trying to remember what those sleazy men had said to me. It was all so filthy, sordid descriptions of depraved sexual fantasies. Shit! Shit shit shit. Is that why Adam has been sleeping with his colleague? Because of me? I hadn't been interested in any of those creeps. All I wanted was someone to tell me I was worth something and that I wasn't going mad. Curious2 was that someone.

'I read all the messages you received,' Adam says.

My hand flies to my mouth. How many times am I going to vomit this week?

'Jules, listen. I wasn't angry, I was... confused. In your post you said you loved your husband, that you were sad because he... I... didn't make you feel good about yourself. I was shocked at first, then deeply ashamed. Not once did you mention wanting to cheat on me.'

'I didn't! I don't!' I cry out. 'Why didn't you say anything?'

'I did,' he says. 'After I realised how you felt, I tried talking to you, asking if you were OK, texting you that I love you, smiling and connecting with you more. But it wasn't enough. It was clear you were falling out of love with me. That you wanted this stranger more than me.'

'No! I didn't. I don't.'

He takes my hand and I think of Dylan, the way he did the same thing in the bar on Saturday, and where his hands ended up. I push the thought out of my head.

'I set up the Kandid account because...' He looks at my hand in his. 'It sounds terrible saying it out loud, but a part of me wanted to test you. See if you'd cheat on me. Then, once we started messaging, I realised... I really missed talking to my wife.'

'So why didn't you talk to me face to face?' I scream. 'I was right here!'

'I didn't know how to!' he shouts back. 'I told you. I tried. It was just... it was *easier* to be someone else, a stranger on an app. I guess that's why you never talked to me either and told a bunch of faceless men how you were feeling instead. The weird thing is that I'd forgotten how much fun you are, how interesting and smart and sexy. It sounds ridiculous because we've been together twenty-five years, but talking to you like you weren't my wife was exciting. I wanted to tell you it was me after the first day. In a way, I was hoping you'd work it out. I even sent you those flowers hoping you'd put two and two together.'

'I thought a stranger knew where we lived!' I shout.

He looks surprised, realisation dawning across his face.

'Oh my God, I'm so sorry. Jules... I... It felt romantic at the time.'

All this time Curious2, the man who was saying all the right things and seemed so perfect, was my *husband*? Adam's eyes are tinged with red. I hadn't noticed how dark the bags beneath them have been getting.

'You don't need to apologise,' I mumble. 'It's not your fault.'

'It is! When your mum got ill, I picked up the slack so you could focus on her. Then when she died, you said you needed some space, and I was happy to give it to you because it was easier to ignore your pain than deal with it. It got to the point where I distanced myself from you so much, I no longer knew how to connect with you. Why do you think I booked a conference on the weekend of her anniversary? I was scared and selfish. I stopped trying. I told myself that what you really needed was me making money, that's how I was looking after you all. And I thought the allotment would be helpful, that I could contribute with food, too. Your mum always said that's what a good husband did, he provided. I was lying to myself because, actually, all you really needed was me to be there for you.'

I take his hand again. He squeezes and my breathing slows down.

'I could have lost you, Jules.'

I shake my head. He wouldn't have. I would never have left him – he's the one leaving me. I'm still waiting for that.

'What about Bea?' I ask.

'Who?'

'The woman you work with.'

'Beatriz? What does she have to do with anything?'

'I thought you two were having an affair,' I say quietly. It sounds stupid now, especially after all he's told me. Adam doesn't look angry or guilty though, he looks amused.

'What? No. Beatriz is work.' He laughs in a sad way. 'Hard work.'

'So there's no other woman?'

'Other... what?'

I feel so stupid. Why have I been so stupid?

Adam smiles at me and this time it doesn't feel patronising. 'Bea is a partner at the company Cedric has spent months closing a deal with. That's what I wanted to talk to you about, and why I've hardly been around. We've sold Atë Innovations. For a lot of money.'

I'm glad I'm sitting down because I can no longer feel my body.

'You finally sold the business? Why didn't you tell me?'

He looks down at his lap and I realise how ridiculous that sounds. So many secrets. So many lies. I haven't told him about my job, about Leah, about the money under our bed, or what happened between me and Dylan. I rack my brain for all the things I told a stranger that I'd been keeping from my husband. My head is spinning. I can't untangle one life from the other.

'Is that why you bought her the bracelet?'

Adam looks confused, then comprehension floods his features.

'You saw the bracelet?' He places his other hand over ours. 'Jules, that was for you. I bought it to give to you on your mother's anniversary, then I saw your post on Kandid and I felt so stupid and angry with myself.'

'It's not diamonds I need.'

I think of Lynsey when I say that; both of us desperate to be adored, not adorned.

'I know that now,' Adam says.

I look at him, really look at him, and we don't need words. His eyes, the same ones I've been staring into for twenty-five years, cloud over and something ignites inside of me. I've said everything I need to say to him already because this is Curious2, the man who understands me. The only one who cares. And he was the man I loved all along.

'I can't stop thinking about those photos you sent me,' he says, his voice thick with the same longing I've been feeling for so long.

My face stings with shame. What must he think of me?

'I'm sorry, I—'

'No.' He slips the strap of my dress from my shoulder. 'They were hot. My wife is so damn hot. Jesus, Jules, I was so turned on. I would lie awake next to you, thinking of those photos, wanting to make love to you, but paralysed because I didn't know how to start. We'd drifted too far apart and the only way I knew how to turn you on, how to connect with you, was by being a complete stranger.'

'I turned you on?'

He laughs lightly. 'You have no idea. You're the only woman I ever think about.'

I take his hand and place it on my thigh, pushing it higher beneath my dress. He gives me a slow smile as his hand inches higher. I close my eyes. I'm scared to talk, to break the spell. This is all I've ever wanted. Adam noticing me, talking to me, touching me.

When I open my eyes, he's stroking my face, his lips inches from mine. 'I nearly lost you,' he says. 'All because I couldn't see how lucky I am.'

Then he's kissing me and it's like getting into bed after a long day. My Adam, my man. The kiss is so familiar it makes my chest ache, yet it's tinged with something more. Fear. Fear of coming close to the end. This is the bridge I've been waiting to cross for so long. I grasp the back of his neck and fall back on the bed. The weight of him is so right, his body that fits so perfectly against mine, two people made for one another.

I'm not going to tell him about Dylan. He doesn't need to know that I *did* betray him, that I *did* let another man bring me pleasure. I'm not going to tell him about Leah either, and the whole sorry mess. He doesn't need to know any of that, it's all in the past. I've sorted it. It's over now.

Except it's not.

'Where are you going?' Adam cries as I run from the room, my phone in my hand.

'It's a work thing. I won't be a minute.'

'Come back to bed!' he says. I can hear the jingle of his belt buckle, his trousers falling to the carpet.

I stand in the hallway and type furiously.

I'll be there tonight. 9pm. You can have all the evidence, just please delete the video. Please!

Two blue ticks show it's been read.

SIXTY-THREE

JULES

I'm curled up beside my wonderful, beautiful husband, my body fitting into his side like we were forged that way from the very beginning. Two pieces carved from the same piece of rock. I'm hot and clammy but I don't want to move. I want to stay in this moment forever. We haven't left the bedroom all day. I don't know whether Leah and Reece are home, and I don't care.

Adam devoured me as if he'd never met me before. As if it was our last day together and he wanted to remember every inch of my body. We re-enacted the fantasy I shared with him, then he told me his, and it was like meeting him for the first time all over again.

'Why has it never been like this before?' I ask.

Adam kisses that special place above my spine that only he knows makes me melt. 'Because we thought what we had would always be there.'

We lie in silence and after a while I begin to unravel, every revelation making me lighter.

'Medusa has been sold to Starz,' I say.

He sits up. 'Steve has sold the business? What about your job?'

I bite down on my bottom lip. 'He retained fifty-one per cent of the shares. He doesn't know whether to relinquish them or not. Either way, I'll probably take redundancy.'

'Do you want to leave? You've always loved it there.'

I shake my head, fat tears I didn't know I was holding back sliding down my face. With everything that's been going on, my job seemed the least important thing to worry about; I've hardly given it any thought. Yet now, now that I know my marriage is safe and my daughter will be too, I realise I *do* care. I love Medusa and I know exactly what it needs to succeed.

'If I could, I'd buy him out. I know I could turn the brand around so quickly.'

'So do it,' Adam replies.

I laugh, a sharp ha! 'Yeah, right.'

'I mean it. Jules, Atë is selling for a lot of money. A lot. Our life is going to change in a big way soon. This is it. This is your chance to be exactly who you want to be.'

I can't process it all. It's too much. I thought I was about to lose everything, and in the last few hours I've learned I could have everything I've ever wanted. This is it, we're on the precipice of a new future. One where Adam and I are happy together, our family stable and content, a life with the mental space and financial security, where I can finally meet my full potential. Isn't that the goal we all aim for, what we're all working towards? Isn't that the whole point of killing ourselves during the best years of our lives?

A fresh start, I say to myself silently as my husband's breathing gets deeper, his chest rising and falling against my back. *Everything is going to be OK.*

I'll take Leah's disgusting evidence to Dylan tonight, he'll delete the video, and I'll never have to think about any of it ever again. Then I can start thinking about what *I* want for a change – like running my own business.

Yet for us to all be happy, to be truly free, I need Dylan to disappear altogether. Tonight I'm going to make that bastard an offer he won't be able to refuse.

SIXTY-FOUR

LEAH

'What the hell is going on?' Reece whispers to me as I sit down at the dinner table.

Mum and Dad are in the kitchen, cooking... *together!* He keeps putting his arms around her waist, nuzzling her and making her giggle.

'I have no idea,' I whisper back. 'But it's making me want to barf.'

'I think it's cute,' Reece says.

'It's demented.'

They've made spaghetti and Mum is saying something about how at least this time we're all here to eat it. Dad says something about being 'curious' and Mum laughs.

'I have an announcement,' Dad says. Reece and I sit up. The last time he said that, five years ago, he'd booked a family trip to Disneyland. Maybe we're going to Hawaii for Christmas.

'Cedric and I have sold the company.'

'So we're rich?' I ask, taking a slice of garlic bread.

Mum makes a disapproving face at me, and Reece mutters something about me being shallow, but Dad looks really proud of himself.

'Yes, Leah. We are in a great financial position, which means things are going to get a lot easier from now on. Apparently, the announcement is already in the business press.'

I doubt anyone I know has seen it. Who cares about tech companies? Reece is asking if Mum and Dad will give him some money to go backpacking and they say maybe, so I try my luck, too.

'If you're giving Reece money, then can I get tickets to Beyoncé?' I ask. Reece's eyebrows fly up. I don't know why he's judging. He's so going to want to come with me. 'I mean, I did miss out on Flying Donkeys.'

'Are you serious?' Mum shouts.

OK. Fine. Too soon. God, you'd think she'd be more chilled considering we're going to be loaded soon.

'It's not been an easy few years,' Dad says in a serious voice.

What's he talking about? He looks at Mum and holds her stare. Reece looks at me, I widen my eyes, he does the same.

'I've been absent,' Dad says. 'I've been a little selfish, a little obsessed with work and my own interests, and I feel like we've all drifted apart. There's been a lot of change lately.' He's stroking Mum's hand and her eyes are swimming with tears. 'And loss. So I wanted to say I love you all, very much. We need each other, OK? Remember that. We all need each other.' He raises his glass. 'To the ones we love.'

Mum's face is completely soaked now but she's grinning like some kind of maniac. I raise my glass of water and we all clink glasses. When Mum puts hers down, I take her hand. She looks up, as if she's seeing me for the first time.

'I love you,' she mouths at me. Dad is giving Reece some lecture about the importance of knowing what career you want but Mum is looking only at me now. It's a bit dramatic, but I don't hate it.

'I love you so much,' she whispers again. 'Fiercely.'

I squeeze her hand, biting my lips together so she can't tell she's making me teary. 'I know.'

She nods in response, like she's gearing herself up to do something big, then stands up.

'Right,' she says. 'Let's eat before the pasta gets cold.'

She signals that we pass her our bowls and one by one we hold them up as she serves.

'By the way, I need to pop out at half past eight.' Her voice is all tight from the crying. 'Lynsey has an appointment and I said I'd keep an eye on the boys.'

'What kind of appointment is at night?' I say.

'Why can't John look after his own kids?' Reece asks. 'He's too hot for Lynsey, by the way. Sorry.'

Dad holds out his empty bowl. 'Want me to come with you?'

'Can everyone calm down,' Mum shouts, serving him a slippery mound of pasta. A load of it slops over the side. 'I'll only be an hour or so!'

We all look at one another and don't say anything. She mumbles something about us having a family game of Uno later if we want, but nobody answers. Mum's been acting really weird lately, even for her.

SIXTY-FIVE

LEAH

'Well, that was intense,' I say to Reece.

'Yeah, what was all that about?'

'Mum's mad.'

'You're mean. Lay off her.'

'Whatever, golden boy.'

We're sitting in his bedroom because he wants to show me pictures on his laptop of some beach in Thailand he plans to go to after uni, and Dad is in the living room talking on the phone to work people. Reece is dressed in nothing but a pair of baggy shorts and some Boss sliders he wears around the house. He loves wasting money on shit no one ever sees. His hair is streaked blonde from his trip to Ibiza and he's still brown, making his eyes and teeth look extra bright. No idea how he pulls off the Californian surfer look when the only time he gets in the water is to record his thirst trap TikToks.

'That's where they filmed *The Beach*,' he says, pointing at his laptop screen.

'What's *The Beach*?'

He smacks the back of my head lightly. 'You're so vacant.'

His phone keeps buzzing, and with every photo he shows

me, he stops to glance at the screen, types something and puts it back down again.

'More drug orders?' I say.

He rolls his eyes. 'You're hilarious. It's just my mates. Listen… this is weird, but…'

'What?'

'Were you talking to any of the guys I was with at Carnage?'

My heart quickens. Did his friends see something?

'No.'

'Good. Stick to boys your own age.'

'I do. There's a new boy in my class, Santi. We were kind of seeing each other.'

Reece links his hands together and rests his head on them, batting his eyelashes like a cartoon. 'Oooh, Santi. Is that short for Santiago? Sexy. Tell me everything.'

'He doesn't like me anymore.'

'I hate him.'

I laugh and lean my head on his shoulder. 'It was my fault. I messed up. I hate boys.'

'Yeah, we're the worst. So… No. Never mind. It's probably nothing.'

I hit his arm. 'What?'

'Are you sure you weren't chatting to Bunny's brother's friends at the festival?'

My stomach twists. This doesn't mean Reece knows anything. I shake my head, but he's looking at me funny.

'Why?'

'I saw one of them, Dylan Ward. He was on our street earlier and I thought it was strange.'

What? Was Dylan looking for me? How does he know where I live? He must have looked in the school files.

'Did he see you? Does he know you're my brother?'

'No. Leah, what… You know him, don't you? Jesus! What's going on?'

'Nothing!'

'Tell me.'

I let out a long breath and flop back on his bed.

'He's my art teacher.'

They say the best lie is one peppered with truth.

'Your *teacher*? He teaches at St Margarette's now? I thought he was still in Watford.'

His phone buzzes again and he looks at it for a long time, looks at me, my hand, and frowns.

'Why didn't you say anything?' he asks.

'I wasn't sure if it was him. He looks different than he did at Carnage. What's the big deal?'

He looks at his phone for the longest time, then holds it up. It doesn't take me long to work out what I'm looking at. It's a selfie of a girl wearing nothing but a red bra. Oh. I know that photo.

'Who's that?' I say, keeping my voice as neutral as possible.

My brother is showing me the half-naked selfie I took. Why does he have a photo of me in my bra? I'm trying not to show any emotion on my face, but he knows I know. He can always tell.

'It's you, isn't it?'

I jump off Reece's bed, but he pulls me back down.

'Get off!' I cry as he forces me to sit.

'What's going on, Leah? I know this is you.'

'How do you know? The face is cut off!'

He points at the screen and then my hand.

'Your ring. The one I bought you that you never take off.'

There's no point running to my room, he'll only chase me, and Dad is downstairs anyway. I start to cry. Reece puts his arm round me, but I shake him off.

'How did you get that photo? Did you take it from my phone?'

'It was sent to me. Dylan sent it to Bunny's brother, who

showed him. Bunny was with me when I had that ring made for you. He recognised it.'

I let out a wail and he pulls me to him. This time, I let him.

'Have all of your friends been talking about me?'

'No! Nobody else knows it's you. I promise.'

He holds me tighter, and I wrap my arms around his neck. I thought the worst thing in the world would be someone knowing about Dylan and me, but now I want to tell my brother everything. He needs to understand that I'm not easy, that it wasn't how it seems, that what could have been wonderful went really wrong and none of it was my fault.

'Did he hurt you?' he says quietly into my hair.

I shake my head. 'Not really.'

'Leah.'

I look up.

'Tell me.'

So I do. I tell him every single thing that has happened. Everything but the door key part. At one point he's on his feet and I have to pull him back down.

'He needs to be taught a lesson,' he's muttering. 'Someone needs to ram a fucking Snickers down his fucking throat and finish him off once and for all!'

'Snickers?'

Is that a euphemism?

'He's allergic to peanuts. You didn't know that? He always has that EpiPen on him. Leah, this is serious. I'm going to have to talk to him.'

I start crying even harder.

'No. Please don't, you'll make everything worse. He didn't even do anything wrong,' I say. 'I lied to him.'

'It doesn't matter. He's a nasty, manipulative pervert.'

'You don't know him like I do. He can be nice.'

'No, he can't. It's all an act. I've been selling weed to him every weekend for years. I told you to keep away from those creeps at the festival. I told you!' He's shouting and I start crying again. It's bad enough my friends and Santi won't talk to me, but I can't lose my brother over this.

Reece sits back down again and hugs me. 'Sorry. I didn't mean to scare you. He makes his money extorting women. A blackmailer. Like that thing we saw on TV the other day. It's normally older women – he seduces them then tricks them into paying him – but... Jesus. I didn't know he had moved on to school kids. Has Dylan asked you for anything?'

I shake my head. 'He genuinely thought I was twenty-one. He had no idea who I was. He keeps telling me to leave him alone.'

'OK. Good. But we still can't let him get away with this. We have to report him to the school. Leah, you said you have evidence. I'll help you. I won't tell Mum or Dad, I promise.'

Reece pulls me up off his bed, and hand in hand we go to my room. I point at Garfield, and he unzips the cat, rooting around inside.

'Where's the condom?' he asks, as if it's the most normal thing in the world.

'It's in the box. In a plastic bag.'

He shakes his head and I push him out of the way.

'It's here, it's... Where is it?'

I slam the lid of the box down.

'Shit,' Reece says under his breath, staring at my bedroom window. It's wide open. I opened it this morning because of the stench of smoke Mum keeps complaining about.

'Did you tell him about the condom?'

'Yeah. I did. Shit! Do you think that's why he was on our street?'

Reece nods. 'He's taken it.'

SIXTY-SIX

JULES

Dylan lives in a small flat up three flights of stairs. When I buzz the intercom, he says the downstairs door is already open. By the time I get to the top, I'm out of breath and he's already standing at the door, barefoot, jogging bottoms so tight I can see the outline of his penis. I look away, but he's already smirking.

'Like what you see?'

'Go to hell.'

'Come in.' He opens the door wider, but I remain in the hallway.

'Jules, get inside. We're not doing this in front of the neighbours.'

I step inside. It smells of turps mixed with expensive coffee. Every inch of the flat is littered with half-finished art. Swirls of bright colours have been splashed on canvases, creating crude nude forms and flowers.

'Coffee?' he asks, nodding at a large machine in the corner taking up half the kitchen counter, if you can call it that. Three jars of beans sit beside the contraption, each one labelled: 'Colombian', 'Ethiopian', 'Bolivian'. He looks disappointed when I say I don't drink caffeine this late in the evening.

The coffee machine spurts and bubbles as he leans against the counter, legs crossed at the ankle, arms propped up either side of him, taking in every inch of me. A gnawing ache forms in my chest at the realisation that this bastard is exactly the kind of guy I'd have fallen for at Leah's age. Attractive, confident, creative, sophisticated – at least to a young mind. I try not to look over to the bed in the corner, try not to envisage my daughter in his home. I want to cry for her naivety, for her stupid recklessness.

He's still looking at me, making something hot and thorny tug in my guts. No, it was *my* stupid, reckless decision that brought me here.

'I don't drink coffee after seven, either,' he says. 'But I'll make an exception tonight.'

He takes his coffee to the sofa and moves a guitar in order to sit down. I stay standing.

'Let's get on with it,' I say.

'Sit. Relax,' Dylan says, putting his coffee down. He picks up the guitar and begins to strum an acoustic version of 'Sweet Child O' Mine'. It's taking every ounce of strength I have to not punch him in the face.

'Here.' I hand him the plastic bag. He looks inside and makes a face.

'Fucking hell!' he cries. 'Seriously, who keeps a used condom? Your kid needs therapy.'

'She's had therapy. She's fine.'

Dylan screws his nose up. 'She's not, and neither are you.'

'She's just a child,' I say.

'I'm more than aware of that.'

He gets back up and throws the bag in his kitchen sink. I watch as he pours lighter fluid on it and lights a match before recording the acrid bonfire on his phone. The bag starts to shrink and darken, the smoke turning from black to white. I open the window. I'm so tired of watching everything burn.

'Give me your phone,' I say once Dylan has finished filming. 'I want that video of us deleted.'

He bats my hand away, scrolls through his phone and shows me as he deletes the recording.

'It's gone.'

'And now you need to go, too,' I say.

'Go where? We had a deal, Jules. No evidence, no video. We're even.'

I didn't think I still had a husband yesterday. I didn't think I had anything left to lose. Now I know I have everything. Perhaps I always did. Dylan is dangerous and he needs to disappear.

'I want you to resign and leave town.'

He laughs. 'Who are you, Clint Eastwood? I'm not going anywhere. At least... not for free.'

I was waiting for this. This vile creep is proud of his extortion racket; I didn't think he'd go so easily. I wonder how many other women like me he's blackmailed. I wonder if he was Fiona's online boyfriend.

'I've done a bit of digging,' he says. 'I even took a little stroll to the nicer end of town this afternoon. You have a big house.'

'Don't you dare go near my house!' I cry, lunging forward.

He laughs, holding a hand up to keep me back. 'I was only looking. For now. You never told me Leah's father was *the* Adam Crow. The same Adam Crow who sold his tech company this week for a *disgusting* amount of money.'

And there it is. But I'm one step ahead of him.

'What will it take for you to disappear forever?'

He raises his brows. 'Everything has its price. I guess it depends how much your family means to you. All the evidence has gone now, all that messy business, so it's just you and me agreeing on a mutually beneficial financial incentive for me to disappear.'

'Call me when you have a figure,' I say, walking out of his

flat without a backward glance. I have physical cash, untraceable money that no one knows about. He'd be crazy to turn that down.

I reach the street and look up at Dylan's window, his silhouette filling the frame. He's watching me, contemplating how much I will pay him. How much is my family's freedom worth?

SIXTY-SEVEN

LEAH

Dylan has been inside my house. In my bedroom. He's taken the only evidence I have that we slept together. I used to imagine what it would be like to have him in my room. Now the thought of him touching my things makes me want to rip his eyes out.

Reece keeps saying we have to report him, but I've made him promise not to do anything yet. Dylan told Ms Willis I have a crush on him, that I'm obsessed with him, and now he's taken the condom it's my word against his. If I make a big fuss, all that will happen is that I'll get expelled, and then I'll have to explain everything to Mum and Dad. No way. It's bad enough Reece knows.

I dressed sensibly for school today, no make-up, hair tied back. I've been looking for Dylan all day. I'm going to tell him I have CCTV footage of him breaking and entering my house. Yeah, that will scare him!

It's lunchtime and my friends are still avoiding me, so I'm sitting in the playground on my own eating a sausage roll. I can see Dylan by the front of the school, holding his stupid coffee mug, talking to Ms Willis. He's smiling and looking happier than I've seen him in a long time.

I throw the greasy wrapper in the bin and head back to the main building, but as soon as Dylan sees me heading towards them, he walks away.

'Leah,' Ms Willis calls out.

My stomach drops. What has he been saying to her? She's giving me a strange look. This isn't going to be good. I don't realise I'm biting the inside of my cheeks until I taste blood.

'Can I have a quick word?'

The bell is about to go in ten minutes. She beckons me closer and leads me away from a couple of girls playing football.

'Are you settling into sixth form OK?'

I nod.

'What about your classes?'

I nod again.

'I was talking to Mr Ward and... Listen, I know some of our teachers are young, and fun, and can feel like one of your friends, but it's important to remember those boundaries we talked about. Do you know what I mean?'

I nod again and she rubs the top of my arm.

'You know my door is always open, Leah. If there's anything you're struggling with, anything at all, you can come to me.'

I nod a final time and walk away.

'Oh, and Leah.' I turn around, arranging my face into a pleasant expression. 'Nice to see you wearing jeans again. Those dresses you had on last week were a little short for school policy.'

I head back in the school building, my cheeks burning so fiercely they feel like I've been slapped. As I near my locker I spot Dylan heading towards the staff room. I pinch his arm as I walk past.

'Ow!' he shouts. A few kids from year seven stop and laugh,

but I stay standing there. 'What do you want?' he says under his breath.

'What did you tell Ms Willis?'

His lips twitch into a semi-smile.

'The truth. That you're obsessed with me.'

'Well, she won't be laughing when I tell her you broke into my house yesterday. I know you stole the evidence.'

He leans against the wall and grins. He doesn't even care that students are rushing past, seeing him act like an evil cartoon villain. 'I never stole anything.'

'You broke into my house, I have it on CCTV. I'm going to the police.'

'You can stop your stupid games now,' he says. 'I won.'

'No, you haven't. I'm going to make sure everyone knows you're a paedo. That you abused your position of power and seduced an innocent sixteen-year-old student. And then you'll go to prison.'

He laughs again, this time so loud and cruel I can see right to the back of his mouth.

'No, I won't. You have no proof anymore, so leave me the fuck alone.'

He takes out his phone and shows me something. It's a video of his sink with a plastic bag in it. He's pouring something on it then setting it alight. My tongue has turned solid, and my throat is closing up. I bite my lips together to trap the sob building in my gullet. I can't let him see me upset; he can't see that I care. The corridor is crowded now. I only have three minutes to get to my next class. Santi is standing by his locker looking over at us.

I clear my throat, but my voice comes out croaky anyway. 'I can't believe you stole from me.'

'And I can't believe *you* stole from *me*,' Dylan says. 'Because I very much doubt you went from insipid Swift merch to vintage seventies punk apparel overnight.'

He's talking about his Blondie t-shirt.

'Is that what you did when I was in the shower, before you let yourself out, Leah? Because Ms Willis told me all about your stalking tendencies and I must say it's all rather sinister.' He sighs and looks down at me like I'm the sorriest thing he's ever seen. 'It's over. Give up.'

'You're not going to get away with this!' I say through gritted teeth.

'Of course, I will. You're not smart and you're not scary,' he says. 'You're nothing but a desperate, horny little girl who's in way over her head. Stay out of my life or it will be *me* destroying *yours.*'

'I'm going to tell my parents everything. They can afford the best lawyers and they'll take you to court and ruin your life forever.'

Dylan keeps acting like this is all a big joke, his grin widening as he shakes his head from side to side slowly.

'Yes, I heard about your rich daddy. Well, you tell your parents I'm looking forward to seeing them at parents' evening on Friday. Maybe I have more than one video to show them.'

Shit. I forgot about parents' evening.

SIXTY-EIGHT

JULES

I'm no longer a shit wife, and I'm no longer a shit mum – it's now time to not be a shit friend.

'What's up?' Lynsey asks, picking up the phone. She's whispering, like her son is sleeping nearby. 'You never call in the day when you're working.'

I can't believe I haven't even told her about my job yet.

'Are you OK?' I ask.

She gives a little laugh. 'It's John, isn't it? He got to you, too. He's worried about me. I've been a bit overwhelmed with the kids lately and I needed a break. I'm fine. In fact, I've decided to go back to work.'

I sigh with relief. I can't believe I ever suspected her of lying to me. Of doing worse than that.

'Are *you* OK?' she asks. 'Because you've been acting really weird lately.'

'Yeah, I'm good. Well, getting better. I was just... Lynsey, do you ever tell yourself that something that happened never happened?'

This morning, Adam sidled up to me in bed, his arm snaking around my waist, and straight away I thought of Dylan.

hate that man; I hate him with all my being. For so long all I wanted was Adam to show me affection, yet when he touches me now, all I feel is guilt.

'Of course, I lie to myself all the time,' my friend replies. 'Remember that pink-haired DJ I kissed when John and I started dating?'

I go quiet. I have no idea what she's talking about.

'See? You've forgotten,' she says. 'Because it didn't happen. Well, it did, but I told myself it didn't, and you promised to never mention it again, so it never happened. How's everything between you and Adam now?'

I let out a half-laugh, but it sounds more like a sigh. 'We're having amazing sex again and he's not having an affair.'

'Of course, Adam was never having an affair!' Lynsey clicks her tongue at me. 'As I said, all you needed was to kick-start the engine again. So, what's the matter?'

'Nothing. Everything's fine.'

And it is. Isn't it? The video has gone, Dylan wants nothing to do with Leah, and Leah can't make things worse again without any evidence. It's checkmate. Game over. I should feel relieved, but I don't. I can't relax because that nasty little shit is still there, in her school, her classroom, our life, and I don't know how much money it's going to take to get rid of him forever.

'You still there, Jules?'

I can hear a soft whimpering in the background. The baby's awake.

'I'm fine. Everything's fine. You go.'

'We'll talk soon, yeah?'

'Yeah,' I say, knowing full well it will be a long time until I decide to tell her everything. Perhaps I never will.

Some things I need to sort out alone.

SIXTY-NINE

LEAH

I let myself into the house and shout from the bottom of the stairs.

'Mum!'

Silence. Maybe she's not working from home today.

I run through every room, doors banging against the walls. Dad is always moaning about that because there are little dents in the plaster from the handles, but I don't care. All I can think about is that Dylan climbed through my bedroom window and stole from me.

'Mum!' I shout again. I hear her slow footsteps on the stairs.

She looks different. Harder.

'Do we have CCTV?'

She looks at me blankly. My chin is wobbling and I'm shaking all over.

'What's the matter?'

'Something is missing from my room.'

'Missing? What's missing?'

'It's private.'

I expect her to start interrogating me but instead she pulls me into a hug, and I let her. I wish I could tell her everything because I need her to make it all go away like she did when I was little and scared of the shadows in my room at night. I start crying huge, hacking tears and she wraps her arms around me tighter. Too tight. I can't breathe. She's right in my face, mumbling something about how everything is going to be OK and how much she loves me.

'I'm fine,' I say.

She's pinning my arms down with her embrace. I can't move.

'Mum, what's going on?'

She keeps hugging me. Why won't she get off me? She's not listening, so I scream. I scream and scream right in her face until she lets go, jumping back like she's been stung. My mum can't help me. No one can. I'm going to have to deal with the sick motherfucker myself.

SEVENTY

JULES

I was stupid to think all my problems would disappear overnight. Adam is being wonderful, attentive and kind, but I can't enjoy it because I know what I did. And I know what my daughter did. And the threat of Dylan will never go away until he does. He's still there, teaching my daughter, and it's killing me. He needs to name his price and he needs to go.

Leah had a meltdown on Wednesday. For some reason, she thinks Dylan broke into our house. That must be the only conclusion she got from the condom going missing, which is better than her knowing the truth.

I also miss Curious2, which is stupid because the internet stranger I was obsessed with was never real to begin with – he's right there beside me every night, saying to my face all the romantic things his avatar would tell me. Perhaps it's not the man I miss, but the thrill of opening a message and seeing his reply. The sharing of forbidden fantasies with a forbidden stranger. The cheap hit of adrenaline. I'm a disgusting person. I don't deserve Adam or my children. I don't deserve any of the nice things I have, because I break everything.

I haven't even got back to Steve about my decision yet and

I'm due back at work on Monday. All of that has changed now, too. I can afford to buy Steve out. It's wild to even think it, but I could own Medusa. Yet I don't trust myself not to mess that up as well.

I took tablets to help me sleep last night, so when a piercing ring wakes me, for a moment I don't know where I am. My phone has somehow worked its way under my pillow. I turn down the volume and look at it under the duvet so as not to wake Adam. It's 2.39am. I'm not going to ignore it – no one calls at this hour unless it's an emergency. My first thought is of the children, my thundering heart cranking up a gear until I remember they are both safely asleep under the same roof as me. My next thought is my mother. I swallow that pain down, too.

I scramble out of bed, fumbling in the dark as I answer.

'Hello?'

The line is muffled. Adam mutters something and I tell him to go back to sleep as I tiptoe out of the room and go downstairs.

'Who's this?' I whisper.

'Robert.'

It takes me a moment to connect Robert from the bar to Dylan.

'It's two in the morning,' I hiss. 'Are you high?'

'I've been thinking about you, Jules. About your proposition.'

Flashes of what we did in the toilet run through my mind again like a technicolour blur and I'm ashamed by the jolt of pleasure I feel at the memory. He really needs to go.

'Say it. How much?' My mouth is so dry it's making my throat ache. I grab a glass from the draining board, my hand shaking as I hold it under the tap. I take a sip.

'Fifteen thousand.'

I'm choking, spluttering so loudly I nearly drop the phone.

'Are you deranged? I can't get my hands on that kind of money.'

'Of course, you can. Don't make me have to tell your husband all the gory details.'

'He wouldn't believe you.'

Or maybe he would. He saw what I was like on Kandid.

'I still have the video,' Dylan says.

I go cold all over, like icy water is dripping from the crown of my head, down my spine and to the floor.

'But I saw you delete it.'

'You old women really are stupid.'

'I can give you ten. Ten thousand. Cash. Then you must leave forever. The school, the county, gone.'

He laughs, a low chuckle like the crackle of a faulty line.

'That will do. For now.'

'I'll bring it tonight,' I say. 'But you have to write the resignation letter in front of me and email it, so I know you're not lying. Every photo, text, telephone number, video, I want it all gone.'

'Saturday,' he says.

'This evening! I want this over with, once and for all.'

'But we're both busy this evening, Jules. Parent–teacher conference, remember? I hope you're as excited as I am.'

SEVENTY-ONE

LEAH

Art is the last class of the day. Dylan isn't in the classroom yet, but I know he's been here already, because his desk is perfectly neat as usual. All the coloured pencils are in colour order; a pencil sharpener, rubber and notebook arranged creatively; a ruler, a pen and a scalpel lined up in a perfect row like some kind of stock photo.

I stare at the scalpel. I imagine taking it and slipping it into my pocket, then making my way to his house, the tip piercing the skin of my thumb, blood staining my blazer. How would it feel to run it along his throat? Would it be like the slip of scissors against silk, fast and silent, or like cutting at a chicken breast before you cook it?

I want to see him bleed. I want to hear the sounds he makes as he lies dying.

'Leah!'

Summer and Santi are in their usual seats at the back of the class. Santi is beckoning me over, and I'm eager to talk to him, but the look Summer is giving me has me taking a step back. I make an apologetic face to him and find a stool right at the back on my own, in the corner, on the other side of the classroom.

Santi is still staring over at me then breaks his gaze as Summer whispers something to him. Are they talking about me? He smiles at my friend and my throat thickens with the strain of trying not to tear up.

'Hello, class!'

Dylan looks different today. Lighter. He's wearing a black Nirvana t-shirt I haven't seen before. It fits tight over his strong arms and loose around his waist; his jeans look new too and have rips at the knee. I don't know how Summer refuses to believe Dylan was at Carnage when he looks exactly the same as all my brother's mates. Not that it matters now all the evidence has gone. I can't believe I have to spend another ten months sitting in his class, watching him act like he's won a battle I never started.

'Instead of our planned lesson today, I have a little treat for you,' he says. 'We're going to watch the movie *Frida*.'

A cheer goes up as twenty-three students celebrate that they have no work to do for the last ninety minutes of the week. I don't cheer though because Dylan is looking straight at me, a smile curling on his lips.

I hate him. I hate him. I hate him.

The lights dim and Salma Hayek fills the screen. I don't realise Dylan is standing behind me until I feel the heat from his breath on my cheek. It smells of coffee mixed with stale alcohol.

'And how's my favourite student doing today?' he whispers. I'm right at the back, so no one can see him talking to me.

I stay silent, staring straight ahead. I freeze as I feel his hand on my waist, his fingertip grazing a line from my hip bone up to my ribs. I shiver. I don't mean to, but it just happens. Dylan laughs softly, hooking his fingers beneath the fabric of my top until his hot hand is stroking my bare skin. It's like he's counting my ribs, his hand climbing higher until he's outlining the curve of my bra beneath my right breast. Two weeks ago, I would have leaned into him, murmured something smutty, maybe even reached behind me and stroked him in the darkness. But not now. Now I hate him, and I know it's that which is turning him on.

'You're really going to miss me when I'm gone, Leah,' he whispers into my ear.

Gone? I stay silent. His hand moves over my stomach, edging towards the waistband of my jeans.

'I'm leaving. I've come into some money. I'm finally getting away from you and your stalking, you messed-up little psycho.'

A single tear travels down my cheek as his thumb circles my belly button.

'Shame you turned out to be so mental because you were a pretty decent fuck.'

On the last word, he nips my ear with his teeth, and I take a sharp inhale of breath that sounds like a gasp. A few people turn around, but Dylan is already standing at the back of the class like a soldier. Eyes ahead. Hands clasped behind him. Everyone continues watching the movie – everyone but Santi. Can he see my tears from the other side of the room? I swat them away with the back of my hand and try and make sense of what Dylan just told me.

Where is he going? How come he gets to escape? How does he get to walk away from all this mess, when I'm the one left with no friends, no boyfriend and a screwed-up family?

I'm not going to let him get away with this. I want him to suffer.

I want the motherfucker dead.

SEVENTY-TWO

LEAH

I know exactly how I'm going to get my revenge. Dylan won't be home for hours tonight because of parents' evening. My parents have the last appointment at 6.30pm, which means I have three hours to do what I need to do until I join them.

I didn't take Dylan's scalpel. I thought about it, as we all filed out of the classroom, while he made some sarky comment about how he couldn't wait to meet our families tonight. I thought about taking the blade and hiding in his flat. Then, as he slept, running the scalpel over his throat and watching his sheets turn crimson. But that's not something you easily get away with.

As I sat watching the movie in class this afternoon, all I could hear was Reece saying how he wished someone would stick a Snickers bar down Dylan's throat, which reminded me of the EpiPen I saw in his flat. Then it hit me – the perfect way to make him pay and still get away with it.

I know the way to his house without even looking up now. I exit the corner shop and follow my feet, avoiding the cracks in the pavement because I need all the good luck I can get. As I walk, I play with the little balls in my blazer pocket. I take one and pop it in my mouth, savouring the sweet crunch as it explodes between my teeth. Peanut M&Ms. My favourite.

I'm thankful the road is empty as I push the downstairs door open and run up the stairs to his flat two at a time. I'm not out of breath, I'm excited. Dylan gave me the idea himself as he was saying those horrible things to me in class, his rancid coffee breath stinging my nostrils, his stupid special mug always nearby.

I'm in his kitchen now. I run my finger over the jars of different coffee beans he has, all neatly labelled. There's no point putting the peanuts in the jars – he'd see them. Plus it would take days to get around to drinking them.

I scoop the M&Ms out of my pocket and place them on the counter. I only planned to use one, but I guess the more the merrier. Standing on tiptoes, I lift the lid of his ridiculous machine and peer inside at the beans, placing one bright yellow M&M in the centre before switching it on. The loud noise makes me jump, then laugh, then whoop. I do it again with a red one and a green one, checking there's no change in the colour of the ground coffee. There isn't. I then throw a few more coffee beans on top and shut the lid, leaving it looking how it did before.

I use a dishcloth to wipe down the machine and use my sleeve to shut the front door behind me. I lock it, and then I throw his key down a drain outside. It disappears into the darkness. It's over. I know Dylan doesn't drink coffee late at night, but he does enjoy one early every morning. I wonder how bad his reaction will be. I hope he really suffers.

Dylan is about to find out he messed with the wrong girl.

SEVENTY-THREE
JULES

Leah is on my left, Adam on my right, and before me is Mr Ward – the man who has single-handedly almost ruined my family.

'Leah is a very talented girl,' he says, smiling at our daughter.

Adam places a hand on my knee and squeezes it. 'She takes after her mother,' he says, giving me a wink.

I'm playing with my wedding ring and Dylan is watching me as I twirl it around and around. 'I don't doubt that. I can see Leah and her mother have a lot in common,' he says.

I want to climb out of my skin and scurry away. A shadow creature blending into the dark corners of the room, leaving behind its crumpled shell like the wrinkled sheaf my daughter was hoarding in her bedroom.

I turn to Leah, but she's not listening. Her eyes are dead, and she's hardly blinking. I met her at the school entrance forty minutes ago. I have no idea where she was before that. We've already spoken to her English teacher and her history teacher. We're only a few weeks into the school term – it's meant to be more about starting off on the right foot than maintaining grades but they've both noticed a change in attitude over the last two weeks. I'm the only one who knows why.

'Leah,' Adam says, 'what do you think?'

I wasn't listening, and neither was our child.

'Huh?' she grunts.

'About Mr Ward offering you one-to-one art classes. He says you have real potential.'

Dylan is testing us, and now he knows I haven't told Adam anything, because my husband is eagerly lapping up every little thing he's telling us about our wonderfully creative daughter. The sick fucker is enjoying himself.

'Leah?' Adam says again.

She ignores her father and stares her teacher dead in the eye without saying a word. I watch, seeing who will crack first. Adam is confused, squeezing my knee to get my attention. I make out I have no idea what's happening.

'I thought you weren't staying,' Leah says eventually.

'It all depends,' Dylan replies, directing his comment at me. 'There are some delicate factors at play.'

Leah hums, like she's contemplating what he's telling us. 'You may be gone sooner than you think. Let's wait and see how things go before we make any plans.'

Dylan looks at his watch. 'Time's up. So wonderful to meet you both.'

Adam shakes Dylan's hand then leads Leah away. When it's my turn to shake his hand, Dylan doesn't let go.

'Don't forget, nine o'clock tomorrow morning,' he says under his breath. 'The sooner I get the money, the sooner I can get away from your fucked-up little family.'

I don't say a word, walking quickly away until I catch up with Adam and Leah.

'Weird guy,' Adam says. 'Don't you think he's a weird guy, Jules?'

Leah says nothing.

I say nothing.
Adam repeats himself. 'Weird.'

SEVENTY-FOUR

JULES

It's half past eight and Adam has entered the living room as I'm about to leave.

'Where are you going so early on a Saturday?'

Shit. I thought he was still asleep like everyone else.

'There's a sale on at that new kitchenware shop. I want to get there before it opens.'

He shrugs and mutters something about the allotment, then leaves. I wait for his car to drive out of sight before I get in my own. I've been up since five o'clock and I've already counted out the cash and bundled it up with elastic bands, stuffing it in one of my many tote bags.

I've had about four hours' sleep in total. All night, all I could see was Dylan's face as he looked at my daughter yesterday, then his face as he pushed me against the toilet wall, then his face lit by the flames of burning plastic. I did a terrible thing, and I've helped him cover up an even more terrible thing, but now I have the chance to get rid of the evil bastard once and for all.

· · ·

My hands are shaking as I pull up outside Dylan's house, my legs weak as I push the ground floor door open and climb his stairs. Every footstep sounds like the beat of a drum. He takes a while to answer when I knock. When he finally opens the door, he's half-naked, a towel around his middle and his hair wet. He's done it on purpose.

'You're early,' he says.

'Only by a few minutes.'

'Come in. I've made coffee.'

His flat is immaculate. He's hung the canvases on the wall, his guitar has a new stand, and his books are in colour order. There's even a pot of pens on his coffee table. This doesn't look like the home of a man who's about to leave town.

'Milk?' he asks.

I wish he'd put some clothes on.

'I'm not staying.'

He places another mug beneath the nozzle of his elaborate machine, and it splutters back into action, the milk dispenser hissing and producing steam. I've never understood why some men get off on these fancy coffees.

'I ordered these beans directly from a plantation in Guatemala,' he says as if I care. 'This is a new blend. I'm very excited to try it.'

What's wrong with Nescafé? I don't answer and he continues talking as if we're old friends.

'I went for a run later than normal,' he says. 'So I'm dying for a coffee. Last night was hideous – so many awful parents, so many talentless children. Please, take a seat.'

I stay standing and keep my jacket on. He places my mug on the coffee table, his towel parting at the thigh. I've never seen his bare chest, arms or legs before. He wants me to notice. He knows his body is worth looking at.

'Your husband seems nice,' he says. 'Totally clueless, but nice.'

Dylan really does love to play games.

'Cut the crap. The money is in the bag. I need to see you delete all copies of the video and send your resignation letter.'

He goes back to the coffee machine and picks up his mug.

'Let me have my coffee first. My goodness, Leah did say you were a nag.'

I clench my teeth together. I'm not going to bite, I'm not going to react, I just want him gone. He puts his coffee on the table beside mine and opens his laptop, motioning for me to sit beside him so I can see the screen. The letter has already been drafted. Very organised. He adds Ms Willis's email address and the subject line 'Resignation'.

'Money?'

I drop the bag on to his lap, hoping it hurts. He gives a wolfish grin and peers inside, taking out the bundles and sniffing them.

'One thousand each. Ten of them,' I say.

'Fast work. I know you're very rich now, but I didn't realise you had wads of cash lying around the house.'

'Press send,' I say.

He does so with an exaggerated flourish, and I immediately feel lighter.

'Now the video and all the text messages,' I say. 'Leah's and mine.'

He picks up his phone and waves it at me. 'A deal is a deal.'

I watch closely as he deletes everything off his phone, this time from the cloud too, and again from a drive on his laptop.

'How do I know that's everything?' I ask.

He shrugs. 'You'll just have to trust me. Most women do... at first.'

'I wish you were dead,' I say.

He laughs and picks up his coffee, closing his eyes with pleasure as he takes a long sip. 'According to the Guatemalan distributors, these beans are meant to have a caramel undertone.

I know people think that...' He clears his throat and takes another long sip. 'Try yours. Does it taste strange to you? A little sweet, a bit—'

He coughs, scratches his arm and takes a third sip. I don't want his stupid coffee.

His phone beeps and he picks it up, showing it to me with a grin.

'It's Leah. See? I told you your child was demented. Utterly obsessed with me.'

With a look of resigned amusement, he clicks on the message as he drains the last of his coffee. He grimaces, his brow creasing with confusion as he looks from the text message to the empty mug in his hand and back. What did my daughter say to him? Dylan clears his throat again. His cheeks are tinged red, and his lips are looking a bit puffy. He drops his phone on to the sofa, the empty mug in his hand falling to the table with a clatter, making the handle snap off.

'Jules,' he says, his voice strangled, his breaths coming in jagged pulls. He's bent double, grasping at something on the coffee table. The cup full of pens. His now swollen mouth is opening and closing but no sound is coming out. He reaches for the pens, scattering them over the table and floor.

'What's the matter?' I cry out.

He's pointing at one of the pens – a chunky orange marker. I look closer. It's an EpiPen.

His eyes are now tiny slits cut into pink mounds, his lips two little pillows, a rash blossoming over his chest. He tries to open the EpiPen but drops it, and it rolls along the rug to the edge of the sofa. Dylan is trying to say something. It sounds like 'please'. He wants me to pick it up and hand it to him. He needs me to help him.

I rush over, intending to pick up the EpiPen, then notice Dylan's phone. It's still open to Leah's message.

DON'T DRINK THE COFFEE

Oh, no. Leah. My sweet child. What have you done?

I delete the text message and place my boot over the pen. Dylan splutters at my feet, clawing at my ankles, his bulbous eyes staring up at me pleadingly.

But Dylan is a bad man who has done bad things to good people. And he isn't going to stop at ten thousand pounds; he's going to torture me and my family for every penny we have. Extort us until there's nothing left, like poor Fiona. This is just the start... but it could also be the end.

He's pulling at my foot, desperately trying to reach the pen, but he's not strong enough.

I bend down so my lips are inches away from his red, swollen face.

'Go fuck yourself,' I say slowly, pushing him off me and kicking the EpiPen under the sofa.

Dylan is dragging himself along the rug, his towel coming away at his waist. He's reaching under the sofa, but his hand doesn't fit. He starts to convulse at my feet, shit dribbling out of his arse, his features now completely unrecognisable.

I could save him. I could retrieve the pen and administer it, or call an ambulance, but he will know both my daughter and I tried to kill him. This is the only way I can ensure he is gone for good, but first I have to get rid of the evidence.

Dylan continues to gurgle face down on the rug as I look around the flat. There are rubber gloves and bleach by the sink. Perfect. I've spent the last seventeen years cleaning up after my daughter and I'm not going to stop now.

By the time I'm done, everything will be gone: the evidence, the money and Dylan.

SEVENTY-FIVE

LEAH

I'm a murderer. I didn't mean it, I tried to stop him, but I did it. I killed him. Yet that's not what they're saying on the news. My phone woke me up early – everyone in my year messaging the class WhatsApp group about Dylan dying, but nothing's making sense. My hand shakes as I scroll through the messages. Mel from my art class is having the best time telling everyone the gossip, like he knows anything at all.

Apparently the police wanted him and that's why he jumped.

Why?

Blackmail. They found loads of stuff in his flat.

How do you know that?

It's all over the news. He even left a suicide letter.

I do a Google search and everyone's right. The latest news article says Dylan confessed to extortion and then jumped from his balcony. I don't understand. So I didn't kill him? He saw my text message in time? I keep scrolling, my fingers getting sweaty, a high-pitched noise buzzing between my ears.

Ngl I always knew Mr Ward was a nonce!

Abdul has had it in for Dylan since he gave him a detention for the comment he made on my birthday. My heart skips a beat. Why are they calling him a paedophile? What have they heard? Mel replies.

What are you talking about, bro?

A million question mark emojis and confused GIFs appear.

That's why he left the other school. He was boning students and their mums then blackmailing them. Apparently, he was trying to do the same at our school. They're asking people to come forward. Some old lady on the news is saying how he conned her out of twenty grand.

I don't hear my mum enter my bedroom until she's right beside me. She passes me a hairbrush.

'Thanks,' I say, brushing my hair and returning it.

'Have you heard?'

I nod. I'm too shocked to say anything else.

'Are you OK?'

I shrug. I'm not sure if I am, actually. Dylan is dead. It's what I wanted, yet I don't feel happy. I feel... terrified. What if the police find out what I did? I've been worried sick all weekend. I don't understand. Why did he jump?

'I'm fine,' I say.

'He wasn't a nice man, Leah.'

She has no idea what I've done. She doesn't know I'm not a nice girl, either.

'Mum.' I want to tell her everything. I want to say I'm sorry and that I love her and that I'm sorry. I'm so sorry.

'Don't say anything,' she says, cupping my face in her hands and kissing my cheek. 'You'll always be my baby.' She pauses and takes a deep breath. 'Which is why we need to be careful now.'

Careful? My heart is pounding so loudly she must be able to hear it.

She reaches for my phone and opens my text messages. The last one is the one I sent to Dylan. I'm frozen. I should snatch it out of her hand, but I can't move.

She deletes it and hands it back to me.

'I made it all go away,' she says, drying my face with the cuff of her fluffy dressing gown. 'You know I'll do anything for you. He can't hurt you again.'

She knows what I tried to do, but how did she make it all go away?

SEVENTY-SIX
REECE

Leah never simply walks through the front door; she always flies through it like she has the police on her tail. She slams the door behind her, drops her bag to the floor with a thud, and throws herself beside me on the sofa.

'What are you watching?'

'*Life. Love. Luxe.*'

'Sounds shit.'

It is. It's a ridiculous reality show about trashy American real estate agents. She throws a cushion on to my lap and lays on me. I push three Maltesers into her mouth. She sits up, coughing, and grabs a handful of chocolates from the box.

'Dick.'

I laugh. 'How was school?'

'Better than yesterday and Monday. It's nearly back to normal now. Paige and Summer are all apologetic and the police have finally stopped asking everyone questions.'

'What about that boy who liked you?'

She shrugs. 'I don't think he's talking to me. He's been off school all week, and he's not replying to my messages. Where are Mum and Dad?'

I point upstairs and wiggle my eyebrows. She pretends to be sick.

It's been like this since the weekend, the four of us only talking about the little things, even though Dad's made us rich, Mum's in legal talks about buying Medusa, and the teacher my sister was sleeping with is dead.

'How can you sell a mansion in those heels?' Leah mutters, throwing a Malteser at the TV.

'Yeah. If I was selling my beachside villa and she scuffed my expensive floors with her stripper shoes, I'd sack her.'

I watch Leah watching the TV. Sometimes I see the woman she's on the verge of becoming, but most of the time I see a silly kid who doesn't know anything about anything.

'Are you really OK?' I ask.

She sits up. We haven't had this conversation yet. I stayed at a friend's Saturday and only came home yesterday. I thought it was safer that way.

'The news is now saying he had an allergic reaction before he died,' I tell her. I can't bring myself to say his name out loud yet but she knows who I mean. 'He managed to find an EpiPen in time.'

Leah is fiddling with the ring I bought her. I was hoping she'd tell me. I knew Mum wouldn't – she'll take secrets to the grave – but Leah and I talk about everything. I did wonder what would end up being the one thing too big for my little sis to confide in me about. I guess attempted murder is up there.

I throw a Malteser into the air and catch it in my mouth. 'I'm just saying that, you know, if anyone *did* sneak peanuts into his food to teach him a lesson, I wouldn't blame them.'

Leah does that long staring thing again and I know. Although I already did.

I was four years old when she was born. I still remember when they brought her home. From day one she was my doll. I never wanted to go to school; I wanted to stay home with Mum and look after her. I wanted to be the one to feed and change and dress her. Our parents said we had a psychic connection because I always knew when she was unhappy way before she started crying. She was only ever truly happy when I was holding her. I haven't let go since. Not really.

She lies back down on my lap and I stroke her hair.

'I didn't think he'd kill himself,' she admits.

He didn't.

I've delivered weed to Dylan every Saturday afternoon for over a year now and last weekend was no exception. I was prepared to feel rage when I saw him, but what I wasn't expecting was to see him looking like that.

'Jesus!' I cried when he opened the door. 'Hello, Elephant Man.'

I kept my cool, thankful he still only knew me as his dealer. He had no idea who my family was.

'Allergic reaction,' he said, unnecessarily pointing at his face, which looked like he'd had ten rounds with both Tysons at the same time. 'I just got back from the hospital. Took ages because they were questioning me about my meds.'

I knew all about his depression and had told him countless times that weed wasn't going to help. Dylan was still weak, lowering himself down on the sofa before sipping at some water. There was a stain on his rug which was damp like he'd been scrubbing it moments earlier.

'Give me the strongest shit you have,' he said.

I'd come prepared, but he was making it so easy for me.

'I have a new strain,' I said.

'Nice. Today has been rough. A couple of bitches fucked me up bad.'

He could have been referring to dozens of women. So many hated him.

I struggled to keep the expression on my face passive. How the hell did they allow this monster to be a teacher? I couldn't stop thinking about Leah, and what he did to her, and what wanted to do to him.

'What happened?' I asked, and he told me.

He said a girl he'd been seeing must have put peanuts in hi coffee beans which gave him a reaction. The news didn' surprise me as much as it should have – a small part of me wa actually proud of my kid sister. After all, I'm the one who gav her the idea. But the rest of his story was pure horror.

'I also had a thing with the girl's mum,' Dylan explained 'She was here when it happened, cleaned up all the evidenc when she realised what her daughter had done, and left me t die.'

He had sex with Leah's mum? *My* mother?

'Don't worry, man. I'll get my revenge on that whole family he sneered.

I stayed calm, even though I was desperate to punch him gouge his puffy eyes out, beat his disfigured face to a pulp. Bu I'm not a fighter – I'm smarter than that, which is why I cam prepared. I'd come to kill Dylan and, unlike my mother an sister, I was going to be successful.

Leah turns the volume of the TV up and I pop anothe Malteser in her mouth. She's safe now. We all are.

'That one's a nightmare,' she says, pointing at the curv brunette on the screen tottering about in a skimpy dress.

'I know. Imagine driving a red Porsche dressed in fuchsia.'

'What on earth is she wearing?' Mum says, walking into th living room. We both sit up. I could ask her the same thing Since when has she started swanning about the house in sil robes?

Dad walks in and stops with a start. 'Oh, I didn't realise yo kids were home.'

'Clearly,' I say, making a face at my sister.

Mum goes straight into the kitchen and starts bangin

about, asking us what we want for dinner. Leah keeps catching my eye and trying not to laugh.

'Mum, sit down,' I say, muting the TV. 'I have an announcement to make.'

Leah frowns at me but I hold a finger up so she doesn't interrupt.

'Good news or bad?' Dad asks, sitting on the other couch. Mum joins him.

'Good news for me, but you might not think so,' I say.

Leah gives a fake gasp and covers her mouth with her hands. 'You haven't got a girl pregnant, have you?'

We all laugh, except Mum. She's already worrying about my big news before knowing what she should be worrying about.

'What is it?' she says.

This is earlier than planned, a year earlier in fact, but after Saturday... well, needs must and all that.

'I'm going travelling. I leave next week.'

'What?' Leah jumps to her feet, scattering Maltesers everywhere. I can't tell if she's angry, excited or jealous. 'Mum! Why does Reece get to skip school and fuck off around the world?'

'Leah!' Mum and Dad say at the same time.

She sits back down, arms folded.

'On your own?' Mum says.

'You can't bail out of your last year of uni,' Dad says.

I have to. I can't stay here. Not after what I did.

'I spoke to the dean, and he agreed going abroad was a good idea,' I say to my parents. 'It's all planned. My trip includes community outreach work, which helps towards my final grade anyway, so it's more than a *holiday*,' I say, looking pointedly at Leah, who sticks her tongue out at me.

In the past, Dad would have said something about my degree being useless, and Mum would have said something about me travelling so far away, or how I never spend enough time with her, or telling me to be extra careful. This time, they stay quiet. Amazing what sex and money can do for the nervous system.

Dad tells Mum not to worry about dinner, we can order pizza, and Mum suggests a game of Uno. Leah actually stays this time and offers to shuffle. And in that moment, I know I did the right thing.

'No cheating,' Dad says as Leah deals out the Uno cards.

She keeps looking at her phone. She's still waiting for that boy to reply to her. It kills me that I can't save her from every man who will break her heart.

Growing the hemlock was easy. My dad has no idea what I do in his allotment; he's just pleased his son likes to share a hobby with him. I made sure to grow my plants and mushrooms in a corner, away from his fruit and veg, nowhere people or animals could touch them. It's a bit macabre, to be so fascinated by poisonous plants, but when you like camping as much as I do, knowing your plants is a matter of survival. As I say, growing it was easy. Harvesting it, grating the roots, drying it and incorporating it into a spliff was a little harder. But it was worth it.

Dylan didn't think it was strange when we went on to the balcony to sample the new weed I brought him. He didn't think it unusual that I had a pre-rolled spliff for him or that it tasted a little different.

He was already weak and collapsed instantly. I left him there groaning and gasping, a crumpled heap on his balcony, hidden behind the brick wall, convulsing, tearing at his swollen face, grasping at his constricted airway.

I used his fingerprint to access his laptop, where I found a resignation letter in his inbox that had bounced back – he'd sent it to the wrong address. I wondered if Mum had paid him off in exchange for that and he'd felt clever tricking her. I re-wrote it as his confessional suicide letter and amended the email address to Ms Willis, but I wasn't going to send it until I was certain he was really dead. Because once his body was found, I knew the police would come to the flat, and they'd look at his things, and they'd find his antidepressants and his weed and all the evidence they needed on his laptop that Dylan was a blackmailing piece of shit.

I cleaned up after myself too – like mother, like son. Wearing his washing-up gloves, I carefully picked up the poisoned joint to dispose of afterwards, then I waited until it was completely dark before I sent the email then used a stool to help me haul Dylan over the edge of the wall. I left the stool there and didn't hang about to watch him hit the ground. It didn't matter whether the impact killed him or not – he was already dead with a substance no pathologist would ever think to test for. A depressed weed addict with a heavy conscience, reeling from an allergic reaction, who sent a suicide letter ten minutes before he jumped? Easy.

The body landed on one side of the building, and I exited from the other. No one saw me on the stairs, no one heard me. By the time I was on the street, someone had screamed, and a few neighbours had come out to investigate. I walked one way; they all ran in the other direction. All except one.

'Hey, you're Leah's brother, right?'

A boy was standing before me. He was sweet-looking. Like a young Leonardo DiCaprio, but darker.

'Were you at Mr Ward's house? Man, I hate that guy. I came here to say something to him, but got scared. You know he's being mean to your sister, right? Were you up there talking to him? You totally should.'

The boy was nervous. Angry. I knew how he felt. He looked over my shoulder behind the trees at the crowd forming, the blue lights, the sirens. Then he looked at me. At my face. I don't know what he was thinking, but he started to run, so I ran after him.

'Uno!' Dad shouts.

Mum takes her turn and tells Leah to concentrate, but she's staring at her phone, her hand shaking and her face pale. I can already feel her pain, like I could when she was a baby. Except it's not so easy to stop her tears now.

'Santi's missing,' she says, showing us a picture on her phone. It's one of those posters you see on social media of runaway kids, teens that turn up safe or dead or disappear forever. 'He's not been seen since Saturday.'

I didn't mean to do it. I had no choice.

I'll be gone before they find him.

A LETTER FROM NATALI

Dear reader,

Thank you so much for choosing to read *My Daughter's Revenge*. It's thanks to readers like you that I get to keep writing books which I hope are entertaining, insightful and thrilling. If you enjoyed *My Daughter's Revenge* and want to keep up to date with all my latest releases, please sign up at the following link. Your email address will never be shared and you can unsubscribe at any time.

www.bookouture.com/natali-simmonds

Although *My Daughter's Revenge* is a work of fiction, the struggles Jules and Leah face are often all too real: women feeling invisible as they grow older, mothers losing their identity, communication issues in a marriage, extortion, and obsessive behaviour in adolescence. If you or someone you know is facing any of these issues, you can call the Samaritans for free on 116 123 or www.mind.org.uk for a list of other mental health services.

I hope you enjoyed reading *My Daughter's Revenge*. If you would like to recommend it to others, I would really appreciate your review. Your comments make such a difference helping new readers to discover one of my books for the first time, plus I love hearing from my readers.

You can also get in touch with me and share your thoughts through social media or my website.

Thanks,

Natali Simmonds

www.njsimmonds.com

ACKNOWLEDGEMENTS

All my book ideas start with a 'what if?' question, and *My Daughter's Revenge* was no exception.

Back in 2017 I had an idea for a book about a teen crush that got obsessive and deadly, fascinated by the idea of the prey becoming the predator. Nothing came of that book, but I never stopped thinking about the concept.

Fast-forward five years and I was telling my agent about this random idea when she asked, 'But how would the mother feel?' and that's how *My Daughter's Revenge* came to life.

As a forty-five-year-old mother of two teen girls, and someone with many amazing female friends who share their ups and downs of marriage and motherhood with me, I really wanted to explore the idea of what it would be like to be the kind of woman who defines herself by her beauty and sexuality – then slowly loses them just as her teen daughter discovers her own. I asked myself how those emotions could lead to making some very bad decisions... and Jules and Leah didn't disappoint!

I'm incredibly lucky to have a wonderful mother, and to be the mother to two amazing girls, with a fabulous husband who sees me, supports me and pays me plenty of attention. No one in this book is based on them! But I do know many women who are not as lucky – women who feel invisible, unwanted and lost as they near their fifties.

This book is for you.

Although writing is a solitary endeavour, its completion and success are the result of the collective efforts, encouragement and support of many individuals.

Firstly, a huge thank you to my agent, Amanda Preston, who totally got this book and backed it from the start. Her insights and ideas shaped it into a story I'm so proud of, and I'm eternally thankful that she also found the perfect home for it at Bookouture. It takes a very special kind of person to not only keep up with my manic intensity but remain a steady and whip-smart guide on this crazy writing journey. I'm so thankful we found one another.

Lucy Frederick, my editor, I'm utterly thrilled to be working with you. Your vision for *My Daughter's Revenge* was spot on and I'm very excited to delve into the world of domestic suspense with you. So much fun ahead of us.

And a huge thank you to the rest of the Bookouture publishing team, including talented cover designer Lisa Brewster, fabulous copy editor DeAndra Lupu, proofreader Deborah Blake and publicist Jess Readett, who have worked tirelessly behind the scenes to bring this book to life and share it with the world.

To Pete, Isabelle and Olivia, for your unwavering love, enthusiasm and patience as I either ignore you, force you to listen to my latest chapter or ask you questions like, 'How would you kill your teacher?' I wish I could say I'm going to stop now, but the likelihood is I'm only going to get worse.

To my mum, Chris, my biggest cheerleader (this book is dedicated to you – you can finally read it now), Bob, Desi, Jemma, cousins, aunts, uncles and the married-ins for being the perfect example of what it means to be in a loving, supportive and totally bonkers family.

To my friends, whose trauma and humour I steal for all my books, thank you for listening to my ideas as if it's the first time I told you them. A special thanks to my bestie and Caedis Knight co-writer, Jacqueline Silvester, who can always be relied on to brainstorm murder techniques with (the best parts of this book were probably her idea). Thank you, Lauren North, for all your help. And a special shout out to all my other talented writer friends, including Anna Rainbow, Isabella May, Emma-Claire Wilson, Teuta Metra, Maz Evans, Alexandra Christo, Emma Cooper, Louie Stowell, A J West and all the countless others I WhatsApp, Tweet and chat to on various platforms and groups. I'd be lost without you!

A special mention goes to Victoria Handford at Woodlands School in Essex. During my 2022 school visit two cheeky lads asked to be in my book and I said yes. Here you go, Mel and Abdul (year eleven) – you're famous now. Told you I keep my promises.

And lastly, thank you to the booksellers, librarians, reviewers, bloggers and, of course, all my readers. Thank you for accompanying me into the twisted minds of my troubled characters and their bloody antics. Your enthusiasm and support mean everything.

There's a lot more to come, so brace yourselves!

Copyeditor
DeAndra Lupu

Proofreader
Deborah Blake

Marketing
Alex Crow
Melanie Price
Occy Carr
Cíara Rosney
Martyna Młynarska

Operations and distribution
Marina Valles
Stephanie Straub

Production
Hannah Snetsinger
Mandy Kullar
Jen Shannon
Ria Clare

Publicity
Kim Nash
Noelle Holten
Jess Readett
Sarah Hardy

Rights and contracts
Peta Nightingale
Richard King
Saidah Graham

Printed in Great Britain
by Amazon